P B NORTH

Girl in the Picture

D1527707

WATERMILL CLASSICS

P B NORTH

PB North was born in Stockton-on-Tees, England. He studied at the University of Cambridge where he received an MA in English. He later went on to take a post graduate degree at Edinburgh University.

He has lived most of his life in Scotland, where he has worked in various roles as a government official, writing many thousands of words for public reports. He is currently based in East Lothian where he lives with his Norwegian wife, his cat and his rescue staffie/dachshund cross. When he is not writing, he tries to grow things, plays golf badly and goes out in his boat.

Girl in the Picture is his second novel, which draws on his time spent in the north of England, as well as exploring a period of British colonial rule in east Africa.

His first novel – *Leaving Pimlico* – was published earlier this year.

GIRL IN THE PICTURE

Dear Reader

This novel is entirely a work of fiction. The names, characters and incidents portrayed in it are the work of the author's imagination. Any resemblance to actual persons, living or dead, is entirely coincidental. The central part of the novel is set against the general historical and geographical background of Kenya in the 1950s, which the author does not claim is accurate in detail. The reader should note, however, that the modern spelling of the name *Maasai* has been adopted throughout, except for *The Masai of Kenya*, which was the actual name given by the East African Railway Company to one of their steam locomotives.

Apologies are offered in advance over the references to Middlesbrough FC playing in The Championship in 2005. They actually did well that season in the English Premiership but the author, a lifelong Boro supporter, ignored that for the sake of the story.

Finally, Shakespeare, of course, only wrote 154 sonnets as far as scholars have determined. Sonnet 155 is entirely the work of the author, as will be painfully apparent.

If you enjoy the book, the author would be delighted to hear from you at pb_north@btinternet.com

ACKNOWLEDGEMENTS

To Inger and Katie, for their helpful comments on the text.

To THB at Watermill Classics for all his work on the cover design and production.

To Whitby, for the memories of childhood holidays.

PART ONE

Chapter 1

Whitby, North Yorkshire, February 2005

Edward Ottaway took out his handkerchief and wiped a round clearing in the layer of dust that fogged the bedroom window. He looked out across the harbour.

'Christ! How the hell did I end up here?' he asked himself. He looked again at the fishing boats tied up at the quayside, bobbing up and down in the choppy waters whipped up by the easterly off the North Sea. 'Christ Almighty!' It was freezing cold and felt like the middle of winter. He was used to a centrally heated flat in Kensington, with triple glazing. He thought he had ended up in Siberia.

He had asked a simple enough question with a simple enough answer. He had lost his job in the city; his wife had walked out on him; and the bank had appropriated his flat when he failed on the payments. Life was bleak, almost as bleak as the view from the window. It had been a year of hell and it looked like carrying on that way. He clattered down the bare wooden stairs to the poky living room of the fisherman's cottage. There was a coal scuttle by the side of the fireplace so he started to lay a fire. He had a distant memory of seeing someone do this, way back in his childhood, but the details were lost and his effort foundered. The damp paper caught fire eventually, then fizzled out, and the room filled with acrid smoke. 'Shit! Damn!' he shouted and kicked the metal scuttle, skinning his ankle in the process. He collapsed into the battered armchair by the window and lit a cigarette. He had taken up smoking again as soon as he could no longer afford the monthly payment to work-out in the fitness centre at Canary Wharf; that is, before he lost his wife and his flat. He began to feel very sorry for himself. He had always regarded himself as a nice guy, friendly, generous and mild-mannered. Now that he had no money, he had discovered his true self, capable of kicking coal scuttles and using four-letter words, despite his public school upbringing and his choral scholarship. As well as taking up smoking again, of course. He was just a miserable bastard, deep down.

He had arrived in Whitby only that afternoon. He had studied the map to find out where it was. The fund manager colleague, who had lent him his folding bed in the living room for the last six months, had never set foot outside London so could not advise him. Edward had been to Edinburgh once, for a freezing cold New Year in Princes Street. Otherwise, his idea of the north was Welwyn Garden City. Now he was following a route map to north Yorkshire, to a God-forsaken little place called Whitby. Who the hell ever went there?

He pulled over his ten-year-old Peugeot into a lay-by somewhere on the A169 and looked at the map. He seemed to be in the middle of nowhere. There was a lashing hailstorm belting in from the east and the only living things in sight were the sheep huddling behind the dry stone walls along the roadside. Everything he owned in the world was within three feet of where he sat: a suitcase, a holdall, and a couple of bin bags, stuffed inside a 206. Fifteen years on city bonuses and this is where he had ended up. And his ex-wife moving in with her personal trainer, the sexual marathon man.

His departure from London was painful but a necessity. He had no home and only a pot from his severance payment to live on. He couldn't keep up with his so-called friends any more. So it came as some sort of relief that his uncle had conveniently died and left him, as the only relative, a property somewhere in the north. Uncle Freddie was an enigma. Edward had no memory of meeting him, although he guessed he must have, and for the last thirty years no one remotely connected with the Ottaways knew anything about him. But then the Ottaways were snobby folk, came from nothing, made some money from metal-bashing before the First World War, and then bought themselves a pedigree by sending their children to fee-paying schools. No surprise then that dodgy geezers like Uncle Freddie were *personae non gratae* and not to be enquired after, although Edward had often harboured a sneaking desire to find out about him. He'd heard he was an artist but of what sort he had no idea. He imagined him with long grey hair, sagging corduroy jacket, smelling of cheap cigars and absinthe. Romantic fantasy.

He'd had a letter from a solicitor in York three weeks earlier, asking him to call in to sign some papers. Edward had hoped there might be some cash but no such luck. He'd signed the papers that morning on the way up from London and Scrivener, for that was the solicitor's apt name, had handed him a brown envelope containing a rusty front door key and an address. Edward, plunged in deep depression, looked out of the car window at the gloomy sheep. He took the paper from his pocket and read it again. It was an address in Henrietta Street, somewhere on the east side of the town. He looked at his map again. According to that, he was in the middle of Goathland Moor, with about fifteen miles to go. He felt as cheerful as the black-faced sheep looked. He turned the ignition key, the cheap little crate lurched into life, and he pushed on into the unknown, feeling as intrepid as Scott crossing the Antarctic. This was no country for Londoners, he thought.

An hour later, after several gyrations round the one-way streets of Whitby, he pulled up outside a small flat-windowed cottage in the cobbled lane called Henrietta Street. His heart sank. This was not Kensington; on his journey round the town he had not noticed a single decent restaurant or wine bar. His thoughts raced: 'Where on earth does one eat?' Was this the promised end to a glittering career, or image of that horror?

He sat for minutes slumped in the front seat of his car, very much resembling the sagging bin bag beside him on the passenger seat, rain hammering at the windscreen, when there was a knock on his driver's side window. A red face stared in at him. He wound down the window.

'You can't park here, son. You're blocking the road.'

'I'm moving in here,' he replied. 'Where can I park then?'

'Round back,' said the red face, pointing over his shoulder to a narrow gap between two cottages. 'You moving in? You

Freddie's nephew, eh? Got summat for you.' He was a man of sixty-five perhaps, with a strong northern accent.

'What's that?'

'Tell yer later.' And with that the red face disappeared into a doorway.

Edward reflected on the long day he had endured. He stubbed out his cigarette on the hearthstone and felt his shin. It was hurting badly. All around him lay his things, half unpacked. He felt knackered and hungry. All he had to look forward to was a cold night in a sleeping bag on the old mattress he had seen in the upstairs bedroom. He looked at his watch. It was six o'clock and it was dark. He was starving. *But where on earth would he eat?* He could not escape that question. Then he remembered his red-faced neighbour. He threw on his Barbour and went out into the street, trying to remember into which doorway the man had disappeared, before taking pot luck. He knocked on the first door he came to on the right. After a while, the door opened. He had chosen correctly.

'Hello, I'm Edward Ottaway, Freddie's nephew,' he said, breathing in the wave of whisky fumes wafting towards him.

'Aye, right. I know who you are. I'm Jim.'

'You said you had something for me earlier.'

'Aye, right. Can't give it to you now though.'

'OK.' Edward paused for thought, somewhat puzzled. 'Fine. Well, is there anywhere to eat round here?'

'Aye, Caedmon Fish Restaurant, down the road. That should do you.'

And the door closed before Edward could say more. But the message was promising; Edward quite fancied a starter of seared scallops followed by, perhaps, a fresh seafood platter and a crisp bottle of sauvignon blanc. After all, he could splash out on that before he took on his sackcloth and ashes. And the Caedmon Restaurant sounded quite classical. The rain had eased and his gastric juices were flowing; life might not be too terrible after all. He pulled up his collar and strode off down the lane. A couple of minutes later he reached his destination and, pushing open the street door, entered the restaurant. It was simple – and empty; but simplicity was often the sign of honest cuisine, he thought. Then he noticed the formica topped tables and the seventies colour scheme of brown plastic chairs and orange light shades. Still, undeterred, and driven by hunger, he sat down and looked around him. Then a girl appeared from somewhere in the back. She was wearing black leggings and a flimsy top; she looked like Maria Sharapova on a good day.

'Hi, can I help you? We're just about to close,' she said.

Edward looked at his watch in disbelief. 'But it's only six-thirty.' What kind of a restaurant was this, he thought.

'Takeaways only after six-thirty,' she said briskly.

'I was told this was a fish restaurant,' he replied, somewhat forlornly.

'It is. We do cod, haddock and skate. That's fish,' she said.

'What about scallops or lobster?'

'That's seafood, or you could say molluscs and crustaceans,' she added with a laugh. 'I suppose we could just about manage a fish tea, if you order quickly.'

'A fish tea? What's that?' Edward asked in bewilderment.

'Which planet are you from? Battered fish, chips, bread and butter and a pot of tea.'

Edward paused, his legs cut from under him, by this Boadicea of the north. This was certainly not a Kensington bistro. Then he summoned a reply. 'OK. Cod and chips. And I'm from planet London.'

'That explains everything,' she said, and disappeared off into the back, from where he could hear his order shouted out. Ten minutes later, she reappeared, planted the order in front of him, and said 'Enjoy' before striding off. His appetite took over and in no time he had cleared the plate, including the bread and butter, and drained the teapot. He found it surprisingly delicious. He put his knife and fork down and, leaning back in his chair, closed his eyes.

'How was it?' came a girl's voice. It was the waitress, who had just turned the open sign to closed.

'It was very good indeed. Best fish I've had in years. Thank you.'

'You sound surprised,' she said, sitting down at his table. 'I'm off-duty now. Dad's opened up the chip shop bit next door, so I can relax.'

'I've never heard a waitress talk about molluscs and crustaceans before. What's all that about?'

'I'm not a waitress. Just filling in before university. Couldn't resist winding you up a bit. I could see you'd never had high tea before. I'm Jane Martin, by the way.'

'And I'm Edward Ottaway. Just moved in up the road.'

'I know, Freddie's nephew.'

'How come everybody knows about me? After all, I'm a traveller from a far-off land.'

'Freddie told everybody about you, before he died. Everybody knew Freddie,' she said. 'He was a gem. Now, what about you? What do you do?'

'I, Jane, am a failed futures investor. I failed to foresee the future and lost the business fifty million overnight. Bet on blue but it turned red and kept on going down.'

'Didn't you have a hedge in place?' she asked.

Edward looked at her with amazement: this dazzling eighteen-year-old also knew about spread-betting. He couldn't believe it.

'Jane, I went out on the booze and missed the closing bell. Where the hell did you learn all this? I bet you got four straight As and are off to read rocket science at Cambridge.'

'Gasworks comprehensive, down the road,' she replied with a laugh, 'and you're almost right, but it's medicine. Good night Ed. Nice to talk to you. See you around.'

'Before you go Jane, who's Caedmon?'

'Good God! Caedmon was the first English poet. Lived up the hill at the abbey in the seventh century. Where did you go to school?'

'Eton, actually.'

With that Jane swung out of the door leaving Edward intellectually gutted, boned and battered, just like the cod he had just eaten. But as he walked back up the lane to his two-up and two-down, he felt a glimmer of enlightenment. Perhaps there *was* life after Welwyn Garden City.

Chapter 2

Edward had an early night, curled up alone in his tight little sleeping bag on the damp mattress in the upstairs bedroom. He didn't feel as miserable a bastard as he had earlier, when he had kicked the coal scuttle. Jane had considerably cheered him up so he fell asleep in reasonable good humour. At four o'clock in the morning he awoke with a start. There was a loud clatter from downstairs, as if a door had been thrown open; then a rush of feet up the stairs. A body flung itself at the bedroom door, which creaked open. Edward sat up in terror, peering into the dark, his hand groping for the switch on the bedside lamp, waiting for the cold steel of a knife to pierce his ribcage, or the dull blow of a blunt weapon to crush his skull. Instead, he felt the weight of a sandbag land on his stomach, squeezing the air from his lungs. There was a loud screech, he finally found the light switch, and there it was: he was gazing straight into the green eyes of a huge black and white tomcat with a head the size of a turnip. He was pinned in shock to the bed; the cat stretched forward, claws digging into Edward's chest and, starting to purr, licked his nose with its sandpaper tongue.

'Christ!' he said. 'Where the bloody hell did you come from?'

For what remained of the night, Edward slept fitfully. The cat seemed accustomed to sharing the bed with a human and was adept at curling up in the exact spot where Edward wanted to put his legs. While the cat slept soundly, Edward struggled. At eight o'clock he could suffer it no longer and crawled out of his sleeping bag to smoke his first cigarette of the day. To his surprise the sun was shafting through the gap in the curtains. He threw them aside and gazed out on to the sunlit harbour. It looked almost picturesque. Across the bay he saw the tall white hotel buildings on the west cliff reflecting the morning sun. The sea shimmered blue and, in the breeze, the brightly painted fishing boats swayed gently at their moorings. For the first time since his arrival, he began to notice his surroundings. He saw, for example, that the windows to the bedroom were full length and opened out on to a narrow verandah hanging precariously over the harbour wall. He pushed them open and stepped out into the yellow sunlight of the February morning. He breathed deeply; the salt air tasted good. It was fresher than Kensington by some measure. Then he heard a disembodied voice from below.

'Aye, right,' it said. Edward peered downwards. It was Jim from next door. 'Fine morning.'

'Yes, Jim. I wish I could appreciate it fully. I didn't get much sleep last night. Bloody great cat slept on top of me most of the time.'

'Aye, right,' said Jim. 'I said I 'ad summat for yer. That's Monty. Me sister brought 'im down from farm last night. Been keeping 'im up there since Freddie died. Let 'im out late on. Probably went ratting down in t'arbour. Lucky he didn't drop one on yer. Brought a live seagull 'ome last year. Freddie wasn't pleased. Neither was seagull for that matter.'

'Bloody hell, Jim. Am I supposed to keep him? I hate cats.'

'Aye, right. Not much choice 'ave yer. Comes with cottage.' And with that, Jim spat over the harbour wall and retreated into his house.

Edward looked downwards. Staring up at him was Monty, blinking in the sunshine and wrapping himself round his legs. 'Oh, God,' he said, but couldn't find the coal scuttle to kick.

Later that morning, after half a packet of fags and three cups of coffee, Edward decided he needed fresh air. Jane the waitress had mentioned the abbey on the clifftop so he decided to explore. He strode off up the cobbled street, which became steeper before turning into an enormous flight of steps, one hundred and ninety-nine in all, if the street name was correct, leading up the hill to the top. Halfway up he paused for breath, leaning on the iron rails, his heart pumping.

'Hi, Ed,' he heard from behind him and there she was, six feet tall, in tight jogging kit, earpiece plugged in, skipping up the steps two at a time, and still able to speak.

'Jane, I'm dying,' he said.

'No, you're not. You just need to get fit,' she replied, and danced off up the hill. 'Come on! I'll wait at the top for you!' she shouted over her shoulder.

Edward staggered upwards. Fifteen minutes later he was lying horizontal on a stone slab on top of a Victorian tomb in St Mary's church yard, trying to get his breath. Jane was doing stretches on the grass.

'I wouldn't fall asleep there, if I were you,' she said with a malicious grin. 'That's where Dracula spent his first night on shore.' Edward looked vacant. 'Didn't Eton teach you anything? Leapt ashore as a wolf and turned into a vampire. Bram Stoker.'

'I'm overweight, bad-tempered, and ignorant,' thought Edward. Then out loud he said: 'OK, young miss. I'll take you on. One week from today, I'll race you to the top. Then we'll see.' He regretted it instantly, but such is manliness.

Edward was slowly beginning to learn that the rules for living were changing. Being a futures investor had been like playing a penny arcade machine with somebody else's money. The way to earn millions was by investing billions; the slightest sliver of a market change, if the stake was big enough, could result in a six-figure bonus at the end of the year. When it was good, it was bloody good and, until recently, Edward had found it good. Until that fateful day a year ago when he took his eye off the fruit machine and three bananas suddenly became two with a melon in the middle. But it had, at the end of the day, been all a game. Life was different now: he had a cat to feed. Monty had fallen in love with Edward and Edward had to reciprocate by feeding him. In a strange way, Monty and Edward became a team; they ate together and they slept together. All in all, life had moved on. He had to win a race against a girl fifteen years his younger; and he had a neighbour who spoke to him in the morning. This had never happened in Kensington, where life flowed smoothly and expensively, but here in the north there were more jagged edges.

Edward started to set his mobile to wake him in the morning, cut down on his cigarettes, and dug out his workout gear from his holdall. He ran up and down the steps. The day of his challenge to Jane was approaching and he secretly felt sick at the stupidity of his behaviour. The day before the race, he doubled his training regime. He had been up the steps to the top and down to the bottom and up to the top again. He was feeling OK. Then halfway down he missed a step and turned over on his ankle. The pain was excruciating, like the searing heat of a red-hot poker. He felt his head turning to cotton wool, his eyes glazed over, and he saw the sky turning upside down. Then he passed out. A spectator would have observed a slow sequence of events: a figure in a track suit grabbing his ankle; the head turning to the sky; the crumpling at the knees; a comic forward roll down the steps; and finally the body disappearing into the open doorway of a jewellery shop. For Edward, it felt slightly different. The moment he lost consciousness was a moment of great joy. The pain vanished and he was looking down a tunnel of golden light. It was a world of utter peace and happiness; his troubles were over. He wanted to stay like that forever. Then slowly he began to make out two of the most beautiful eyes he had ever seen, deep brown and almond-shaped; then he smelt an exquisite perfume; and best of all he could feel the warm yielding flesh of two beautiful breasts snuggling down on top of him. 'If this is death,' he thought, 'let me stay dead. I am in heaven.' Then he heard a voice and felt a blow on his cheek.

'Edward, wake up! Look at me! Look at me!'

Edward regained consciousness. He was lying flat out on the floor of the shop and the owner was crouching over him, looking into his eyes.

'I think you've broken your ankle,' she said.

'How did I get here?'

'You just rolled in,' she replied. 'I'll call an ambulance.'

'How did you know my name?' Edward asked.

'Freddie told us you would be coming,' she replied. 'My name's Juliana. Call me Julie.'

'Pleased to meet you, Julie,' he said, before passing out

again.

He woke some time later to find one paramedic holding his legs in the air and another taking his blood pressure.

'You'll be alright, mate. Blood pressure collapsed. Need to get the blood back into your brain.'

The next thing he knew, he was lying in the back of the ambulance on the way to the general hospital for an X-ray. Julie was sitting next to him.

'Thought I'd better come with you,' she said. 'You haven't got anybody, have you?'

Edward looked away. 'No,' he thought with a sudden wave of gloom, 'I haven't.'

Four hours later, Edward hopped on crutches up to his front door. His ankle was in plaster and he was bunged up with pain killers. Julie opened the door and escorted him in. The living room was unrecognisable. The bags that had littered the floor had disappeared, the carpet had been hoovered, the cobwebs and dust had vanished and a bright coal fire burned in the hearth. Monty sat on a cushion on the sofa, blinking. A short round woman came through from the kitchen with a teapot in her hand.

'Who are you?' asked Edward.

'This is Ruby,' answered Julie, before Ruby could speak. 'She's Jim's wife.'

'Just tidied up for you, Mr Ottaway. Used to do for Mr Freddie. There's new bedding for you up the stairs, if you can manage them. Well, I'll be off now,' she said and toddled off to the street door. Edward was dumb-struck but at last found his voice.

'Thank you Ruby. Thank you very much.'

'Aye, right,' she replied, which seemed to be the family motto, and disappeared into the street.

Edward collapsed in the fireside chair and laid his crutches down. Julie poured some tea and handed him a cup.

'You're very lucky, Edward, you know,' she said, with a wicked smile.

'Lucky? You must be joking. I've just broken my ankle!'

'Better than a heart attack, which is what you would have

had if you'd tried to beat Jane up the steps. She's the English Schools high jump champion. At least you got out of that!'

For the first time in an age, Edward laughed out loud, even though it hurt like hell. 'What I don't understand, Julie, is how everybody knows about me. Is this some sort of conspiracy I've wandered into?'

'You mean a carefully constructed plot to get you to fall into my shop? I'll call in tomorrow to see how you're getting on.'

With that she stood up and went out through the street door. Edward was in a daze by the pace of events. He couldn't wait to see what the next day would bring. He hadn't felt like that for a year.

Chapter 3

Juliana had been in business for three years in her little shop on the staircase leading up to the abbey. One half of her front window was given over to simple jewellery in jet, for the tourist trade. She needed to make her money in the summer months to pay the bills in the winter. The other half displayed her real work, which took shape in the back of the shop where she crafted minute and ornate pieces in gold and silver, working to commissions. These, however, were few and far between. She had an exquisite artistic talent and a lively imagination, which had made her a star student at the Glasgow School of Art, but were less influential in earning her a living in the harsher climate of the marketplace. Her most regular customer had been Freddie Ottaway, who commissioned pieces twice a year, paid for them, and then gave them back to Juliana so that she could sell them on at a large profit. He had been her true sponsor. But he had walked through the door on two legs, unlike his nephew, who had rolled in sideways.

Juliana thought she had better look in on Edward that morning. It was a breezy February day. The herring gulls wheeled noisily overhead and across the harbour she watched a swarm of them follow a fishing boat into its berth. She didn't expect to find Edward up and about but, to her surprise, a push on the front door yielded an entry. Edward was sitting by the fireplace with his foot up on a stool.

'How are you, Edward?' she asked. 'Sleep alright?'

'Not bad, thanks, Julie. And thanks for yesterday. You couldn't make me a cup of tea, could you?'

'Of course,' she replied, and threw a teabag into a mug. 'You know there's a scrunched up packet of Silk Cut on the worktop here.'

'Given up,' he replied.

She looked at him sideways. 'Not Jane's influence, I

hope.'

'In a way. But I'm not about to chase an eighteen-year-old, if that's what you think. Jane will need a combination of Superman and Einstein to keep her happy. Just thought it was about time to make a fresh start. Forget about London. That's over with. Got to move on. My near-death experience showed me a whole new other world. I've seen the other side and returned,' he added with mock mystery.

'And you've got a cat.'

The kettle had boiled and Julie handed him his tea. She sat down opposite him on the other side of the fireplace. For the first time Edward was able to study her at his leisure, outside of his supernatural encounter of the previous day. She was really beautiful. Her eyes were as tender as he had noted in his semi-conscious state, dark and soft. She was as graceful as a tulip and as slender. And she spoke with a delightful northern accent, quiet and flat toned. He felt himself slipping.

'Tell me about Freddie. He was my uncle but I never knew him. Jane called him a gem.'

'She's right,' Julie said. 'Freddie was everything rolled up in one person. He was kind, generous, funny. He looked after all of us. Kept my business afloat in the bad times. Picked Jim out of the gutter more than once; and made sure Jane knew what ambition could achieve for the daughter of a fish and chip shop owner. We all loved him.'

'I knew he was an artist but I never saw any of his work.'

'The tourist shops in the town are full of Ottaways – seascapes, fishing boats, cliff tops with abbeys on them. They sell pretty well. But that was only his income, what he called his fripperies. He once told me he couldn't paint honestly any more. I think he meant he had no soul left to put into his work. A strange thing to say and I often wondered if that's what he meant. He never expanded on it.'

'Perhaps something happened, in his life,' said Edward.

'Maybe. I often felt there was a hidden side to Freddie. Now, can you walk on those crutches?' Julie asked abruptly.

'I think so, slowly.'

'Good. It's a fine Yorkshire day by the sea and I'm going

to show you the town. Don't worry, we're not going far.'

Julie took his arm and helped him up, handed him his crutches, steered him out of the door and down the street towards the swing bridge linking the two halves of the town that faced each other across the harbour. She put her arm in his and together they made steady progress. On each side of the narrow street stood ancient asymmetrical cottages, leaning and balancing against each other, soft sandstone facings eroded by the salty gales off the sea. And there was no traffic.

'You still haven't told me how you all knew I was coming,' he said, as he hobbled along.

'Freddie said you would, that's all.'

'What did he tell you about me?'

'That you were his nephew. He asked us to look after you,' she added with a smile. But for the life of him, Edward could not work it out. Freddie had hardly known him.

When they reached the swing bridge over the Esk, flowing onwards into the grey North Sea between the sandstone moles of the harbour, Edward had to stop to rest, leaning on the balustrade in the sunshine. He turned to Julie and said: 'You know, Julie, this is really very beautiful. When I left London I thought this place would be a hell-hole. But actually my life in London was crap all along. I was never any bloody good at it.'

'So what do you think you *are* good at? Everybody's good at something.'

'I haven't found it yet, I suppose.'

'Come on. Better get you back before you become too philosophical. We'll stop at *The Caedmon* for a cup of coffee. You never know, you might be able to feast your eyes on Jane in her black leggings. Her Dad tells me business has perked up since she started working there, mostly old chaps.'

It was only a short haul to the restaurant but it was uphill and a struggle on a pair of crutches. Edward flopped down on the first chair he could find, leg stuck out in front of him, just as Jane breezed through from the back.

'Good God! What happened to you, Ed?' she asked.

'He was practising a Fosbury Flop down the abbey steps,'

said Julie with comic malice. 'Broke his ankle and ended up in my shop. You must stop egging these men on Jane.'

'So our race is off?'

'I'm afraid so,' said Edward. 'My career as an athlete was short-lived.'

'Never mind, Ed. I'll bring you some coffee and a jam doughnut. How does that sound?'

'It should help reduce the pain, slightly.'

Later that day Edward found himself alone in the cottage. Julie had disappeared back to her shop but Ruby popped in from time to time to see he was still alive and there was a constant flow of tea and cakes. A brown pot appeared around five o'clock, which Edward took to be tea-time in the north. He lifted the lid and saw two large dollops of something floating in a sea of thick gravy and lumps of meat.

'Beef stew with dumplings,' said Ruby. 'That'll sort yer.'

'Thank you very much, Ruby. Much appreciated,' replied Edward but, to be honest, Monty showed greater interest in getting his head into the pot than Edward did. Still, Edward was moved by all of this. These people were treating him as if he were a novelty from another world, an exotic creature from another clime, to be looked at, humoured, but essentially inferior. Nevertheless, he felt safe and, above all, wanted. He remembered Julie's statement: but did he really need looking after? Perhaps he did. After all, he hadn't distinguished himself in his chosen career. With much effort he struggled to his feet, wobbling across the floor on his crutches. Over the fireplace was a mirror with the silver faded and in it he caught the reflection of his face. He looked at it carefully, as if he had never seen it before. *Was he really such a failure?* He had always thought of himself as *à la mode* in the city. He had strong blonde hair, parted on the left, which flopped over his well-bred forehead, rather like Boris Johnson's; he wore striped shirts with braces; and at weekends turned up at The Stoop in cavalry twills and Barbour to consume pints of Fuller's *London Pride* while Harlequins knocked hell out of London Irish. But in this mirror he looked different. His trousers were too tight and a roll of belly flopped over his belt; he had acquired another chin to add to the original; and his face was a florid red. He looked thirty-three going on fifty. Perhaps he was a loser after all.

His spirits were in the descendant at these thoughts. He longed for a cigarette, but Julie had helpfully thrown them in the bin which Ruby had emptied that morning. He took a turn round the room. By the window overlooking the harbour stood a small writing desk with two drawers. He pulled one open. Inside was a clutter of pens, paper clips, and bits of paper. A bottle of Quink had turned into powder over the years since fountain pens had last been in fashion. He opened the second. Among the detritus of a man's private bits and pieces was an old exercise book. He picked it up and the pages fell open, a litter of newspaper cuttings falling on to the desk top. Prominent among them was a cutting from *The Financial Times* which Edward recognised immediately. The painful memory hit him like someone stamping on an old wound: *City investor in futures scandal; HB Index loses £50m overnight.* Edward did not read on; he knew the story from the inside: the painful appearances in front of the chief executive, before he learned he had escaped with only a lost job; the hasty enforced exit from the glass and steel office tower, with only a cardboard box; handing in his pass and keys at the front desk. But most shocking of all was that Uncle Freddie knew all about it and more, actually seemed to care enough to give his unknown failure of a nephew a house to live in and a set of unpaid guardians to hold his hand. He had always had a yearning to find out about the elusive Uncle Freddie but he had never thought it would look like this. He felt ashamed: he'd had all the chances and he'd cocked it up, sloping off to a champagne bar on a Thursday night and forgetting to get back before the end of trading. He really was a fool. By the time he remembered the stew, Monty had picked out all the meat, but left the dumplings. He could not face trekking down the road on his crutches for fish and chips so he resigned himself to an abstemious night at home. He felt a deep creeping gloom around him; life seemed to be taking one step forward and two backwards. I must improve, he said to himself. He found a piece of notepaper in a desk drawer and sat down, like Gatsby, to write himself some rules. When he had finished he propped up the note behind a candlestick on the mantelpiece so that he would see it first thing in the morning and remember to do better. The rules were:

1. *Stay a non-smoker*
2. *Stop using four-letter words*
3. *Get thin*
4. *Find something to be good at.*

Edward did not realise it then, but this was the first time in his life he had ever set himself a target. But it wasn't going to be easy. The next morning he slept in and only surfaced late in the morning. As he woke, he felt grim, his ankle aching and throbbing.

'Christ, I need a fucking fag,' he said out loud.

'Well, that's two rules broken already,' came a voice.

Edward craned his neck to look around him; Julie was standing by the bedroom door.

'Brought you some tea,' she said. 'Couldn't help seeing your four commandments on the mantelpiece. But never you mind, Edward, it's a good start!'

'It's time I grew up, Julie.'

'You're probably right. Drink your tea.'

Juliana was twenty-eight years old. She had lived in her tiny flat above the shop in Henrietta Street for three years. Her father had named her Juliana because he was an Anglo-Saxonist and Juliana meant "youthful" in Anglo-Saxon. He had learned this while studying Old English at London University at the end of the seventies. He had shown a particular talent in poking about in the deeper recesses of *Beowulf*, even better at analysing the various shades of meaning of "tulke" in *Sir Gawain and the Grene Knight,* and on this recommendation had found himself teaching Middle English and Anglo-Saxon literature at Hull University. A junior lecturer's salary was very small and he could only afford to buy a little brick house on the south bank of the Humber between Barnetby-le-Wold and Scunthorpe. Admittedly, this was not the most glamorous part of the world, but the sunrise was early over the flat eastern plains and the sky was wide open. Moreover, Doctor Allington could drive very easily over the Humber Bridge to deliver his lectures and classes to the eager students of Hull and return, in the evenings, looking southwards across the flatlands of Lincolnshire where Anglo-Saxon began. He felt at home. But Juliana preferred pictures and shapes to alliterative verse. Her paintings and drawings always took pride of place at the annual school art show, where she had fallen in love with the silver-haired head of the art department at the age of fifteen, and had been pursued into the art stockroom by a long-haired twenty-two-year-old art teacher when she was seventeen. At eighteen, after one-too-many Harvey Wallbangers at an ill-judged *soirée* following her A Level exams, her friends had persuaded her to enter the *Miss Scunthorpe* competition advertised in the window of the local newsagent. She won, hands down. Her local reputation thus destroyed, she fled to Glasgow to study real art. And she made beautiful things in silver and gold. She was tall, with shiny dark hair and soft brown eyes. It was not difficult for her teachers to grade her work highly.

One morning, a lifetime later, she was bent over her workbench in the tiny back room, when a body rolled through the front shop doorway. It seemed to be dead. She put down her soldering iron and quickly went across to the corpse. It was breathing but its eyes were closed. She bent down and put her head to its chest, her breasts brushing the face. It was still alive. She gently slapped the man's cheek.

'Edward, wake up! Look at me! Look at me!' she shouted.

The eyes opened slowly and a relaxed smile gradually spread across the face. So this was Edward, she thought. Freddie had told me he might be coming. No one else could have rolled in that way. She dialled 999 to call the ambulance and, while she waited for the paramedics to arrive, she held Edward's hand and looked into his eyes to try to keep him conscious. He had a nice face, she thought, if a little podgy, and two light blue eyes sitting beneath a flop of blonde hair. He looked a bit red in the face but, on the whole, he was presentable. Then his eyes rolled upwards into his skull and he was gone again. She wondered what to do next. An image came to mind of Trevor Howard, emerging from the steam of the up-train, wielding a pristine white handkerchief in the blinking eye of Celia Johnson, saying 'Stand aside. I am a doctor'. Then the paramedics arrived, hoisted his legs in the air, and the podgy face came to life again. But it was far from love at first sight. Juliana Allington had had enough love at first sight to last a lifetime.

But things can change. A month is a short time in the history of the world, just enough for it to turn on its axis thirty times or so, for the sun to get higher in the sky, for the seasons to change from winter to spring and for the green things of the earth to return. More importantly, it was long enough for Edward to kick off his plaster; walk up and down the abbey steps, once a day, then twice, then thrice; for his trousers to get loose round his waist; for his double chin to become single once more; and for him to fall head-over-heels in love with Juliana. He still craved for tobacco, but that was receding, and he still used the 'F' word, but only silently and in a contemplative fashion. But he hadn't found the words to say anything to Julie.

Then one day something happened that changed everything. Edward's rule number four had said: *find something to be good at.* This had been a difficult precept to follow, rather like not coveting your neighbour's goods when he has just bought an Aston Martin, and for a while Edward thought of crossing it off the list as just too demanding. But at last he thought he had succeeded. Julie had told him about Uncle Freddie's *fripperies* that could be found in the tourist shops in the town, easy-going watercolours and acrylics of the harbour, Caedmon playing a harp with the wind in his hair, or the abbey in the sunset, or the *Stella Maris* setting sail into the rising sun. So, with walking stick in hand, he set off one morning down Church Street, across the swing bridge, past *The Smugglers* pub and through the fish market. Between the amusement arcade and the seats at the end of the west pier, just before *Gypsy Rose's Parlour*, he found a glittery, blingy little shop full of the kind of junk that trippers want to take home with them; and half a window full of Ottaways in gilt frames, selling at knock-down prices before the summer holidays arrived. The shop was owned by a stringy middle-aged fellow, with nicotine-stained fingers from too many roll-ups, and worry beads round his wrist. He was more than happy to knock a few quid off the Ottaway Edward chose: it was a fishing boat heading out to sea. It was like the front cover of *The People's Friend* : cosy and comforting. 'I could do that,' thought Edward. So he bought a box of watercolours, some heavy paper, and a bundle of paintbrushes.

Later that day, he was sitting with the french windows thrown open, looking across the mouth of the Esk, paintbrush in hand. He was making a mess of the sea.

'Let me help you with that,' said Julie, who had entered unannounced, pulling up a kitchen chair to sit down beside him. 'Do it like this,' she said, guiding his hand in light sweeps across the paper, but by this time Edward had lost himself, his head had been turned sideways by some invisible force, and he was drawn irresistibly towards the goddess seated beside him. He leaned across and gently kissed her ear.

'You have the most beautiful lobes,' he said.

At last he had found the words he had been searching for. Julie did not react at first; she thought he had said "globes" but then, he had kissed her ear, which suggested it had been "lobes". This was the only time she had been wooed aurally but the experience was not unpleasant.

'Do you always kiss girls on their ears?' she asked.

'No. I don't think I've done it before, in fact,' he replied. 'Would you like me to kiss you somewhere else? It's just that your ear was handy. And beautiful.'

'Well, why not kiss me somewhere else,' she replied.

The debate lasted only seconds longer. Edward was decisive and Juliana receptive. Their heads came together against the background of a failed seascape. In the weeks that followed, Edward's watercolour technique improved by leaps and bounds. He painted dramatic waves breaking on rocky coasts; ragged clouds racing across windswept headlands; ruined choirs with the setting sun shafting through broken archways; and valiant fishing boats butting against the fierce North Sea. He had found something he was good at; and he had found someone he loved; and the coincidence of the two seemed to him miraculous. Not only had his artistic repertoire widened, he had also kissed Juliana in several different places. He threw away his list of life rules.

As for Juliana, she had never meant it to be this way. But she was content enough to drift into the deeps with Edward without worrying too much about the direction in which their little voyage was taking them. Monty's nose was often put out of joint when he discovered there was no room for him in the bed while, on other occasions, he had the bed all to himself. The residents of Henrietta Street were not deceived. Ruby had predicted the course of events a while ago while Jim had used the family motto to agree with her. Jane, who knew how the world worked, was above it all. By the time summer came, Edward had gathered together a collection of watercolours which he framed using a clever little tool he had bought from Screwfix. He used a sophisticated pricing scheme: big ones £20, little ones £10. He displayed a few in Julie's window and, to his surprise, had to replenish them regularly. Julie thought they weren't half bad. Edward wondered if he had inherited something from Uncle Freddie, as well as the cottage, that is. He had never been so happy in his life.

One morning in May, Edward set off in his car to buy a cat basket. He had not driven his clapped-out tin Peugeot much since his arrival in Whitby and not at all during his enforced inactivity with the broken ankle. The car had spent most of the time since February in the gap between the cottages in Henrietta Street and the salt air from the sea had turned the tiny stone chips on the bodywork into rusty blotches. In the old days he would never have held on to a car for more than two years; and he wouldn't have been seen dead in anything as feeble as a 206. But the old days had gone and he viewed the rusting heap as a kind of triumph over the self-indulgence of his past life. He remembered what a miserable bastard he had been when he first realised he had no money. Now he was a thin non-smoker, happy to be driving a rusty car, rejoicing in the simple life of the artist.

The journey to buy the cat basket had a story attached. Monty was fretting: he had become jealous of Juliana when he was kicked out of Edward's bed. And then he seemed to pine when Edward disappeared up the street to spend the night above the jewellery shop. He displayed his misery, when Edward was not looking, by spraying vertical objects in the cottage: table legs, curtains, wellie boots. He once sprayed Edward's trousers when they were hanging on the back of a chair, a fact that only came to light when Edward emptied the bar of *The Smugglers*. Jane, who was well-informed on animal psychology, suggested that Monty needed a place to call his own, as he was clearly suffering an identity crisis. And so the idea was born that he needed a designer cat basket. But for Edward, the issue was more pressing than that: he could not possibly persuade Julie to move in with him unless the problem of Monty had been addressed. The fact that he had not considered tying a brick round his neck and chucking him in the harbour showed how far Edward had progressed from his rugby club days in London.

Edward had taken Jane with him, as a sort of basket

consultant, and she sat next to him as they headed out of town to *Pets at Home* in Pickering. Julie was working on a commission in her shop and Jane had a day off. He wanted to pick her brains.

'How long have you lived in Whitby, Jane?' he asked, as they drove up the hill out of the town.

'All my life,' she replied. 'That's eighteen years.'

'And your Dad?'

'All his life in Eskdale. That's fifty years. But only in Whitby since I was born, I suppose.'

'What can you tell me about Freddie? I've really begun to be fascinated by him. He's a complete mystery to me and I'm his nephew. What did he look like, for example?'

Jane turned her head towards him. 'Well, he looked like you, Ed. That's why everybody knew who you were when you first came here. Freddie had told us you would be coming. But when you did appear, there was no doubt who you were.'

'But why would he tell everybody I would be coming? He didn't know me.'

There was a long pause. The car had cleared the outskirts of the town and was rolling along through the bracken-clad hills. Jane seemed uncomfortable about something. At last she spoke. 'He told us you were in trouble. That you were to get the cottage when he died. We all assumed you were coming here. That's why we weren't in the least surprised to see you.'

'Did he say what kind of trouble?'

'No, but the story was money trouble. From what you told me, it was kind of true, wasn't it.'

'Kind of. Fifty million kind of true.'

'You should talk to my Dad. He knew Freddie from way back, when he first landed up here.'

'Thanks Jane. I will.'

Edward knew it wasn't fair to lumber Jane with too many deep questions. She *was* a genius but she was only eighteen and had her own life to worry about, although that seemed to be going swimmingly. In Pickering they bought a fancy *pied à terre* for Monty and stopped off for lunch on the way back at a pub on the moors. Edward could feel the eyes looking at

Jane as they walked in. 'Hope they think I'm her father,' he said to himself, 'and not some old letch.'

They were back in Henrietta Street by three in the afternoon. Jane could sense that this was a moment of truth for Edward.

'I hope this works,' he said, looking round the room for the most desirable location for Monty's place-to-call-his-own. 'If he doesn't go for this, my future will be in doubt. Our relationship will be off.'

'With Julie, or the cat?' Jane asked, with that sophisticated smile that showed how much she really knew.

'Possibly both,' replied Edward.

As it happened, the plan was a success. Monty was coaxed into his new basket and slept there for a day, only emerging to catch harbour rats when the sun went down. Juliana was no longer a threat to Edward's relationship with his cat. That evening, he cooked supper for her. They were sitting on a battered sofa with their feet on the coffee table, drinking wine, while the pasta came to the boil.

'What would you do if you had to choose between me and Monty?' she asked.

The question was never answered but left hanging in the air, as Edward went to stir the bolognese. The fact was he was happy to have both. 'I don't answer hypothetical questions,' he said, which for him was surprisingly subtle. Julie seemed satisfied.

Later that evening, Julie put down her sketch pad, where she had been planning a new piece for a very promising client, and looked across the fireplace at Edward. He had been very quiet for some time. 'What's up, Edward?' she asked. 'Not like you to be so lost in thought. Anything the matter?'

'I asked Jane about Freddie today. She said you all knew it was me because I looked like him.'

'Well, you do. There's nothing wrong with that. Freddie was *quite* handsome.'

'But that could be how he knew about me, don't you see.'

'You mean, he might have seen a photograph of you. How would he do that? You said you and he had no contact.'

26

'But I *was* in the papers, wasn't I!'

Edward stood up and went across to the writing desk and pulled out the exercise book. He shuffled through the cuttings he had discovered a long time ago. He read again the *FT* article; there was no picture of him. But then, stuck in the back of the exercise book was another, from the *Sunday Telegraph* finance pages.

'Look at this,' he said, handing the cutting to Julie. She looked at it and saw in the newspaper photograph the face that she had come to know so well.

'Poor Ed,' she said, 'you look lost.'

'I was,' he replied.

She stood up, put her arms round him and kissed him. 'Don't think about it. You made a mess but it's over. You're a different guy now.'

'I hope so. But maybe that's how he found me, eh?'

'Of course. He must have known your name. He might have known you worked in the city. You look just like him and you're called Ottaway. How did you learn about the will from the solicitor?'

'Come to think of it, I got a call to my mobile from one of the office secretaries. That's it! The solicitor only had my office address from Freddie. That's *how* he did it. But I still don't know *why* he did it.'

Julie began to feel impatient. 'Tell me Ed, why are you so interested to find out?'

'Because,' and he hesitated as if embarrassed by the admission, 'I'm not used to people giving me anything. Where I come from it was take-take, not give-give. What do you think it was like, working in the city? Bloody jungle!'

'Come down from your tree then and give me a kiss, on my ear if you like.' She was laughing at him inside but she knew what he wanted and she sympathised. 'OK, Edward. Tomorrow we shall start to think about what to do.'

Tomorrow was Saturday. The sun was shining and the summer visitors were beginning to flow. The winkle stalls appeared by the fish market and you could buy little paper bags of pink shrimps and plastic tubs of cockles in vinegar.

The fishing boats were home for the weekend and they lay moored, two or three abreast, against the harbour wall. The swing bridge opened to let the yachts from the new marina head out to the sea for the weekend regatta. Whitby was bustling.

Edward had woken first and got up to make the tea and reassure Monty that he still loved him. Juliana was slower to become human. She poked her head above the bed clothes to greet the day.

'We need to think,' he said, as he handed over the mug of tea.

'Not yet, Edward. Too early. I'm going to take you somewhere special today, where we can think,' she said.

'What exactly are we thinking about, by the way?'

'Oh, whatever we were talking about last night.'

Later that morning they set off along the footpath leading out of town along the side of the Esk. After half a mile or so the path left the river bank, cut across a couple of fields deep in early summer wheat, and emerged in a little village with a mill and a weir.

'Where are we?' asked Edward.

'This is Ruswarp,' said Juliana. 'I used to spend my summer holidays here when I was a kid. My uncle has the boat hire business. Can you row?'

'I was the coxless pairs champion at Eton,' replied Edward.

'That's a "yes" then?'

Juliana's Uncle George was a leathery middle-aged man in empire shorts. He greeted Julie with open arms and shook Edward's hand vigorously.

'Got your favourite boat for you Julie,' he said, as he hauled a varnished wooden skiff up to the landing stage. 'You've always had *Primrose* for as long as I can remember.'

The sun shimmered on the dimpled surface of the river. A dipper skimmed inches above the water and moorhens and mallards paddled around the tree roots that reached down into the darkness. The willows and aspen fanned out in the breeze; summer flies hovered; and lazy trout rose to the surface, leaving gentle concentric rings. Juliana lay back in the boat, her hair blowing and her hand trailing in the water. Edward rowed smoothly, rejoicing in the heaven that was the world he now lived in, a surprisingly successful seaside artist, with his beautiful girl. Life was complete. He could hear the sound of harps as the minstrels made their way to Camelot.

'You should talk to Dan,' Julie suddenly said.

'Who's Dan?'

'Jane's Dad. He knew Freddie longer than anybody.'

'OK. Is that our thinking over? That's what Jane said.'

'She would.'

Edward rowed on, the prow of the skiff cutting smoothly through the water, and round a bend in the river they drew to a halt under a leaning sycamore that dipped its boughs into the river. A dappled light fell upon them through the rippling leaves. The rest was the stuff of dreams.

The sun was beginning to descend in the sky and the air above the river was warm as Edward rowed them slowly back to the landing stage. A boy appeared from the wooden shed that served as an office and, on their approach, seized the painter and pulled the skiff gently into land. He handed Julie ashore.

'Grandad says call in for tea,' said the boy. This was George's grandson, who earned pocket money working on the boats at the weekend and during school holidays.

Juliana took Edward's arm and together they walked along the narrow country road by the side of the river. A quarter of a mile from the landing stage they came to a white cottage with a small lawn leading down to the water's edge. A garden path led round the side of the building to the river. There, under a parasol shading a garden table and chairs, Uncle George sat reading a paper and smoking his pipe.

'Julie, my dear,' he said, rising to his feet. 'Come along in. And Edward, isn't it? Come and have some tea.'

Uncle George was sixty-five years old, with a thick mop of totally white hair and a sun-tanned face from his outdoor life. His khaki shorts gave him the air of a Second World War army officer in the desert campaign. He was lean and wiry.

Julie and Edward sat down and at that moment a woman appeared from the door of the house with a tea tray and a cake, setting it down and departing without speaking. Julie showed no sign of surprise, so Edward followed suit. George poured the tea and handed round the cake.

'Now, Edward, what brings you to this neck of the woods?' began George.

'Well, I've just moved into a cottage in Whitby, a couple of doors down from Julie, which I inherited from my uncle. A bit of an escape from London, in fact. You might have heard of my uncle, Freddie Ottaway. He painted pictures.'

'Of course, everybody around here has heard of him. So you are an Ottaway too? And do you paint?'

'Just learning,' replied Edward, 'with Julie's help.'

There was a pause, while Julie topped up the tea cups. Then George spoke.

'You say you inherited a cottage in Henrietta Street. But what about Angelus House?' he said.

'What's Angelus House?' asked Julie.

'It's where Freddie lived before he moved to Henrietta Street. It probably got a bit remote as he got older, I suppose, and he felt he should live in the town. I'm talking about twenty years ago. As far as I know, he never sold it. Last time I was over that way, it was looking a bit ramshackle. It's up the top of the moor beyond Egton. You should take a drive there. It's beautiful country. Here, I'll show you on the map.'

George shot off into the house. While he was gone, Julie turned to Edward, whispering: 'That's his hobby. He's written the definite guidebook on the domestic architecture of north Yorkshire. Published it himself. Medieval latrines to Victorian almshouses. It's all there. Loves it. He used to be an architect. The woman's his girlfriend. Say nothing! He thinks the family don't know! But she's not his housekeeper.'

George reappeared with an Ordnance Survey map, spread it on the table and with his leathery hand pointed out Angelus House. 'Local legend has it there was a religious community there in the tenth century, but I've never found any evidence for that,' he said.

'You say this was Freddie's property?' said Edward, 'but I heard nothing about it from the solicitor. That's strange.'

'We should take a look,' said Julie.

'Why don't you go now. It's not more than half an hour away and it's a beautiful day for a drive in the country,' said George.

'But my car is in Whitby. We walked here this morning,' Edward replied.

'Borrow mine,' said George.

He took them round to the other side of the house and flung open a pair of rickety garage doors. Inside were two cars, an XJ6 and beside that Edward saw the long low bonnet of an English sports car, British racing green, with the hood down.

'It's my Spitfire,' George said. 'The keys are in it. It gets me from A to B – most of the time,' he added with a grin.

It was a glorious day to be driving in the English countryside with the top down. The rush of warm air drowned out the sound of the engine and it felt as if they were gliding, except for the times when they bottomed out in a hollow in the road, or when the back end worked hard to hold on as they careered round a sharp bend. Most alarming of all, was the feeling of flying, when the long bonnet seemed to point to the sky as the car reached the crest of a rise. Hedgerows rich in hawthorn, elder and dog-roses rushed by, often rising high above the cockpit, as the narrow road followed the route of a medieval sunken cart track. After thirty minutes of lurching, shaking and cornering they reached the hill up to Egton Grange, a single-track road rising steeply upwards and upwards. Edward flung the car into second gear and put his foot down. The trees cleared, the hedges receded and the wide blue sky of the moors opened before them. There, up a pot-holed track, behind a five-barred gate, stood Angelus House in all its dilapidated glory. There was a sign that read: "Private. Keep Out."

'I wonder if I own this,' said Edward.

'Perhaps you're a medieval squire,' suggested Julie.

'More likely the bastard son of the abbot.'

Julie had been right when she said that Saturday would be a good day to do their thinking about Uncle Freddie. But the simple question of *why* Freddie had deposited his limited assets on an unknown nephew had become a lot more complicated by Uncle George's revelation about Angelus House. An element of real mystery had been introduced. The question now was why Freddie appeared not to have endowed Edward with *all* his property; from having been truly generous but on a small scale, he might actually turn out to be truly mean on a large scale.

The *Private Keep Out* sign had immediately encouraged both Julie and Edward to bound over the five-barred gate like gazelles, in their enthusiasm to explore what was, in truth, a rather plain-looking Yorkshire stone house from the early nineteenth century, albeit now infused with the frisson of the unknown. It stood on a green hill above the gate and the track took a wide curve before coming to a stop before the front door. At five hundred feet above sea level, it was not an ideal location for a garden, although there were the remains of flower beds in front of the house. Most of the vegetation was overgrown shrubs and wind-bent Scots pine and hawthorn. A copse of stunted firs stood away to the east of the house and a small stream trickled down the slope, seeking a route to the Esk in the valley below and onwards to the sea. Sheep had penetrated the fence around the property and the grass was close-cropped.

Julie and Edward walked slowly up the track to the front door. They didn't know what they were looking for but nevertheless they could not resist the temptation. The weather-beaten oak door, with massive iron ring handle, was locked tight and surprisingly the front windows on either side had survived the weather and intruders. They slowly wandered round the back of the house. There an ugly single-storey extension, of the kind added in modern times, stuck out brazenly. The side door was off its hinges and Edward levered it open.

'In here, Julie,' he shouted over his shoulder, disappearing inside. Julie followed, grabbing his hand, and pushing up close in fear of the unknown that might be shadowing her in the gloomy interior. They pressed forward intrepidly. The scullery was unremarkable, with twin stone sinks from the 1920s. The kitchen was a relic of seventies bad taste, with sharp-edged flat-pack wall units, brown tiles and a stainless steel sink. Cork tiles still stuck to the floor with their edges curling up in the damp. Tongued-and-grooved panelling, daubed with polyurethane varnish, closed off awkward corners. Next came the living room, with windows on two sides, to the east looking across to the distant blue sea and to the north across the Esk valley to the Cleveland Hills.

'Look at this,' said Julie, pointing to the floor. There below them, on the bare boards, were splashes of paint in profusion. 'This is where Freddie must have painted,' she said. 'It makes sense of course; light from all angles and wonderful views.'

'Let's go upstairs,' said Edward.

A narrow winding staircase led to the first floor. There was no grandeur, simply a curved handrail bolted to the walls in brass rings, opening on to a small square landing with four bedrooms extending from each corner. Three were nondescript but in the fourth Edward felt something was unusual. He paused, silent.

'What strikes you about this room?' he asked after a while.

Julie looked around her but could see nothing out of the ordinary.

'Count the sockets,' said Edward. 'Look at them. I've counted eight double sockets. There must have been a reason to supply so much power to this room. Why? What's been going on?'

Julie looked vacant. She was excused from making an ill-informed reply by a scuttling noise from downstairs. A sense of trespass froze her solid. She looked at Edward. Before she could speak he had clattered down the stairs and back the way they had come.

'Edward! Don't leave me,' she shouted, feeling the primeval fear of the child left alone in a dark bedroom when something goes clunk in the night. Then her instinct kicked in, telling her to get out into the sunshine as quickly as she could. She tumbled down the stairs, hurled herself through the ground floor rooms and out through the rickety back door. She tripped over the threshold and fell headlong into the arms of the returning Edward. He held her tight against him for a minute. When she had caught her breath, she said: 'Edward, what was that?'

'Gloucester Old Spot, or might have been an English Middle-White. Definitely not a Tamworth.'

'What on earth are you talking about?'

'Pigs,' replied Edward, 'there's a flock of them in the field at the back.'

'Flock? Do they fly?' said Julie.

'In the city I often saw pigs flying. That's probably why I never made a fortune. Come on. Let's get out of here. There's something strange about this place.'

They drove back to Ruswarp through the blazing afternoon, leaving the car with George and promising to return soon. It was six in the evening before they had crossed the golden wheat fields beside the footpath to Whitby. As they walked alongside the widening Esk, herons flapped clumsily into the sky, mobbed by the gulls. The tide was out and the mudflats along the river estuary glistened in the dying light of the sun. The yachts had returned to their marina moorings long ago and the harbour pubs were filling with yachties in need of refreshment. That night, in the romantic light of the *Pearl Dragon* Chinese restaurant, across a platter of *dim sum*, Edward held Julie's hand and looked into her deep brown eyes. She was stuffing a dumpling into her mouth at the very moment that Edward found his true voice and told her he loved her.

On Sunday, Juliana moved in with Edward. Monty looked

a little downcast.

On Monday, Edward phoned Scrivener, the York solicitor. 'How do I find out who owns a house?' he asked.

'You mean you want to buy it?' asked Scrivener.

'No, I want to find out if I already own it,' replied Edward.

Scrivener thought Edward had lost his marbles. There was a long pause. 'Surely you would know that yourself, wouldn't you?' he replied.

'Well, I don't. It's called Angelus House and it's above the village of Egton Bridge.'

'Leave it with me. I'll have a look at the Land Registry and get back to you,' and the phone went down quickly.

Edward decided it was time to talk to Dan Martin, Jane's father. It is a miracle of human life that, while two wrongs never make a right, two little fat people can make a six-foot supermodel like Jane. That was the thought that passed through Edward's mind as Molly led him through to the back room of the *Caedmon* where Dan was tidying up. Monday was a day off, after the weekend tidal wave of fish teas, and Jane had said it would be a good time to talk to her Dad. Edward was becoming desperate to fill in the gaps about the enigma that was Freddie.

'Aye, I've known Freddie all my life,' Dan started. 'I owe him everything. Gave me the money to rent this place for the first couple of years. Till we started to make a go of it. That was in the eighties, if I remember right. Yes, must have been 1987.'

'What did you do before then, Dan?'

'I was born in Egton, you see, so I've known Angelus House since I can remember. Us kids used to play all around there on the hills. Can't remember a time when Freddie wasn't there. I seemed to have grown up with him. Used to see him outside in the good weather, always painting. Or walking the moors.'

'Did he live there on his own?'

'He had a dog − border collie − and his sheep. Aye, wasn't a sheep farmer but he taught himself to keep sheep. Rented a couple of hundred acres of moors off the Grange lot. Built up quite a nice little flock of Black Faces. Crossed them with Suffolks later on. That's when I got a job.'

'You worked for him?'

'Aye. Used to keep the garden beds in those days and work with the sheep. Helped out at lambing, that kind of thing. It were great. Not much money but I liked it. But he gave it up just before I came here. Too much for him, I expect. Moved to the town, to your place now. I followed him here. That's when I rented this place and got married to Molly. Wouldn't have coped without him. No jobs around really.'

'Did he ever mention me?' asked Edward.

'Not that I can remember. But he did have a visit from his brother, only once though.'

'His brother?' Edward stopped to think. 'How do you know it was his brother?'

'Looked like him. Looked like you as well. But you're more like Freddie. Spitting image in fact. Stayed a couple of days. Freddie painted his portrait.'

'How do you know that, Dan?' asked Edward, becoming more and more intrigued.

'Cos he gave me it before he died. Had a whole pile of them. Said to choose one. So I did. Liked the pier in the background.'

'Do you still have it?'

'Aye, it's on living room wall. Come up and have a look.'

Edward followed Dan up the narrow staircase to the tiny flat above the restaurant. There, on the wall above the fireplace, against the background of the east pier, he saw the face of his father looking down upon him.

'Good God!' he exclaimed. 'So Dad knew where Freddie was all along. Can you remember when his brother visited him?'

'Well, Molly were pregnant, I seem to recall. Our Jane's eighteen, so it must have been 1987. Why?'

'Oh, just interested, Dan.'

As Edward walked back home his mind was racing. He was doing his sums. In 1987 he was fifteen years old, second year at Eton. In 1988 his father went bankrupt, the metal-bashing business which had sustained the Ottaways for a century, finally succumbing to the competition from the far east. A year later he was dead. Mother had had to sell up and move down market. There was no money. And yet, as Edward now realised for the first time, somebody kept paying the school fees. His father must have gone to see Freddie to tell him he was bust; and he must have asked Freddie to see him through school. He knew he was dying and had no means of raising any cash. Freddie had saved Juliana's business, given Dan a livelihood, seen Jane pointed in the right direction and now baled out Edward.

Halfway up Henrietta Street a small square opened out with a view of the harbour. It had been an old fish market. Edward wandered aimlessly towards the harbour wall and sat down on a metal capstan. He seemed to sit for ages, looking at the shining water, soaking in the peace of it all. But at the back of his mind there was a nagging thought: while he had been mucking about wasting his chances, Freddie was watching him from a distance, ready to help him through.

Edward felt a hand on his shoulder and he awoke from his dream. It was Julie.

'Why are you sitting here like a little lost boy?' she asked.

'You remember my saying it was time I grew up?' said Edward.

'I remember.'

'Well, I just have,' said Edward.

'Come on, Ed,' she said, 'time to go home. You can tell me on the way.' And she took him by the arm. 'But don't become too grown-up, will you?' she said with a smile, as they walked on up the cobbled street.

Behind them a black and white cat suddenly appeared from a narrow vennel leading from the water's edge: Monty returning home from a ratting expedition.

Chapter 7

It was several days before Edward heard anything from Scrivener. During this time, he occupied himself with his art business, while Julie was busy with her fine craftsmanship in the back room. Life fell into a pleasing, predictable routine, which was a welcome novelty for Edward who soon forgot the pain of his London career: the endless drive to succeed in something he knew he was no good at; the constant striving to keep in with people he thought were his friends. His background had hung round his neck like an albatross, although he had not known it at the time. Now he had cut the cord and flung the decaying carcase into the sea. The air in this wind-swept north-east corner smelled sweeter by far than the money-laden *mistral* that had scoured the hard streets of the city and drove people mad.

It was a Thursday morning when his mobile rang.

'Scrivener here. That house you were asking about. According to the Land Registry, Angelus House belongs to a company based in London. It's called VSM Holdings. They're listed on the London Stock Exchange but not the FTSE 100. But they're obviously pretty big in metals and mining.'

'That's interesting. Why on earth would they want to own an empty house in the middle of nowhere?'

'No idea, Mr Ottaway. Do you want me to look further into it?' asked Scrivener, with a tone of voice that was meant to invite a negative response.

'No. Thanks though, Mr Scrivener. That's very helpful of you.' And Edward put down his mobile. 'I don't suppose you have a computer, Julie?' he called through to the backroom. 'I need to check something out.'

'Try Jane,' came the reply. 'What are you up to, anyway?' She didn't really want an answer, too busy watching the tip of the finest of flames transform a tiny piece of silver into a swan's neck in a mould she had carefully shaped for that purpose.

Edward slipped out into the summer sun. He could feel the heat of its rays on his back as he walked down Henrietta Street. Dan was outside his restaurant cleaning the windows.

'Jane in, Dan?' asked Edward.

'Back garden,' replied Dan, nodding towards the open door. 'Go through.'

Molly was in the back of the restaurant, cleaning shelves and re-stacking.

'Come to ask for Jane's help, Molly. I need her detection skills.'

'I'm sure that'll please her,' said Molly. 'She's getting bored here. Needs to be off and doing something.'

Edward walked through the open back doorway. Jane was sitting under a sunshade with her laptop closed in front of her.

'Great,' said Edward, 'just what I need. I'm hoping you can help me out, Jane.' Edward explained about Angelus House and the information he had received from Scrivener. 'What can you tell me about VSM Holdings?'

'Hang on a minute, Ed. I'll just do a search,' and she put down the book she was reading. Edward pulled his chair round so that he could see the computer screen. Several clicks later and a few scrollings up and down, Jane brought up the VSM website. There was not a lot of information to be absorbed. VSM claimed to be the world's leading producer of nickel and palladium and one of the biggest of copper. The offices were located in the City of London, near Island Gardens, and there were lots of glossy shots of stylish open-plan offices and panoramas over the city sights from the top of a sky-scraper.

'Doesn't tell us much, does it?' said Edward.

'Not a lot,' replied Jane. 'Why don't you leave it with me and I'll see what I can find out,' she added. 'I need a challenge. Serving fish teas is beginning to pall. I'll call round later.'

The sun sets late in a northern summer. Edward and Juliana had formed the habit, when the day's work was done, of flinging open the french windows in the cottage and watching the sun trace its downward course until it disappeared behind the buildings on the west cliff overlooking the harbour. It was their happy hour, when beads of condensation formed on their chilled white wine glasses, as they contemplated the meaning of life, consistently postponing the final answer until the next day. While thus engaged, Jane appeared, clutching a small sheaf of notes. 'It's not a pretty sight,' she announced, pulling up a kitchen chair to the window and taking the glass of white wine Edward gave her.

'I'm all ears,' said Edward.

'OK, here we go. VSM is a mining company, based in Siberia. Head office Moscow but business with the west is done from the London office. The company was built up on a Soviet mining set-up which started in 1935 and continued after the war with slave labour from the Gulag. It was run by guess who? – NKVD!'

'Who are they?' asked Julie.

'Later known as KGB,' replied Jane. 'In 1993, when the Soviet empire collapsed, the KGB set up a joint-stock company which was bought up four years later by a certain Viktor Sergeyevich Malinov. Get it?'

'Don't get it,' replied Edward.

'VSM – his initials. And dear Mr Malinov turns out to be no other than a former top gun in the defunct KGB. Owns 51% of the shares in the company. And listen to this!' Jane was getting more and more excited. 'VSM employs over 90,000 workers world-wide and has an annual revenue of over £12 billion.'

'Jane, you are a genius. How did you find out all this?'

Jane smiled that sophisticated smile of hers. 'Oh, natural investigative skills, a lot of googling and Wikipedia!'

'Of course, the poor man's Oracle at Delphi,' said Edward.

'But why would VSM want to own Angelus House?' asked Julie. 'It just doesn't make any sense.'

'I thought about that,' said Jane. 'What if Angelus House is left over from another age? In other words, the KGB age, and the officer who handled Angelus House was none other than Viktor Malinov. Easiest thing in the world to roll it up later in the property of the London-based arm of VSM.'

'Are you suggesting that Uncle Freddie lived in a KGB property in Yorkshire?' said Julie.

'And that Uncle Freddie was working for the KGB!' said Edward.

'Stranger things have happened,' replied Jane. 'What I haven't been able to do is find out where Malinov himself lives. Most of these Russian oligarchs seem to have a house in Mayfair or somewhere but this one is keeping his cards close to his chest. I thought you might be able to ask him about Freddie, if you knew where he lived.'

'You mean, if I bumped into him accidentally on purpose in the local Waitrose?' suggested Edward.

'Precisely,' said Jane.

The three looked at each other over their glasses of Chardonnay. Was this as far as it went?

It was not. Three days later, Edward was looking across the harbour from his narrow verandah, drinking his morning tea. He could smell the upward drift of tobacco smoke from below and looked down on to the balding top of Jim's head.

'Morning, Jim,' he said. The nose below tilted upwards. 'Fine morning.'

'Aye, right,' replied Jim, true to form, but with the gloomiest of tones.

'You don't sound too jolly, this morning, Jim,' said Edward.

'Aye, right. I blame that bugger Malinov. Interfering bloody bugger. Just sold Boro's best striker to bloody bugger at Chelsea. Bloody Russians!'

Edward suddenly realised that Jim was talking about football. And, more than that, Malinov was a name he recognised.

'Who's Malinov,' asked Edward innocently.

'Bloody bastard who owns Boro,' replied Jim, who spat over the harbour wall and disappeared into his cottage.

Edward was plunged into deep thought. So the bugger who owned VSM was the bloody bugger who owned the Boro. He wandered back into the living room where Julie was slowly coming to life over her morning tea.

'Julie, what is the Boro?'

Julie looked at him with a vacant stare. 'The Boro, Edward, unbelievably no doubt to someone of your background, is the only reason many men in the north-east stay alive. They are a football team! Ask Uncle George. He's on the board of directors at the club. Now let me drink my tea for God's sake!'

But in the rapier-like mind of Edward Ottaway a plan was taking shape which involved a visit to Ruswarp. When Julie had rediscovered her inner self, Edward made a suggestion. 'Julie, it's a lovely day. Why don't we take a stroll across to Ruswarp again. It would be a good time to go on the river. And we can always call in to see George.'

'What are you up to?' she replied. 'You have that certain look on your face.'

'Angelus House, Julie. Malinov of VSM is Malinov of the Boro! Can you believe it! Ex-KGB and football club owner. If Malinov spent some time at Angelus House in his KGB days, maybe he went to watch the Boro knock them in on a Saturday afternoon. Maybe he developed a soft spot for this part of the world and that's why he hung on to Angelus House. How do you fancy a seat in the directors' box for Middlesbrough versus Scunthorpe United?' Edward said, warming to the chase.

'OK, I see what you're getting at. I could wear my Miss Scunthorpe outfit,' she replied.

Edward looked bewildered. 'Miss Scunthorpe? What's all that about?'

'Oh, didn't I ever tell you?' replied Julie, off-handedly. 'You're not the only one with a past you know.'

That afternoon they retraced their footsteps across the fields to Ruswarp. George met them enthusiastically at his waterside cottage and once again they sat in the garden running down to the river. The topic of conversation was Angelus House.

'I'm amazed,' said George. 'I assumed that Freddie must have owned Angelus House all those years.'

'It seems not,' said Edward. 'My man Scrivener tells me it's never been in his name.'

'And what kind of a coincidence is it that Malinov's company owns the house and the football club? This is all too mysterious,' added George.

'Especially with the KGB connection,' said Julie.

'There's a room in that house that looks as if it's been set up as a communications centre of some sort, electric sockets everywhere, quite unlike anywhere else in the building.'

'The question is,' said George, 'what the hell was Freddie doing up there on his own, in a house that seems to have been in the ownership of some cold war enemy?'

'That's where I hope you can help, George. Julie and I were wondering if you could smuggle us into the presence of Viktor Malinov when you watch the Boro. You know, directors' box, prawn sandwiches at half time, that sort of thing. You never know, we might manage to learn something,' said Edward.

'Might manage to get nobbled by his Moscow hoods as well,' said Julie in a gallows tone. 'A *we know where you live* kind of conversation comes to mind.'

George rubbed his hands together. 'Well, I'm up for it,' he said, his hand rubbing his knobbly knees in excitement within the voluminous flaps of his shorts. 'Malinov is a shit. We didn't win the war to have our football teams bought up by Russian mafia! I'd like to see him exposed.' And he looked distinctly like Baden-Powell in his determination to see right triumph.

'Steady, Uncle George, don't get carried away!' said Julie.

'Sorry, my dear. I do apologise. I'll take you as my guests next Saturday. Not sure who they're playing.'

'Scunthorpe,' said Julie. 'Last match of the season.'

George looked at her amazed.

Chapter 8

Viktor Sergeyevich Malinov looked at himself in the mirror of the luxurious bathroom suite of his London apartment. He examined his skin tone carefully. Despite his great wealth and his fine dining in all the best Michelin-starred restaurants in the south-east of England, he worried that a lurking greyness from his days in the Siberian wastes betrayed, to the discerning eye of the English, *la nouvelle richesse* of his new identity. He had tried so hard to conceal the fact that he was, deep down, a peasant turned KGB thug, that he wondered if the effort was wearing him out. And things hadn't quite gone to plan. While other comrades-in-arms luxuriated in the owners' boxes in the highest realms of the English Premiership, his team had lost ten games on the trot the moment he had shelled out his roubles, and he was now getting ready for his helicopter to fly him to a half empty ground in the Championship to watch a match against Scunthorpe United, whoever they were.

It was a long way from the Talnakh Mountains of Siberia and in his dreams he often returned there, to hear the tinkling bells of the horses drawing the sledge across the frozen snow, to see the shimmering moon rise full across the vast Russian wastes and to smell the sweet incense smoking in the swinging burner behind the golden altar screen. He thought of his mother, the icon of the Madonna and Child in the village church and the smell of cabbage soup, all in one confused bewildering moment. Yes, he was rich and powerful; but deep down he was alone and sad. He wanted someone to love him; instead he had a gold-digging blonde society girl from Moscow, wielding a string of his credit cards the length of her arm in every over-priced shop in the West End.

Viktor Sergeyevich Malinov was five feet eight inches tall, with very little hair on his shining head, and eyebrows that met in the middle of his face. Apart from his fortune, he had very little going for him.

At half-past eight his chauffeur called for him in the Overfinch Range Rover with the tinted glass, Holland and Holland veneered gun cabinet in the boot, eight matching crystal tumblers and champagne flutes, and number plate VSM 1, to drive him to the London City airport, where his helicopter waited to whisk him to the Riverside stadium, two hundred and forty miles to the north. He always arrived there early now, to avoid the possibility of being struck by a hot pie thrown in protest at the poor form of his team. This had happened once recently and fortunately he had been wearing his Russian fur hat at the time. This week he had a surprise for the fans. True, he had sold their favourite striker to Chelsea but he was about to reveal a secret weapon, a new signing from an unheard of club in Mongolia. He was quietly confident that this would unsettle the Scunthorpe defence.

He travelled alone in the helicopter, seated beside the pilot. It was a few hours each week of insulation from the outside world, the magic of flight that creates a limbo between departing and arriving. He looked down upon the unrolling east coast of England. He had spent most of his life confused about this country. He hated its stuck-up politicians and exaggerated sense of its own importance while a sense of his own inadequacy had made him admire the English way of life. His trips by air to the far-flung outposts of the Championship had made him fond of this funny little island that could be circumnavigated in a few hours. It was a clear day and the sun glinted on the placid waters of the Wash a thousand feet below, where he had been told some forgotten English king had lost the crown jewels and the tide raced in at the speed of a galloping horse. And the ordinary people seemed to like him: a taxi driver had called him Boris only the day before; and a barrow boy, selling bananas on the street corner, had explained what weighing fruit by the pound meant in the fight against European oppression. He would have liked to be one of them; to be able to stand shoulder-to-shoulder on the terraces and eat his meat pie like a true worker. But he was damned by his riches to a life of perpetual apartness.

'Just about to land, sir,' announced the pilot over the headphones and the helicopter took a wide swing across the Tees. Viktor caught a glimpse of the white water of the barrage with its salmon ladder and then the green oval of the stadium rose up to meet them. As he stepped out on to the hallowed turf he looked at his watch: one hour to go, just long enough to chat to the team coach and then settle down to a White Russian or two in his private suite under the main stand.

In the meantime, George was pulling his XJ6 into the directors' reserved car parking spaces in front of the main entrance. Edward and Juliana got out. They were unrecognisable. Edward, wearing a business suit and Old Etonian tie, looked like the chairman of Barclays; Julie had modelled herself on the most famous WAG she had heard of, Victoria Beckham, with her natural artistic talent expended on creating an image of irresistible seductiveness. It was as much as either could do to avoid dissolving in laughter the moment they looked at each other, so alien were their appearances. George wore his blazer and club tie, as befitted a member of the board, and gathered his team into a huddle before they entered the stadium.

'Now, remember,' he said. 'We are here to entice and fascinate our man,' pausing as he looked at Julie's low-cut dress and long legs, 'which shouldn't be difficult. The key is to get Malinov to want to talk to us. So we must be subtle!'

'Absolutely,' said Edward, 'Julie and I do subtle very well.'

And so saying they followed George through the private entrance, signing in as his guests for the day. It was almost kick-off time so they made their way through the corridors of the stand and up the steps to the directors' box, the buzz of the crowd growing louder the nearer they drew to the daylight. They took their seats in the second row. George pointed to the centre seat of the front row. 'That's Malinov,' he said.

Julie and Edward followed his finger to the little man with the bald head who, to all intents and purposes, might have passed for Bob Hoskins. Julie gulped: she would need all her Miss Scunthorpe charms to handle this.

The first half got under way. For ten minutes there was a lot of route one football. The tall Mongolian centre forward wandered aimlessly up and down the middle of the field while beefy defenders booted high balls in his direction. The crowd became restless, fearing yet another Boro defeat, and began to whistle. Then another high ball was hoisted towards the Scunthorpe goalkeeper. The Mongolian trundled forward and pretended to head the ball but instead head-butted the goalkeeper, who dropped the ball into the net: 1-0.

Edward turned to George. 'Wasn't that a foul?' he asked.

'Of course,' replied George, 'Yakult, or whatever he's called, should be off the field!'

Another ten minutes of aimless meandering passed. Julie resorted to counting the beads on her necklace. Suddenly, the ball was in the air in the Scunthorpe penalty area, the goalkeeper rose to catch it, and the Mongolian rabbit-punched him from behind. The Scunthorpe goalkeeper turned and delivered a stinging upper cut. The referee pulled out a red card, sent off the goalkeeper and pointed to the penalty spot: 2-0, and the visitors down to ten men. When the occupants of the directors' box trooped into the hospitality suite at half-time, Boro were 4-0 up.

The plates of fishy canapés did the rounds in the red and white themed salon. Julie and Edward rubbed shoulders with the local business men, clutching their glasses of dry white wine, while George kept a weather-eye on the gyrations of Malinov who was expatiating on the strengths of his new centre forward. He overheard him saying to the owner of a local DIY chain: 'Yes, and I got him for only two hundred thousand and a herd of yaks for his father as a gift!' At last George spied a gap and steered Edward and Julie towards Malinov in the corner of the room.

'Ah, Viktor,' he said, 'I would like you to meet my niece, Juliana.'

Malinov turned, his eyes scanning up and down. 'Delightful,' he said.

'And this is Edward,' added George. 'He's a top

metallurgist from London University.'

'Really, how fascinating. You must tell me all about your research. I too have an interest in metals.'

Edward glared at George, who shrugged his shoulders, as the warning bell sounded for the start of the second half.

'For God's sake, George! I thought you said subtle!' muttered Edward between his teeth, as they walked back to the directors' box.

'He's interested, though,' replied George. 'Just make it up. You Old Etonians have been bull-shitting for centuries. We've got a Government full of them to prove it.'

George was right; Malinov *was* interested. When full-time came, with Scunthorpe down to nine men, and Boro six goals up, Malinov was on his feet joining in the ecstatic applause of the crowd. He turned and shouted across to George: 'Come and have a drink in my suite. Bring your niece and her friend.'

Malinov's suite was the height of bad taste. There were three large red leather sofas, the kind that are advertised every Christmas on TV, and a fluffy deep-pile white carpet. Photographic portraits of past chairmen adorned the walls. A whole corner was enclosed by a curved cocktail bar, behind which stood a young barman, ready to mix drinks.

'What would you like, madam?' he asked.

'Oh, anything except a Harvey Wallbanger,' she replied. Trays of drinks were produced and the party sank back into their red leather receptacles.

'Well, Edward, and did you enjoy the match?' asked Malinov.

'Oh, very much,' replied Edward with mock enthusiasm. 'I thought your new player was very striking, in more ways than one, but the referee was rather generous at times.'

'You think so?' said Malinov. 'If you look out of that window behind you, I think you will see that I can be generous too.'

Edward levered himself into the vertical and walked across to the window, which looked out over the officials' car parking area. There he saw the referee getting into the driver's seat of the largest of the Mercedes saloon range.

'You see what I mean, Edward? That's how we win matches in Russia! Have another drink.'

Another tray of cocktails appeared and disappeared and appeared again. The afternoon turned into early evening. Malinov showed no signs of drawing the gathering to a close. Julie began to become restless as the little Russian gradually slid nearer to her on the deep sinking sofa until a fleshy hand rested on her knee. George, who was seated on the other side of the room, leaned across to Edward and whispered: 'We're getting nowhere! We're sliding down a snake. Time to throw a six!'

'What do you want me to do?' asked Edward, totally lost by George's snakes and ladders metaphor. But events swept him along. Malinov continued to consume his favourite cocktails. Without letting go of Julie's knee, he slid further into the yielding leather sofa until he was almost horizontal. It was when he began quietly and tunelessly to sing in Russian, and tears ran gently down his cheeks, that George decided the game was up.

'Viktor, I'm afraid we must leave you. Thank you so much for your hospitality.'

'No, Georgiy, on the contrary,' said Malinov, staggering upwards on shaky legs. 'It has been my pleasure to have met such charming young people.' He swayed alarmingly and his speech was slurred. He flung out an arm and hooked it round Edward's shoulder to stay upright. From this position of relative security he lurched forward and gave George a manly Russian embrace. When he had done with this, he turned optimistically to where he thought Julie was positioned and held her in a clinging overdone hug. Remembering vaguely that there was another person in the room, he pivoted towards Edward and shook him vigorously by the hand. And then, by a most remarkable chance, the deadlock was broken. The snake of the drunken afternoon became a ladder of opportunity.

'By the way, Edward, I do not think I can remember your surname,' Malinov said. Edward seized the moment to set the hare running.

'Ottaway. My uncle Freddie Ottaway lived not far from here, in Angelus House in north Yorkshire. You might have heard of him.'

There was silence. Julie glanced at her uncle, George studied his feet, and Malinov swayed backwards and forwards as if suspended from a high wire. His mouth dropped open. His eyes became focused on a fascinating object apparently located between Edward's eyes. For a moment, he had the look of a hunted animal, as if a memory from the deep hidden past were stalking him. Eventually he spoke. 'Well....well....Na Zdarovye!' he said. He stepped backwards and collapsed into the soft, yielding cushions of the sofa. The young barman, who had witnessed all from afar, stepped forward.

'Please don't be concerned. This happens after most home matches.'

In the car drive back home, there was a thoughtful silence for some miles. Then, as the urban sprawl of Middlesbrough gave way to the rolling hills of the moor road to Whitby, George finally spoke. 'Well, I think we're getting in up to our necks now!' he said with a grin. 'That was lucky, Malinov asking you your name. Brilliant move, Edward!'

'He must have realised we know something,' added Julie with impressive perception. 'What happens next?'

'That's up to Malinov,' said Edward, 'but I can't imagine that's the last we'll hear from him.'

A few minutes later the car began the long descent into Whitby. The town lay spread out below them, sparkling in the setting sun. On the east cliff the ruined aisles of the abbey cast long shadows across the green sward, as they had for almost a thousand years. Edward looked across the bay.

'Where did this mysterious new life of mine come from?' he asked himself. Beside him, on the back seat, Julie rested her head against the window, fast asleep, her long dark hair falling over her eyes.

Later that evening, when Edward and Julie lay semi-conscious on the sofa, recovering from the ordeal of the day, the mobile rang. It was George. 'Just seen the ten o'clock news. The police have arrested an FA referee called Pratt on charges of corruption. If you've still got the match programme, Edward, can you check the name of the referee today?'

Edward scrabbled around for the programme which he found scrunched up in the kitchen bin.

'Got it here, George,' he said. 'Yes, it was a Pratt!'

'Let's hope they don't arrest Viktor before he gets back to us!'

Chapter 9

Edward was right in predicting that Viktor would get back to them sooner or later but the manner of his so doing came as an alarming surprise. Later that week he was sitting at the open french windows overlooking the harbour, turning out a few more watercolours to replenish the stock in Juliana's shop window, when there was a knock on the street door. At first he did not react. The process of applying sweeps of paint in light and airy brush strokes was mesmeric. It was as if he had returned to that magical age when tiny corners of the illustrations in his childhood books revealed treasures that enslaved the imagination and excluded the real world. Such, he thought, must be the power of art. He could recall still the fear of those sharp little weasel faces hiding in snow drifts, as Ratty and Mole braved the terrors of the wild wood in the book his parents had bought him when he was seven. They seemed as vivid to him now as they were when he had first encountered them. Despite the constraints of his bourgeois upbringing, he suddenly realised he lived for the visual. He had no logic but he could see and feel. His paintings had started as copies of Ottaways, which sold readily enough, but recently he had begun to branch out. A new figure began to infiltrate his compositions, that of a slender, beautiful girl, who readily took on the *persona* of whatever scene he was painting. Juliana had not only entered his life but had taken control of his pictures. He began to wonder if he was turning into Freddie, or what he thought Freddie might be, and he felt for the first time that he was part of a great human tradition: the artist and his muse. Why on earth his twisted, over-priced education had thrown him into the cauldron of the city, to be rendered down as so much useless blubber, he could not explain. Then the knock on the door summoned him again.

He opened, to be confronted by a figure straight out of *The Godfather*: dark suit, white shirt and shades.

'Mr Malinov presents his compliments and would be pleased if you would join him.'

'What, now?' said Edward, taken aback by the barked instruction.

'If you please,' replied the shades, pointing to a long black car parked in front of the cottage.

Edward felt for a moment that this might be his last journey, to be dumped into a flooded quarry with a concrete block tied to his legs. Then he remembered that this was Whitby on a sunny day in May and Jim and Ruby were looking at the whole scene through the net curtains next door. So he said OK and got into the car.

Earlier that morning, Viktor had floated to the surface like a corpse which had been dumped into the sea. His head finally bobbed up out of the water, to face for another day the agony of living. The sea in which he had been floating was the sea of his despair; his drowning, the self-inflicted overdose of vodka cocktails. He could remember something from yesterday: kind English Georgiy, so much at ease in the world; a beautiful young girl, gentle and soft, unlike the brassy blonde who had followed him from Moscow; and then Edward, who had said something that had stung like a wasp. Yes, he remembered now, Freddie Ottaway and Angelus House. He reached out his hand to the bedside phone and told his security man to call George Allington: 'Find out where Edward Ottaway is living and get him over here today.'

Edward sat back in the luxurious rear seat of the limousine. He had no idea where he was going but he hoped he would return in one piece. Then he dismissed this stupidity: it was entirely based on the supposition that Viktor was an ex-KGB thug intent on doing away with him. For what reason? He could think of none. The car swept silently and smoothly along the winding roads of north Yorkshire, rising steadily upwards away from the sea, into the green valley of the Esk and onwards to the open moorlands. This was a world unknown to Edward, the city boy plunged into a new and still mysterious existence. At last the car reached the top of a rise and before him Edward saw the most exotic of buildings beyond a green paddock and round a curving gravel drive. Two fantastical stone lions guarded the pilastered front door of a Georgian sandstone house, miraculously wedged between two wings of what must have been Edwardian facsimiles of Elizabethan manor houses. The overall effect was neither fish nor fowl but it had obviously been of sufficient fascination to Viktor to entice him to part with his money. As the car drew to a halt, and the driver opened the rear door, Edward felt a sudden panic: he had not done his homework. He had not read the pages Jane had printed off for him. He knew bugger-all about metals.

The driver led Edward into a large square entrance hall, with black and white marble tiles chequering the floor and alabaster vases standing on tall plinths at each corner. A double staircase ascended to a first floor gallery and, as Edward looked upwards into the towering glass cupola, he saw the round face of Viktor Malinov looking down upon him.

'Welcome to my house, Edward,' he said, and descended the staircase to the lower hall. 'You are most welcome. The nephew of Freddie is most welcome.' Viktor threw his arms around the dumbstruck Edward and kissed him on both cheeks. Then he took him by the arm and led him through a grand doorway and along an endless corridor which finally opened on to a sun-drenched terrace with steps descending to an ornamental lake. There, on white wrought-iron garden chairs, they sat down amidst a spread of Royal Worcester cups and saucers, plates and cake stands. 'I love cucumber sandwiches,' said Viktor, 'and chocolate eclairs.'

Edward was lost for words. He waited for Viktor to take the lead. There must be some reason for this summons to a scene from *Alice in Wonderland* but it was not going to appear until the charade was played out. At last, after his English tea, Viktor pushed back his chair and spoke. 'You must be wondering why I invited you here, Edward,' he said.

Edward thought it better not to suggest that "invited" might not be the correct word, nor that Viktor was too right in his supposition.

'I'm very pleased to be here,' he replied. 'It was very good of you.'

'You see,' and he paused for a long time, 'when you mentioned Freddie's name yesterday, it brought so much back to me. I have so many memories.'

'Memories of what, exactly?'

'Oh, of happy times long past,' Viktor replied, 'and not so happy times, too.'

Edward thought he could discern a shining in the eyes as Viktor spoke. 'You know that Freddie died, don't you?' he said slowly.

'Of course. I couldn't attend his funeral. I hadn't seen him for many years. But I missed him always.'

'You knew him when he lived at Angelus House?' asked Edward, keen to press home the investigation while he could.

'I used to visit him there.'

'But you own the house, Viktor, don't you?'

'I suppose you could say it fell to me to own it, yes.'

'I'm not sure I understand. Why was Freddie living there? What was he doing?'

'He was living and painting. It was the least I could do for him. You see Edward, he was like a father to me, not in flesh but in spirit. I had never known such a thing. He saved me from my own stupidity. It would have been the end for me. It was the least I could do, you see, to help when times became hard for him.'

Viktor looked across the sweeping lawn that led down to the shimmering water of the lake where mallards and moorhens paddled among the lily pads. 'Freddie loved this sceptred isle, as he called it, more than anywhere in the world, but it made him hate it at the same time!' said Viktor.

'I don't understand, Viktor,' said Edward. 'What are you saying?'

Tears had filled Viktor's eyes. 'It was betrayal, Edward, betrayal. That was the cause of it all. Don't ask me to say more. For our different reasons we lived and worked with betrayal. It was what you call our bread and butter. But when you work so close to the edge, sometimes you fall over, and sometimes the fall is a very long way down.'

Viktor did not speak further. Edward and he sat opposite each other for several minutes, gazing outwards to the distant horizon, their thoughts spinning beyond. Edward rose to his feet and touched Viktor on the shoulder, to signal his leave. Malinov seized his hand and held it firmly. 'You see, Edward, to be a rich man is also to be a lonely man. How do I trust anyone? I trusted Freddie and he trusted me. We trusted each other with our lives.'

Edward felt sorry for this strange little man. The afternoon had taken a course he had failed to predict. He had set out half expecting to be kidnapped or assassinated and now he found himself comforting the billionaire owner of an international metals company and the local football club. But he did not want to lose the chance of finding out more about Freddie. What Malinov had said that afternoon had simply muddied the pool: Freddie as Viktor's spiritual father; Freddie saving his life; and then betrayal. What did it all mean? He had to know more and so he came out with a blinder.

'I say, Viktor, we should have a drink together next time you're up here. I could take you to a real English pub. What about that?'

Viktor's eyes lit up. 'I would like that very much Edward. I can see that we can become friends, just as your uncle and I were.'

'I think we could,' replied Edward, surprised at the feeling of warmth he suddenly felt towards this unlikely acquaintance. He began to understand how Freddie might also have felt the same, the way that emotions can play tricks and steer you in strange unexpected directions.

And then it struck Edward. This had been the whole point of the exercise: to get Edward to say that. It was what Viktor wanted all along but had not known how to do it.

Edward wandered back through the house, taking wrong turnings into kitchens and sculleries, until he finally found himself in the chequered hall again. The driver sat waiting by the front door. He said nothing but opened the front door for Edward and led him to the car. On the drive back to Henrietta

Street Edward tried to work out what he could say to Julie and to George. In the end, he could only recount what had happened and let them make sense of it. Neither could add much to clarify Edward's confusion despite long and meandering discussions. Jane, who had got in on the act, came up with an instant analysis. 'Obviously gay,' she said. 'That explains the betrayal bit. Gay men are always getting betrayed. Viktor and Freddie were obviously in a gay relationship.'

'How do you know?' said Julie.

'Experience,' said Jane.

Edward was half-inclined to go along with this theory, having witnessed the tearful Viktor at first hand, but he knew there had to be much more to the story of Freddie than that. The word "betrayal" haunted him; the mystery of Angelus House compounded the resonance; and the love between the two men lingered as an unresolved question. Alone that evening with Julie he said: 'This is not simple at all, Julie. There is so much more to be told.'

It was the next morning before Julie responded to Edward's statement. She sat over her breakfast coffee in silence. 'Edward, it's time I told you something else about Freddie. I thought when you came here that you would already have heard this. I think everybody who knew about you assumed the same. That's why nobody has said anything to you. But I know now that this is the last thing you would have heard about your uncle.'

Edward became alarmed by Julie's unusually sombre tone. 'For God's sake, what is it?' he asked.

'The fact is, there was some doubt about Freddie's death. I mean, how it happened.'

'Go on.'

'They found his body along the coast. He was an old man and he could easily have slipped. There's a cliff footpath that goes past the abbey and on to Hawsker. It passes very close to the edge at a place called Saltwick Bay. Sheer drop for a hundred feet or so on to rocks. That's where they found him. Dead, of course. There was a police investigation and a coroner's inquest. The verdict was accidental death. But nobody knows for certain what happened.'

'You mean did he fall, or did he jump?' said Edward.

'Or was he pushed?' replied Julie.

'Why do you say that, Julie?'

'It would never have entered my mind until you told me about Angelus House and who owns it.'

'You can't think this has something to do with Freddie and Viktor and the KGB,' said Edward, becoming very serious and a little pale.

'I don't know what I think,' she replied.

Life returned to its simple pattern after the upheaval of the encounter with Viktor Malinov. The football season was well over and Boro had escaped the drop to League One. The sacked Scottish manager had left the club via the back door, disguised as a cleaner, while the fans gathered at the front door to cheer the next manager up the steps to the scaffold. The *Evening Gazette* football correspondent ran a series of articles on the Mongolian striker, with a fascinating photograph of him playing football as a boy on the Mongolian plains, kicking a stuffed sheep's stomach as a ball. Jane had disappeared from the *Caedmon*, taking her earnings with her on a trek to the Himalayas, before preparing to descend on the callow unsuspecting males of Cambridge in October. There was no word from Malinov, who had returned to London and his lonely life in the city. Meanwhile Julie, Edward and Monty had formed a peaceful *ménage à trois* and the two artists, one real and one pretend, plied their trade successfully to the summer tourists. George was a regular visitor, his housekeeper had begun to speak in public, and the idyllic stretch of the river at Ruswarp, where the water nymphs played in the summer evenings amid dragonflies and kingfishers, regularly drew the young lovers irresistibly to its bosom. And so life would have remained, had it not been for one thing: Edward had grown attached to the legend that Freddie had become in his mind. It was more than an attachment, perhaps a fixation.

One evening, with the sun sinking behind the hills, Julie

took him to see the place where Freddie had died. The narrow cliff-top path wound precariously in and out of hollows and indentations for a mile past the abbey, past the rocky extrusion of the Nab, thrusting itself into the breakers of the North Sea, until the semi-circle of Saltwick Bay spread out beneath them. Julie stopped and bent down to clear the long grass from a stone in the meadow a few yards from the cliff edge.

'I carved this,' she said. Edward knelt down and with his fingers traced in the smooth surface of the stone the letters that spelled Freddie's name. 'You and I are the only people in the world who know this is here,' she said.

'It's as if Freddie meant you to bring me here,' said Edward, 'just as he meant me to live in his cottage and meet you. Perhaps there really is a divinity that shapes our ends, rough-hew them as we will.'

Chapter 10

The golden days of summer drifted towards the mellow glow of autumn. Before he knew it, September had arrived, but the questions surrounding Freddie still troubled Edward's mind. Then, one day, came the most remarkable discovery: a set of beautiful paintings, the like of which no previous Ottaway had ever resembled. They were large, unframed, oil on canvas, and they had never been displayed. They came to light by chance, as a Roman horde casually resurrects itself under the glancing blow of a spade or ploughshare, while the discoverer grows more and more amazed by the swelling grandeur of his find. There was no spade and no ploughed field; simply a ladder reaching up into an unexplored loft in Henrietta Street. Edward set out the paintings, one by one, six in all, against the livingroom wall and looked at them. To his inexperienced eye they were magnificent in their concept; to Julie, they were astounding in their skill.

Edward gently brushed off the thick layer of dust. The paint lay in rich swathes across the rough surface of the canvas. He ran his hand across the swirling textures, the combination of palet knife and brush applied with abandon but absolute precision, and he could almost feel the beating heart of the artist yearning to translate into paint his deepest emotions. But there was one fact about these paintings that struck him between the eyes and Juliana, who was standing beside him studying the pictures, saw it too.

'There's a girl in all of these paintings, Edward, and it's the same one,' she said.

'I know,' replied Edward, 'and it's very worrying.'

'Worrying?'

'You see, Julie, just as you have taken over my paintings, the girl in the picture took over Freddie's. I'm beginning to feel like Freddie's *doppel-gänger* and I've never even met him! I inherited his cottage, his cat, and now I'm even copying his paintings. What's happening to me?'

'Nothing's happening to you, Edward,' she replied. 'You are yourself. Do you remember I told you that Freddie had lost the will to paint. This is why. This is his real art; this girl was his muse. The girl in the picture. And my guess is that the reason he stopped painting from the heart was that she disappeared from his life. Who was she?'

'Well, she may be standing on the east pier at Whitby,' said Edward, 'but it doesn't disguise the fact that she's not a Yorkshire herring girl.'

'True. I've never met a black one before,' said Julie.

'We should show these to George. Perhaps he remembers something from the past. He might have met the girl. Who knows?'

As it happened, George drove across later that week and called in to Henrietta Street. 'Never seen her before,' he said, 'but, by God, she's beautiful. No wonder Freddie couldn't stop painting her. If she'd been in Whitby, she would have stopped the traffic.' George pulled at his pipe and took a gulp of coffee. 'By the way,' he continued, 'Malinov will be up on Saturday for the match. His man phoned me to remind you about a real English pub, whatever that may mean.'

'I remember,' said Edward. 'That's good. I need to ask him more about Freddie. Perhaps he knows about the girl in the picture. A few pints of Yorkshire bitter should be more effective than thumbscrews in getting the truth out of Victor. I want to get to the bottom of what the hell Freddie was doing in a KGB house in the middle of Yorkshire.'

'Good luck,' said George, with a pessimistic look.

Edward decided he needed moral support for his meeting with Victor so he recruited, under some coercion, a reluctant Juliana, who still harboured vivid memories of Malinov's manual dexterity. Edward had phoned the number George had left him and got Viktor's man on the line. Mr Malinov would be happy to be collected on Sunday and looked forward to a visit to a real English pub. He expressly hoped, said his man, that he would be able to sample the famous pickled eggs he had heard so much about. Edward put the phone down.

'This is madness,' he thought.

Sunday arrived and Edward, full of self-doubt, drove his clapped-out Peugeot, Julie at his side, across the rolling hills of Eskdale to the unlikely country seat of Viktor Malinov. Ponsonby House, as it was called, was as bizarre as he remembered it. Julie and Edward had turned themselves out as they hoped Viktor would have expected of an English couple going to the pub on a Sunday lunchtime. Nevertheless it was a bit of a shot in the dark and neither felt particularly comfortable, Edward in his corduroy trousers and navy pullover and Julie in her designer jeans and horse brasses scarf outfit. But when Viktor appeared, they felt under-dressed. He wore a pair of crushed raspberry corduroy trousers, a striking mustard waistcoat, a checked shirt and a windsor-soup-coloured tweed sports jacket. The crowning glory was his silk club tie, in bold stripes, and his shining silver tie-pin, in which the letters H, C, E and G were intricately interwoven in the style of an Elizabethan knot garden. He greeted them cordially, kissing both Edward and Julie on each cheek. Edward looked at his humble little car parked beside Viktor's black limousine and wondered if this outing was going to be a success after all. Edward knew enough about the clubs that one ought to join to realise that Viktor must be a member of the prestigious Muirfield Golf Club where Faldo had won The Open some years before.

'I see you are a member of Muirfield, Viktor,' Edward remarked as they drove across the moorland road.

'The Honourable Company, dear boy,' he replied. 'But it was not easy, you know. No Russian has ever been admitted as a member before.'

'How on earth did you manage it?' asked Julie from the back seat.

'I bought the captain a house,' Viktor replied, with a smug grin.

'But didn't he have a house already?' she asked.

'Of course, but not the one overlooking the first tee. He was very happy. We both were. It was what you call in business "win-win".' Viktor rocked with laughter, his round face smiling, as he looked across at Edward. 'You British, I love you.'

Edward felt the hairs stand up on the back of his neck; he felt as if he were sitting next to a grotesque parody of Bertie Wooster, the Russian idea of the typical Englishman.

The pub he had chosen nestled in a sheltered valley on an old drovers' road in the hills above Whitby. In past centuries, sheep and cattle had passed through on their way to markets in Pickering and Malton but now the spit and sawdust of the drovers' drinking den had become the Sunday ride out for the urban commuters. *The Drovers* was what every foreign tourist wanted to see in an English country pub: red-faced locals at play, sitting casually on bar stools, quaffing pints of warm beer, at peace with themselves, while the rest of the world bickered. And this profusion of *bonhomie* was all housed within the charming, tumbling, crumbling sandstone house that had stood sentinel against the north-easterlies for three hundred years. Edward bought Viktor and himself a pint of Marston's and Julie a glass of wine. Then they settled in a snug corner to tackle their pickled eggs. It was a scene of bucolic charm that might have graced a Claude landscape where classical figures picnicked on ambrosia and drank of sweet nectar from horns.

Viktor had a rapacious appetite for English beer but not much of a head for its effects. Edward and Julie took care to stay behind him in the drinking stakes and, while they were simply mellow, Viktor rapidly became effusive, then amorous, then tearful. Julie looked sideways at Edward, hoping to God Viktor was not going to start singing about Mother Russia. The look said: *do something quick!* Edward got the message. 'Viktor, tell me, how did you get to know my uncle? You see, I know so very little about him.'

Viktor studied the bubbles in his pint glass, as if looking for inspiration. Finally he spoke. 'My dear Edward. There is much that I will not tell you about those years. It is best forgotten. The world has moved on and we all have changed. We are not the people we were. But I will tell you this. I first met Freddie many, many years ago. I was a keen young fellow, just doing a job for my country, far away from my home. I was lonely and very naïve, I suppose. Freddie was more than ten years older and he became my friend. He taught me all he knew about the world, which was a great deal. He took me in, you see. He had suffered a terrible tragedy. He was in love with a girl.'

'Who was she, Viktor?' asked Julie.

'Oh, she was younger than him and oh, so beautiful, he told me. I knew how he felt. I too had been in love many times. Oh, yes, my dear Juliana, I was not always this fat little left-over that you see now, buying his way in the world with money that fell from the sky.'

Julie felt a sudden compassion for Viktor in his lonely isolation and his absurd desire to be something he was not. She took his hand in hers.

'Go on,' she said, 'what was her name and what was she like?'

'Her name was Amala Mohammed. Yes, an unusual name but, you see, she was the daughter of a Maasai woman and a Pakistani trader. That was the problem. She was black, even if she was a daughter of a rich man. That's where it all went wrong.'

Viktor paused, his eyes filling with tears, and took a sip from his beer. Juliana turned to Edward. 'Of course, the girl in the picture,' she said. 'You see, Viktor, we've seen this girl in Freddie's paintings. We know what she looks like.'

'Did Freddie bring her here, do you know?' asked Edward.

Viktor put down his glass and wiped his eyes with a handkerchief. Then he spoke. 'He couldn't, could he? You see, she was dead.'

There was silence. Even the sounds of the pub goers became muted as the harsh truth fell upon Edward and Julie. So this was the tragedy; this was the loss that had buried Freddie in his anonymity; that had caused his retreat into the little world of Henrietta Street, where he had painted his secret paintings of the girl he would never see again, against the empty sea and sky of the cruel world he had inherited. He had poured himself into them so that there was nothing left to give his art.

'How did it happen?' Edward at last was able to ask.

'He gave up his life in Kenya for Amala. There was an incident and he had to leave in a hurry. That's what it meant to go with a native girl. They wanted him out, you see, the British. He was a threat to their way of life. It was not what one did in Africa. He had to leave his job with the colonial service, in a hell of a hurry. And then, when the worst happened, Freddie was alone and with no money. We gave him a job.'

'*We* gave him a job!' said Julie. 'What kind of a job? And who are *we*?'

'A job he wanted. He came to work for us. It was to take his revenge on the country he loved. I leave the rest to your imagination.'

Suddenly, the pieces fell into place but for Edward the shock of the picture they made was overwhelming. And then he remembered Viktor's words: it was betrayal, all about betrayal. Their conversation had come to a natural conclusion and no one had the desire to take it further. Edward drove back to Ponsonby House in silence; Julie rested her head on her hand and stared out at the empty landscape; while Viktor, overtaken by his memories, half slept in the passenger seat.

At Ponsonby House, Edward stepped out of the car to help Viktor into his house. He was drunk but quiet, unsteady on his feet on the gravel. He held on to Edward's arm with a desperate grip. Edward had one more thing to say. 'But why do you want to be like us, if you hate us; how can you love us, if you worked against us? I don't get it, Viktor.'

Viktor swayed gently in the breeze, his eyes screwed up against the light. 'Edward, dear boy, let me tell you one thing I've learned: life is a mystery, just a fucking mystery. I can't explain why things are the way they are. Don't try to make sense of it. But don't let go of Julie; just love her, my boy, and don't think too much.'

Viktor's man appeared from nowhere and took his master's arm with the confidence of a well-rehearsed routine.

As the tragi-comic little Russian billionaire struggled up the steps of his preposterous mansion, Edward tried to make sense of the man within: the music hall English gentleman and the calculating secret agent. But he came to the same conclusion as Viktor: life was indeed just a fucking mystery. As they were driving back, Julie turned to Edward. 'What did Viktor say when you left him?'

'Oh, not much. Just to love you.'

'And do you?'

'I do.'

PART TWO

Chapter 1

Cambridge, May 1950

Freddie Ottaway sat in the airless cavern of the Senate House and looked at the examination paper before him. He looked around at the other two hundred undergraduates, arranged in rows and columns like a Victorian counting house. Most of them were already scratching away, composing elegant paragraphs on the metaphysical techniques of John Donne's poetry; the Christian symbolism of *The Faerie Queene;* or the nature of wit in Elizabethan love poetry. But Freddie could not bring himself to tackle any of these questions. Not that he did not know the answers; he knew them very well. It was just too boring to have to tell some dog-eared university examiner what he already knew. The fact was that he had a brilliant mind but no desire to display it in a brilliant degree. He was an artist and all he wanted was to paint but his father had insisted he complete his studies on pain of losing his allowance. And it was the allowance that permitted him to live among friends in the artistic end of Bateman Street in Cambridge, with the time to paint and the money to eat and drink. In his mind, completing his studies did not include passing his finals, although he had already dashed off five papers with relative ease. It was just this sixth one that stuck in his throat; he wanted to go out with a grand gesture. He picked up his pen and wrote a title: *Sonnet Number 155.* He had three hours to compose fourteen lines, arranged in three quatrains rounded off by a rhyming couplet. It was a triumph of literary skulduggery, which he signed *William Shake-speare,* exactly as it was in the original. It bristled with images of summer days, wilting lovers, lurking sexuality and slow laments. The final couplet was a paradox of hope and despair. At twelve o'clock he marched out of the hall into the blazing sunshine, happy that he had served out his time according to his father's *diktat* but even happier that he had pulled off such a flamboyant act of independence. When the lists were posted on the college noticeboard ten days later, he saw, to his horror, that he had been awarded a starred first. He could not imagine how that had happened but it was simple: it was just another case of boredom.

It was late at night in the gloomy study of Dr Roderick Fotheringay, lecturer in English and lover of fine wines. A tower block of examination scripts teetered at one end of his desk. He was blinded by the banality of the answers he had waded through and graded. He was dying of boredom. He opened another bottle of wine, poured himself a glass and, thus anaesthetised, forced himself to open the final examination script. His eyes lit up as his brain engaged with what he read. It was pure beauty, fourteen lines of Shakespeare he had never seen before and, as he read it over and over again, he had an idea.

The day after the results were posted, Freddie picked up a note from his pigeonhole in the porter's lodge. It was from Fotheringay:

Mr Ottaway

Please come to my rooms at three this afternoon.

Dr Fotheringay.

Freddie was not happy. The last time he had visited Fotheringay was for a supervision and, while Freddie was reading out his essay on Keats, Fotheringay had put his hand on his knee. Another student had reportedly encountered a trouserless Fotheringay at the door to his rooms and fled back down the stairs, flinging his essay on Shelley over his shoulder. But this was Cambridge and such things happened.

At one minute to three that afternoon Freddie climbed the stone steps that led up to Fotheringay's first floor rooms on E staircase. He paused outside the main door and took a deep breath. Then he knocked and pushed the door open, entering the short hallway that led to his tutor's study. He knocked at a second door and heard a voice shout 'enter'. Freddie opened the door and saw Fotheringay sitting behind his desk by the window overlooking Front Court. Through the square-paned window he could see the clematis and wisteria in full bloom against the soft sandstone of the quadrangle. Fotheringay looked up from his papers and removed his small round glasses, which he polished on his tie.

He had a look of disappointment in his face, for he carried with him twenty years of scholarly near-misses that had prevented him from winning the glittering prizes every academic craves. His career had at first rocketed like the initial moments of a moon shot but somewhere along the line the curve had flattened, his research had turned sour and dull, and worse qualified but more lively young brains had taken the top jobs that he thought by rights were his. In fact, he had never left the college he had attended as an undergraduate, and now he was a long-serving fellow of whom not much was expected, beyond a trickle of little-read papers published in the journals. He needed a bomb to wake up the establishment. He thought he had found it.

Fotheringay beckoned Freddie to take a seat by the desk. 'I must congratulate you on your Tripos result, Ottaway. Your final paper was outstanding.'

'But I didn't answer any of the questions,' replied Freddie. 'How could I have got top marks?'

'Never mind the questions. What you did was most imaginative. Pure genius in fact. The most remarkable piece of work I have ever read.' Freddie looked bewildered. He could not understand where this conversation was leading. 'It was so fascinating,' continued Fotheringay, 'that I think we could take it further.'

'I'm not sure I understand,' said Freddie.

Fotheringay paused, running his hand through his unkempt flop of hair. 'Consider the effect, if your fourteen lines of manuscript, became fourteen lines of Elizabethan folio. Then add a little aged, yellowing paper. What would you think then?'

'I don't know what I would think,' replied Freddie, staring at Fotheringay as if he were insane.

'And what if a letter from a known source were to be found, referring to the sonnet, providing provenance?' Fotheringay was clearly becoming excited by the prospect. He stood up and began pacing the carpet before the fireplace.

'You mean a forgery?' said Freddie. 'But I only wrote the thing as a joke. No one would be fooled into thinking it was a long-lost Shakespeare sonnet, would they?

'Why wouldn't they?' echoed Fotheringay. 'You captured the tone and style to perfection. Literary critics would argue over it for decades, just as they have over who wrote the plays. Don't you see, Ottaway, we are surrounded by gullible fools, ready to be taken for a ride.'

'We? You expect me to get involved in this?' asked Freddie, feigning indignation but secretly rather amused by the idea. 'What if I say yes? What's in it for either of us?'

Fotheringay stopped pacing and leaned against the fireplace while he lit a cigarette. 'For me, Ottaway, I would be the star of the show. I would be the true scholar whose painstaking research threw up a faded, humble manuscript hidden for centuries in the household papers of some minor aristocrat living on the south bank of the Thames in the sixteenth century. It would be fame and attention, don't you see, everything I have deserved over the years but never received?'

'And for me?'

'For you, you get to keep your starred first. Mum's the word, eh, for both of us!' Fotheringay leered through his nicotine stained teeth and rubbed his hands together. 'Open door to wherever you want to go in life!'

Freddie thought for a moment. He suddenly saw Fotheringay in a new light, as a man of enterprise. And then he thought about his father. At first Freddie had planned to shaft his despotism by failing his exams; now he saw he could really shaft him by exceeding all expectations. The shock might even kill him! What a ruse this could be.

'OK, but there's one problem, Dr Fotheringay,' he said at last. 'Who's the forger who will do all this?'

Fotheringay leaned forward to deliver his *coup de grâce,*

for all the world resembling a grotesque Fagin. 'The head porter's brother-in-law, Ottaway. He's in Wormwood Scrubs doing time for forgery and I'm his prison visitor. What could be simpler?'

Three months later *The Times Literary Supplement* devoted a whole front page to the astounding discovery of Shakespeare's Sonnet 155. Eminent scholars from all over the world endorsed the authenticity of the manuscript. Several papers appeared in critical journals setting out the results of textual analysis which proved *beyond doubt* that the hand was Shakespeare's. An American from a mid-west university gained a PhD by a statistical analysis of the frequency of the letter "o" in the first 154 sonnets and compared that to Sonnet 155, proving *even further beyond doubt* that the poem was genuine. And Dr Fotheringay was given a special chair at Cambridge in recognition of his great scholarship.

In the meantime, Freddie was sailing to Africa on the *SS Aurora*, to pursue a life of leisure and painting as Assistant District Officer for the Colonial Service in a remote corner of Kenya. He had put his academic distinction to excellent use. He found that doors opened wherever he went and a Knight Commander of the Royal Victorian Order, whom his father knew, recommended a career in the colonies, where a bright young man could distinguish himself away from the dusty streets of London and return to the old country as a latter day Wellesley or Clive or even Churchill. The idea appealed to Freddie, not because it offered glory and status, but because he might find a quiet part of the world where he would be left alone. He stuck a pin in the *Times Atlas* he found in his father's study, and the first pink country he struck other than Wales would be his destination. And so he found himself standing at the rails of the *SS Aurora* as she sailed into the setting sun. The bows of the ship carved through the blue waves of the Indian Ocean as it neared Mombasa; sea turtles paddled in its wake; and bottle-nosed dolphins leapt for the simple joy of living. Freddie felt the same; the old world was left behind, like yesterday's newspaper lying in the gutter, while the free fresh air of a new world fanned his cheek. The unknown, the uncharted, the unpredictable, the thrill of it all!

He had been in Kenya for six months when a letter arrived for him with a London postmark. It was from Fotheringay and marked Cell 155, Wormwood Scrubs. Obviously, something had not quite worked out.

Chapter 2

The *SS Aurora* gently sidled into the old harbour of Mombasa. The wind off the sea had faded and Freddie felt for the first time the full blast of the equatorial sun on his back. The hawsers at bow and stern were thrown and secured before he looked over the ship's handrail at the quayside below, where a turbulent army of officials and porters awaited the lowering of the gangway. The moment the wooden planks hit the concrete, amid a cacophony of whistling and a barrage of shouts, a surge of figures poured down the steps to meet the approaching tide of humanity on the shore. It seemed to Freddie that the whole of Africa must be assembled on the quayside, creating a dervish dance of activity; it was his first taste of the African way of doing things. He was dressed as befitted an Assistant District Officer of the British Colonial Service (Administrative Section), in cream tropical suit and wide-brimmed hat and, although he may have appeared to those around him the essence of cool calm, inside he was beginning to wonder if he had made the right decision at all.

By dint of his excellent academic qualifications, and the intervention of his father's tame KCVO, Freddie had skipped the ignominy of serving for two years as a District Officer Cadet. This had allowed him to travel at His Majesty's expense in a first class cabin; and to be met at the quayside by a uniformed driver in a black Morris Ten. But as his eyes lifted to the horizon, from the top deck of the ship, Freddie could see nothing but rolling forests and hills stretching forever into the blue haze of the interior of this vast alien continent.

He was shaken from his ponderings by an African voice. 'Mr Ottaway, sir! I am Horatio and I am here to take you to meet the District Officer.' It was the driver from below, who had already organised a pair of native porters to stagger down the gangway with Freddie's trunk and easel. He bowed.

'Welcome to Kenya. Please to follow me.'

Freddie bowed back, not knowing yet how a white man should behave in this new world, and did as he was told. He was planted in the back seat of the Morris Ten, sweat pouring down his cheeks, his legs sticking to the burning leather of the seat. The engine started, the horn sounded, and Horatio carved his way through the quayside throng like a ship parting the waves.

'Where exactly is the District Officer, Horatio?' Freddie asked.

'Oh, not far, sir,' Horatio replied vaguely.

'How far, exactly?'

'Oh, two days, maybe three at most.'

Freddie lay back in his seat and looked up at the roof of the car. He groaned inwardly. But his fears of being imprisoned in the back seat for three days were dismissed a few minutes later when Horatio drew up in the yard of Mombasa railway station. The building was unimposing, a single-storey brick construction with a corrugated iron roof. There was no platform, simply a flat expanse of dry hard-packed earth, with a few flower tubs dotted here and there, and the occasional bench. The railway tracks ran through the middle. A hole in the wall indicated the ticket office. Flies buzzed in the sun and there was such a silence as if nothing had ever happened here, or was likely to again. Horatio unloaded the boot of the car and carried Freddie's luggage to a bench.

'I say goodbye now sir,' said Horatio. 'I have tickets for you to Nairobi and on to Nakuru. You will be met there with a car.' He handed them over.

'So you're not travelling with me?' said Freddie, slightly alarmed. 'How long is the journey?'

'To Nakuru, one day, but you have first class compartment with a bed. Make sure you get off at Nakuru or you will end up in Lake Victoria.' With that, Horatio bade Freddie goodbye, climbed into the Morris, and drove off in a cloud of red dust.

Freddie sat down on the bench and waited. During the

course of the next hour, amid the incessant drone of flies and the pulsating heat, he noticed a slow accumulation of passengers. A clergyman with a dog collar and a panama hat stationed himself in the shade; an Indian in an expensive suit appeared, complete with servant carrying his bags; and a small number of native Kenyans, men and women, gathered at the far end of the station building. Suddenly, from nowhere, a shrill whistle sounded and a column of steam shot up into the air a quarter of a mile down the track. The clanking of a steam engine grew louder and the ground began to shake as the mighty *Masai of Kenya* locomotive, in East African Railway livery, hauled itself to a halt before the waiting crowd. There was a sudden rush of feet, as if a hundred people had been waiting in hiding for this moment, and Freddie found himself surrounded.

'Don't worry, old boy, follow me,' and he felt a hand grip his elbow. The clergyman steered him towards a carriage door and handed him up the steps. A native porter, without instructions, had magically grabbed his luggage and was already placing it on the racks in the first class compartment. 'That's how it works here,' said the clergyman. 'It's not like trying to find a porter at Waterloo. Just give him a shilling and he'll be happy. New to this country? Best place in the world, believe me. Hugh Porter, pleased to meet you. Come on, let's get a seat and have a pink gin. I'm parched.'

'Freddie Ottaway, Colonial Service. I'm going to Nakuru, wherever that is.'

'I'm going there too,' replied Porter. 'We can share the ride.'

The train pulled slowly out of the station. Freddie and Porter had settled into window seats in a first class compartment, which they had to themselves, but when he put his head out of the open window to look along the carriages, Freddie saw nothing but white-clad figures clinging to rails and sitting on carriage roofs. The train was laden with native passengers.

'Most of them travel for nothing,' explained Porter. 'That's why there was the sudden rush when the train arrived.

Nobody does a thing about it but after a while you don't notice it.'

'And have you been here long,' asked Freddie.

'Half a lifetime, or so it seems. Surrey seems a long way away. I would hate to go back. The sun rises here at the same time every day of the year and sets at the same time. There's the short rains and the long rains, but we know when they're coming and when they're going. This is a country where you don't need a clock, Ottaway.'

And it seemed that the railway company did not need a timetable either, as the train trundled slowly through the empty landscape as if arriving today or tomorrow didn't really matter either way. The steward served the drinks and Freddie sat back in his dusty seat. This felt like his kind of country. At Nairobi, which they reached six hours later, what seemed like a field kitchen was assembled at the side of the tracks, and a squad of Indian cooks loaded large containers of aromatic food on to the train.

'That's dinner,' said Porter. 'Most of the cooks here are Indians so I hope you like curry.'

Half an hour later, with the train puffing its way slowly through a red-brown landscape of rocky outcrops and forests of grey-green eucalyptus and acacia trees, Porter and Freddie made their way to the dining car. Over an array of dishes, the like of which Freddie had never experienced before, Porter began to relate the story of his life. Freddie looked at him as he talked: he was thin, with lank hair slightly over his collar, a mouth that seemed to droop a little, and a bony frame that seemed too small for his jacket. It was as if the relentless heat of equatorial Africa had drained the life out of him. And yet the two were drawn together in a way that could never have happened in England. Freddie realised, for the first time, what it meant to be white in black Africa: the unspoken bond of loyalty that held white people together, despite their incompatibilities, simply because they were white within a sea of black faces. One would have to do something truly awful to break this bond, he thought.

Porter droned on, from his schooldays in Surrey, to a

provincial theology degree and a curacy in a country parish in Suffolk. Then a mysterious jump to become the vicar of St James' Anglican church in Nakuru; but nothing was said about the suddenness of it all and Freddie did not ask.

The steward cleared the dinner things away and the two men smoked over a brandy. Away to the west the vast African sun slid quickly below the horizon. Not the long withdrawal that Freddie had become used to in East Anglia, where the world seemed to slip into an eerie half-light for hours before the darkness thickened. Here the golden ball vanished in minutes, leaving only a splinter of brilliant yellow light playing on the tree tops for a few last moments. Then the blackness of Africa enveloped all, sudden and complete. 'This is a magic land,' he thought.

At ten, exhausted from the day, Freddie turned in. He fell instantly asleep on the crisp white linen of his fold-down bed in the mahogany cabin. The water in the jug swayed gently as the slow train rolled over the iron rails at twenty miles an hour and the sweet warm air wafted through the open window, carrying with it a continent of enchanting scents. Freddie was not the first Englishman to be beguiled and bewitched by the splendours of Africa.

Hours later he was jolted out of his deep sleep by the violent shunting of the train. He rolled up the blind. It was not light yet but he could make out a few low grey buildings along the track, as if the train were being shunted into a siding behind a station. Then there was a knock on the compartment door. It was the steward.

'Nakuru, Mr Ottaway. Disembarking in half an hour.'

Freddie looked at his watch; it was only five o'clock in the morning. Then he remembered Horatio the driver telling him to make sure he got off in Nakuru but he hadn't explained it would be in the middle of the night. He might well have ended up in Lake Victoria. He gathered his things together and made his way to the restaurant car where the steward was serving tea. Hugh Porter was already there and nodded gloomily to Freddie when he entered. 'Sleep well, Ottaway?'

'Thank you, yes. Lucky I woke. I could have ended up at

the other end of the country.'

'Don't worry, the steward knows why you're here. The Africans are like that. Nothing goes unnoticed.' He took a sip of his tea. 'I say, Ottaway, before we part, it's been jolly good talking to you. Next time you're in Nakuru, you must come to stay.' Freddie detected a note of sadness in his voice, as if he were a lonely man seeking a friend. Porter handed him his card. Time was marching on. Together they descended on to the low platform, bags in hand, and walked to the station yard. Dawn was approaching but the air felt chilled. Freddie could see a driver standing by a car with a British flag on the bonnet. He turned to Porter and shook his hand.

'Thanks for introducing me to Africa,' he said. 'I will come to see you, I promise.'

The driver approached Freddie. 'Mr Ottaway. I'm here to take you to the District Officer, Mr Gordon. If you follow me, sir.'

Freddie got into the back seat, the driver stowed the luggage, and they set off along a dusty road into the centre of town. The early morning light suddenly increased and Freddie saw to his amazement the sprawling expanse of huts and shacks that lined both sides of the road. Stray dogs wandered here and there, chickens scratched in the dirt, men cycled precariously along the pot-holed surface and women stood by open doorways. And the town went on and on. It was only when the car had driven a mile or so that stone buildings began to appear, as they neared the centre. The driver took a sharp turn down a wide road lined with tall trees. White detached houses stood apart on each side and they drew up before a villa with a Union Flag hanging limply from a pole in the front garden. As Freddie mounted the front steps, the door opened and a solid black housekeeper greeted him.

'I have some breakfast for you, Mr Ottaway. Mr Gordon will be down to see you in about an hour. If you follow me.'

She showed Freddie into a large dining room, served him coffee and pointed him in the direction of the dishes on the sideboard. There was a copy of *The East African Standard* on the table. Freddie looked at the back page: Hutton had scored a century for Yorkshire. He looked around him, at the white table cloth, at the sideboard with eggs and bacon and kedgeree, and at the framed photographs of colonial officers on the walls. He could have been in a gentleman's club in Picadilly, that is, if he could discount the acres of slums that surrounded this oasis of other-worldliness.

At half past eight, District Officer Gordon entered the room. Freddie rose to his feet, as befitted a junior in the presence of his senior. Gordon was a red-faced Scot from Aberdeen. The African sun had turned him puce not brown and he had squeezed his over-weight body into a bulging white suit. His grey hair was smoothed straight back over his head which created the effect of a boiled egg. His speech was short and decisive, in a clipped Aberdonian accent that was as hard as the granite of the city of his birth.

'Good trip, Ottaway? Trust the *Masai of Kenya* treated you well?'

It took a moment before Freddie realised Gordon was referring to a steam train and not a noble race of savages.

'Oh, yes, thank you. Travelled with a very decent fellow. You probably know him – the Reverend Hugh Porter.'

Gordon looked at him for a moment. 'Porter?' he muttered. 'Oh, him!' Another pause. Then: 'Handicap?' he asked.

'I beg your pardon, sir,' replied Freddie.

'Golf! You do play, of course?'

Freddie racked his memory. A fleeting vision of a shanked seven-iron in a drunken college match flashed before his eyes.

'Oh, yes, golf, of course. Never bothered with a handicap actually. Too busy.' Freddie realised before he had closed his mouth that this was the wrong answer.

'Fine course here, Ottaway,' said Gordon. 'Everybody plays. Not quite a Scottish links mind you, and you need to look out for the odd angry crocodile in the water hazards, but on the whole pretty good if you hit straight.'

'Sounds wonderful,' said Freddie, filling with gloom at the thought of eighteen holes with Gordon, who was looking at him sceptically over his scrambled eggs. Another hour of tedium stretched out before Gordon actually broached the subject Freddie had been waiting to tackle.

'I expect you want to know where you're going,' he said. 'Well, it's up country. Place called Lodwar, in Turkana County. Hussain will show you the way. Not much there but pleasant enough, apart from the snakes. Last man had to have his leg amputated. Just in time – the poison was on its way up.'

'Sounds interesting,' said Freddie. 'I wonder, sir, if you could brief me on my duties there. What are you wanting me to do, in fact?' Freddie realised the question sounded naïve but the answer showed his real naïvety.

'Do? We don't want you to do anything, Ottaway. That's the whole point. Don't do anything and don't let anything happen. If it does, stop it. That's what the Colonial Service is all about. Preserving the *status quo*.'

'I see,' said Freddie, thoughtfully. 'I'll do my best, sir.'

'Take a sand wedge with you. You can practise your bunker shots. Start first thing in the morning. It's a day's drive.'

Chapter 3

Hussain was a diminutive Indian who had lived all his life in Kenya. His father had taken a boat from Bombay across the Indian Ocean to set up a shop in Nairobi and Hussain and his six brothers and sisters had grown up as African Asians, with nowhere to call home, excluded from the tribes of Kenya and exiled from their homeland. Working for the British, the biggest outsiders of all, was a logical arrangement. He drove a car for the District Officer, washing and polishing it every day for want of something to do. Today he had a mission to fulfil, to drive the Assistant District Officer up the rift valley to the outpost of Lodwar, overlooking Lake Turkana, the furthermost reach of Kenya.

They set off at first light in the new service Land Rover, just shipped in from Mombasa. The canvas top was rolled back and the red dust of the road swept over them as they drove, until Freddie's eyes and ears were clogged and his hair had turned ginger. The main road north out of town soon left the shanty shacks behind and turned into a rutted track which, in the rainy season, would be impassable. After an hour the African sun rose on the right, throwing the sweeping plains of the valley into sharp relief. Herds of grazing animals, water buffalo and zebra, wandered casually across the road, interspersed with wildebeest and the occasional giraffe. Maasai tribesmen strolled languidly behind their grazing herds, chiding them gently. It was a world of wonder and majesty as if Noah had flung open the doors of the ark and released his treasures. They lurched along, axles bouncing across the parched mud, until Freddie's arms and shoulders ached from holding the door post. At noon they stopped under the shade of a wide spreading tree. Hussain lit a fire and brewed some tea in an aluminium pot.

'What kind of tree is this, Hussain?' Freddie asked, as he stretched out his legs on the dry ground.

'This is called an epiyei tree, sir, in Turkana but it has many different names in Kenya. The farmers use its juice to treat pink-eye in their cattle. It is a very good tree.'

'It is indeed, Hussain, and a very shady tree too, and this tea is also very good.'

'Yes, sir, my sisters pick these leaves every day, where they live.'

Freddie breathed in the aroma of the steaming tea, mingled with the scent of the epiyei tree and the sweet taste of the dusty earth in his mouth. In his mind he framed the pictures he would paint of these sweeping plains, the flat-topped trees and the wide blue sky with its fleecy clouds. And, according to Gordon, he had all the time in the world to do so.

At dusk they reached Lodwar on the banks of the Turkwell river and passed through its main street to a hill overlooking the small town. There on the top stood Freddie's house, a low wooden building with a corrugated iron roof and a verandah, for all the world resembling the pavilion of an English village cricket team. Desmond, his African servant, came out to meet the car as Hussain drew to a halt.

'I am Desmond, sir,' said the servant. 'Welcome to Lodwar. I will lower the flag now that you have arrived.'

The sun had vanished quickly and darkness surrounded the house. Desmond showed Freddie his bedroom, with simple cane furniture and an iron bedstead; then his living room, which resembled the conservatory of a bungalow in Epsom; and finally his office, with plain deal desk and wooden filing cabinet. Freddie pointed to a metal cupboard bolted to the wall and secured with a heavy padlock.

'What's in there, Desmond?' He asked.

'That is secure gun cabinet, sir. The key is in your drawer.'

Freddie pulled open the drawer of his desk and took out a keyring with a couple of keys hanging from it. He opened the gun cabinet and looked inside. There he saw a double-barrelled shotgun, a hunting rifle, and a Browning pistol. He had never fired a gun in his life and the thought of taking aim against any living creature filled him horror.

'What are they for?' he asked.

Desmond looked at him in disbelief. Then he answered. 'Shotgun is for shooting dinner, sir. Rifle is for shooting lions, sir. Pistol is for shooting intruders, sir.'

'Intruders?' queried Freddie. 'What kind of intruders?'

'Many bad men in Kenya, sir,' replied Desmond. Then he turned and disappeared into a back room. Freddie followed him into what turned out to be the kitchen, with a stove burning wood. On the top was an iron pot with a chicken cooking slowly. 'Dinner is ready, sir,' said Desmond.

Freddie returned to his living room and sat at the small table in the window where Desmond had set a place for him. Presently, the chicken arrived, on an oval dish, surrounded by roast vegetables which he could not identify. He had forgotten he had not eaten all day and suddenly hunger overwhelmed him; his first meal in his African home was the most delicious he had ever tasted. Later that evening, he strolled around his new house. Hussain had found a camp bed on the rear porch, where he could spend the night before driving back to Nakuru the following day; while Desmond was seen vanishing up a narrow path to a native hut in a glade behind the house. Two black women sat on the doorstep, grinding maize with heavy wooden mortars.

Freddie slept soundly and woke late the following morning. Desmond brought him the freshest coffee he had ever tasted, with a plate of fruit and flat corn bread.

'Tell me, Desmond, now that Hussain has left, how do I get about?' he asked.

'You have very fine horse, sir. Name is Phoenix. Mr Latimer bought him when he was here. Used to ride him everywhere, before he lost his leg. I show you.'

Freddie followed Desmond across the green lawn in front of the house. There, under a straw roof on four posts, stood a brown horse tugging at a suspended hay bale. The creature looked at him sideways and carried on eating. Freddie had never ridden a horse, except for a donkey on the beach at Margate, but he recognised that Phoenix was far from thoroughbred. He had the look of a camel, without the hump, and very long teeth.

'Phoenix very fine horse, sir. He take you everywhere.'

'I'm sure he will, Desmond.'

'Just don't stand behind him, sir.'

Freddie looked beyond the shelter where Phoenix was tethered, towards a clearing in the bushes some twenty yards away. He saw what looked like the bulbous nose of a car protruding from the encroaching vegetation.

'But isn't that a car over there, Desmond?' he said, pointing off into the bushes.

'Oh, yes sir, but Mr Latimer never used it. There are no roads out of here you see, only the road to Nakuru. Mr Latimer always use horse.'

'Well, I'm going to use it!' said Freddie. He strode across to the thicket and started to pull the overgrown bushes away from the bonnet to reveal a black Austin A40. It was covered in dust and chickens had made a home in the back seat but, apart from that, it looked in reasonable order. He jumped into the front seat, turned on the ignition and pulled the starter button. There was a click and nothing else. Forcing his way to the back of the car, he found a starter handle in the boot, shoved it into the hole in the front bumper and started to crank the engine as hard as he could. Desmond looked on in amazement as the Assistant District Officer broke out into a sweat with his exertions in the full heat of the African morning. But eventually, with a series of shakes and jolts, the engine spluttered into life. 'There you see, Desmond!' Freddie shouted in triumph. Desmond cheered loudly and clapped his hands, while three chickens flapped their way in panic out of a rear window. The bond between the two was sealed from that moment of shared satisfaction. Desmond had never met a white man like this.

Later that day Desmond came into Freddie's office with a note. It was from a Doctor Owen, written on headed notepaper, with the address *Lodwar Clinic* in the top right hand corner:

My Dear Ottaway
Come to supper this evening at seven. Will introduce you

to the locals. No need to reply.
Yours
David Owen.

Freddie thought it rather odd that Dr Owen assumed he would appear that evening. Then, after a moment, he realised it wasn't odd at all: nothing else happened here, and if it did, everybody would know about it. Freddie looked at his clothes, grubby from mucking out the car.

'Desmond, I need a clean shirt and tie for tonight and press my suit, please.'

'Yes, sir,' said Desmond with enthusiasm, and scuttled off to see to it.

Freddie sauntered out into the sunshine to look at his clean new car. Instead of chickens in the back, he saw the flashing eyes of three black children, who jumped out when they saw him and ran off in the direction of the hut at the back of the house. Freddie wondered how many more natives the British Colonial Service was supporting in the cause of doing nothing.

That evening, a little before sunset, Freddie started up the car and set off to find Dr Owen's house. Desmond had given him some directions but, amid the arm wavings and digressions, he had failed to form a clear picture of where he was going. As Lodwar was a very small place, however, he thought it would be easy enough to find his way, providing he was generally heading in the right direction. After a few minutes he reached a crossroads in what seemed to be the centre of the village. A general store stood on one corner, with the name *Mohammed* painted in faded black on the crumbling plaster walls; and on another, two petrol pumps stood like twin sentinels before a pile of empty oil cans. There was not a soul in sight. He chose a road that he thought must be in the right direction and set off. Soon it narrowed to a track and the bush on each side grew denser as the twilight thickened. Freddie began to realise he was lost but pressed on in the hope the track would swing round in a more promising direction. He turned a corner, headlights piercing the darkness, when before him he saw a sudden movement, and another, and a man was waving him down from the roadside. His face shone black in the headlights and Freddie saw the glint of a long steel blade in his hand. Fear struck and he put his foot down to the floor; the engine raced, rear wheels spinning before the tyres bit, and then the car leaped forward leaving the men behind in a cloud of dust. Freddie was shaking and could do nothing but drive ahead with no thought but to escape. By some miracle, the track curved round through the bush and, after a mile or so, he realised he was looking once more at two petrol pumps, but from a different angle, while Mohammed's store was now behind him. An Indian stood in the doorway, under a dull yellow light bulb. Freddie shouted across to him. 'I'm looking for Dr Owen's house!'

The Indian did not speak but pointed towards the only road of the four that Freddie had not already sampled. 'Of course,' he thought, 'stupid of me.' But his hands were still shaking as he tried to change gear. He was late in arriving at Owen's house. He knew he must be at the right place when he saw a post with a house name in Welsh. The lights were blazing out into the night and his host came to the door as the car pulled up.

'Sorry I'm late,' Freddie said. 'Got lost. Met a fellow waving a long knife at me, actually. Gave me a hell of a fright.'

'Did you shoot him?' asked Owen.

'Good God no,' replied Freddie.

'Well, you should have,' said Owen in a matter-of-fact manner. 'You need a whisky. Come along in and I'll introduce you.'

Owen was a short Welshman of middle-age, thinning on top, with a physique that would have passed muster on the front row of a Welsh male voice choir and the avuncular presence of the mature GP who has seen everything a body can throw at him. He thrust a large whisky into Freddie's hand and steered him into the main room.

'Now, everyone,' he said loudly above the general chatter, 'this is our new man Freddie Ottaway. Gordon wired to say you would be here, Freddie. He said you're a very fine golfer.' Every face in the room turned to look at Freddie. He felt as if he were being sized up to see if he would fit the empty space left by his predecessor. 'Already had a run-in with one of the troublemakers,' Owen continued.

'Did you shoot him?' asked one of the guests, Inspector Dalrymple of the Kenyan Police, a tall wiry figure with a military moustache.

'No, I didn't have a gun,' replied Freddie, wondering if it was par for the course to have to shoot one's way to a dinner party in this part of the world.

'You must always carry a gun,' said Dalrymple. 'Never know when one of those fellows is going to jump you.'

'Come on, let's have dinner,' announced Owen, leading the way through a set of double doors into the dining room. The table was set for eight. Owen sat at the head with Dalrymple's wife on his right hand, a tall thin woman with a beaky nose, wearing the kind of outfit Freddie remembered his mother wearing, severe and unwelcoming, with large shoulders. On his left sat a mousy little page-boy of a woman, Miss Spencer, who turned out to be the headmistress of the local school. She said little and ate like a bird. Then came Dalrymple himself, blazer and club tie to the fore, and opposite him a tall, blonde haired Norwegian, Knut Larsen, who ran the fish canning plant on Lake Turkana. He spoke in correct English with a strong Bergen accent, bringing the fjords of western Norway to the heart of Africa. At the foot of the table, Owen's daughter presided, with Freddie on her right hand and Sister Celestine on her left, a member of the religious order who staffed the clinic run by Dr Owen. She peered across the table at Freddie like a pair of eyes looking through a diving mask, her head encased in her order's wimple. Owen's daughter was called Morgane and, like the character in Arthurian legend, seemed to cast a spell on those she encountered, with her dark eyes and celtic hair. She was eighteen years old and had just finished her time at the Sacred Heart Convent School for Girls in Nairobi. She was spending six months with her father in Lodwar before leaving for

London. For Freddie, she was the only redeeming feature of the evening, a single spark of optimism and joy within the dreary drone of colonial attitudes buzzing round the table. Before the men left to smoke on the verandah, she had asked him what he liked doing best.

'I'm a painter,' he said. 'I suppose I shall have time out here to paint a lot. At least, I hope so.'

'I'm sure you will,' Morgane replied. 'Would you paint me?'

'I would love to,' said Freddie, before he was dragged away for the compulsory brandy and cigar. Morgane was entangled with the ladies for the rest of the evening but she came to the door when the guests were departing.

'Remember your offer,' she said to Freddie, who nodded in assent.

'Make sure you take the right road this time, Ottaway,' shouted Dalrymple, on the way past him.

The drive back to his house took only twenty minutes, but long enough for the smoke of the evening's events to clarify in his mind. As he drove into the clearing before his bungalow he saw a single light burning on the verandah. It was Desmond awaiting his return.

'You should not have waited up for me, Desmond,' said Freddie.

'I wanted to see you home, Bwana. There was trouble on the other side of the village tonight. Bad men about.'

'I know, Desmond, but I'm safe now. You go to bed.'

Freddie went into his office, took the keys from his desk drawer, opened the gun cabinet and took out the Browning pistol. This time he kept the keys on his person. He looked at the heavy piece of metal in his hand and he was struck by the grim brutality of it. With some concern, he realised he was beginning to think like the others, and Desmond had called him *Bwana*, as if his master were quickly blending into the African way of doing things.

Chapter 4

That week Desmond taught Freddie how to ride a horse. He led Phoenix round and round the clearing with Freddie in the saddle. In truth, there were only two things to learn about riding this horse: first, that Phoenix would never move at more than a walking pace, unless frightened by an armadillo or a warthog; second, that he would always wander off into the bush if he were not tethered. After two days, Freddie was confident enough to set off on his own, with sketchpad and pencil, to capture the beauty of the African landscape. He trekked to the edge of the rift valley from where he could look down upon the vast expanse of shimmering water that was Lake Turkana, stretching away to the north as far as the mysterious land of Ethiopia. He sat down on a rocky ledge, tied Phoenix to the branch of a spreading tree, and began to assemble his rapid sketches, simple impressions of the majesty of this ancient world. He was an instinctive artist able to capture the essence of place in a few untutored strokes.

After an hour or so, he saw a cloud of dust away in the distance and, through the heat haze, the moving shape of a horse and a man. After his experience on the road that night, he was filled with alarm. He checked his saddle bag for the pistol and waited. In a few minutes, the traveller was upon him, wide-brimmed hat shielding his face from the sun. He was a white man and, when he took off his hat, Freddie recognised the blonde hair of Knut Larsen.

'Good day, Ottaway,' he called out in his Bergen accent. 'What are you doing up here?'

'Making sketches for my paintings,' he replied. 'I didn't expect to meet anyone out here. It's a pleasant surprise to find someone I know.'

'I often come this way,' said Larsen. 'We have a fish-canning plant down there on the shore. Riding out from the office in town gives me a chance to see the country.' He dismounted and sat down next to Freddie. 'Tell me, how did you enjoy the other evening, at Owen's? You were lucky enough to be next to Morgane, I noticed. Quite a girl that.'

'To tell the truth, Larsen, there was quite a lot I didn't understand. Everybody seemed decent enough but they didn't seem to have much good to say about the natives. It was almost as if we were doing them a favour by being here. You know, our great duty to develop them and educate them and so on. I can't help thinking it's their country after all.'

'That's a pretty dangerous opinion for a white man to express out here, Ottaway. I wouldn't spread that around. But I know what you mean. I can see it from the outside. I'm a Norwegian trader. Unlike the British, we don't have a tradition of empire, apart from a bit of rape and pillage a thousand years ago. They close ranks because they feel under threat.'

Larsen took out his leather tobacco pouch and filled his white curved pipe. The sweet blue smoke hung in the still air. He pulled a flask from his pocket, unscrewed the top, and handed it to Freddie, who took a swig. It was warm from the heat of the day and the liquid burned his throat.

'My God, what was that?' he asked, catching his breath.

'Norwegian aquavit. The best you can get,' he replied, taking a mouthful himself.

'You say they are under threat, the British? But they run the show. They've got all the money and all the guns.'

' "They"? ' asked Larsen, turning his pale blue eyes on Freddie. 'I thought you were one of them, being British.'

Freddie was silent, lowering his head and studying the dry earth beneath his feet. 'I thought I was, before I came out here. I'm not quite sure what I am now.' He paused, before adding: 'Why do you say they're under threat?'

'They're sitting on a volcano, Freddie, and don't know what to do about it. That chap you met the other night on the road, with the long knife, he wasn't alone you know. There's a ragged army of them, mostly from one tribe, trying to frighten the rest of the country into kicking out the imperialist British. Everyone of our nice tame houseboys and girls knows all about it. But nobody wants to say anything! Very soon this country will be theirs again and we'll all be back in our cold, wet little kingdoms in the north. Look at the blue of that sky! Doesn't it bring tears to your eyes?'

Larsen pointed the stem of his pipe across the rift valley into the burning heart of the African sun. He stood up, stretched his arms, and mounted his horse. 'Why don't we ride back together,' he said. 'My house is on your way. You can have an ice-cold beer. You see, I have a fridge, borrowed from the factory, which is more than the British have given you! And you can tell me about Morgane. I bet she's made a date with you.'

'I'm going to paint her, actually,' answered Freddie. 'How did you guess that?'

Larsen looked down from his saddle, his face creasing into a smile.

Freddie arrived home late that day, just as the sun was setting. He was aching and slightly confused, not only about the politics of the place, but also about Morgane, the mysterious Welsh princess. Larsen had set hares running in each direction. Desmond met him on the steps and took Phoenix to his shelter for the night. Later, he served Freddie at his table in the window. It was a tasteless fish.

'Did this fish come out of a tin, Desmond?' asked Freddie.

'No, Bwana, it came out of the lake, then went into a tin.'

He broke into a broad grin at the joke before disappearing back into his kitchen.

Over the next few weeks, Freddie's life fell into a pattern. His official duties were routine and undemanding. For the most part he endorsed identity cards and passes with the official rubber stamp; occasionally he issued permits for the native population to move from one settler farm to another; at other times he issued warrants to the police to deal with squatters who had exceeded their stay on farms. Once a week a letter arrived from Nairobi containing amendments to standing orders, which Freddie filed away in his wooden cabinet. But all the time he was aware of a certain rising tide of resentment among the natives. He heard rumours that many natives were swearing an oath to an organisation aiming to overthrow the ruling powers; and acts of violence against settler farmers and their native workers increased day by day. Army patrols began to pass through Lodwar in camouflaged Land Rovers, six men at a time, armed with sub-machine guns and rifles, and British officers at the head of troops from the King's African Rifles became a regular sight. And all the time, his telephone remained silent; Gordon never telegraphed instructions from Nakuru. It was as if the world of Lodwar were an island of irrelevance in a sea of disregard. Freddie had been told to preserve the *status quo*; in this he had no option, no tools to do differently. Yet all around he heard the clock ticking its ominous beat towards the hour of midnight.

One morning, as he sat at his desk, he heard the sound of a horse's hooves on the path outside his house. He stepped out on to the verandah. There, on a tall grey horse, sat Morgane. 'I've come to have my picture painted,' she said. She took off her hat and her long black hair cascaded below her shoulders. 'You said you would,' she added, before dismounting. She wore a pair of moleskin jodhpurs and a white shirt, open at the neck. Her skin was radiant from the African sun.

'I will, Morgane. The verandah would be best, because of the light. Come and sit here,' he said, pointing to a wicker chair. 'I'll make some sketches first.'

Morgane sat down and crossed her legs, looking out into the bush. Freddie took up his pad and a piece of charcoal. With a few quick strokes he etched in the high cheek bones, the sweep of the hair, the curve of the breast against the white shirt and the line of the bare forearm resting on the knee. She was holding her head at an angle, as if she were studying the very blue of the sky. Then she turned and looked towards him, the slightest suggestion of a blush rising on her cheek. 'Do you want to kiss me, Freddie?' she asked.

She was eighteen years old and ready to explore life. Freddie put down his charcoal and dropped the sketch pad on the side table.

'You're a very beautiful girl,' said Freddie. 'Any man would, of course. You know that.'

'Are you any man, Freddie?' she asked.

'I suppose I am.'

She stood up and walked towards him. She put her arms round his neck and held her body against his, turning her face upwards. He kissed her lips and then slid his hand inside her shirt, feeling the warm mound of her breast. There was no way back from this. He took her into the bedroom and closed the door. They made love several times with an urgent passion. At the end, Freddie lay quietly, aware that it was not he who had driven Morgane on, but her simple desire to feel what it was like to be a woman. Later, as she lay in the crook of his arm, he said: 'How did you know all this, Morgane? What did the nuns teach you at the Sacred Heart?'

'They told us what not to do, so we did the opposite, I suppose,' she replied with a laugh. 'We used to hold readings from the *Kama Sutra* in the dorm at night. Amala used to draw diagrams, some of them quite complex.'

Freddie looked puzzled: 'Who's Amala?'

'Amala was my best friend at school. She's half Muslim; half Maasai. She's in Nairobi, studying law. Her father runs the Mohammed business and has made a fortune.'

There were several further sittings before the painting was completed and each ended in the same way, in a riotous encounter on Freddie's bed. Freddie learned a lot about sex during those weeks and months. One day, Morgane announced she was visiting friends of her father's in the Highlands. It was a day's ride away and Freddie was to come with her.

'Tell Desmond you'll be away for three days,' she said. 'You can show me how well you ride. I want to let you see the real Kenya, Freddie, before I leave for London.'

The Highlands were the richest farmland in the country. They lay in the cooling uplands above the valley, where the white settler farmers built their wealth on the cheap wage-labourers of the native population. Freddie had heard about it but had never seen it in reality. Morgane and he rode for a day beneath the African sky, pausing to rest under the wide canopies of the trees of the valley, with the calls of a thousand exotic birds in their ears.

'Will you return to Kenya?' he asked Morgane, as their horses carried them slowly higher and higher.

'I mean to return as a doctor here,' she replied, 'when I finish in London. But I want to work in a different way from my father. The days of benevolence will be over; and the days of entitlement will have arrived. I want to work with the Africans as equals. My father doesn't understand that. Do you?'

'I do. You make me feel worthless, Morgane. You have such a mission in life.'

'You're an artist, Freddie. Paint the beauty of the Africans. Let the world know!'

And that was how the seedcorn of an ambition was planted in Freddie's mind, seduced by an eighteen-year-old girl with the world at her feet.

At dusk they reached Marlborough Farm, a thousand feet up in the clear, dry air. From a distance the white wooden walls of the low farmhouse shone in the setting sun and the horses, sensing journey's end, put their heads down and pushed upwards along the dusty track. A glade of fruit trees sheltered the short driveway which wound through green lawns to the main door. At the sound of the horses' hooves, a young black boy emerged from a side door and took the reins as the travellers dismounted, shaking the dust off their clothes and hair. Freddie looked westward towards the setting sun. The Highlands were not what he expected; they were rolling hills, like the rounded hills of north Yorkshire. But they were bright lime green, with waves of swaying bushes covering every inch. Tall trees grew at intervals between fields and, beyond a copse in the distance, he could make out columns of blue smoke rising from the native fires in the Kikuyu village.

'It's tea,' said Morgane, 'all for export to Britain and all picked by the women and children of that village down there.' She pointed to the rising smoke. 'Sixty years ago, the natives owned everything you can see. Now they own nothing. And all because we want our tea. Are you beginning to understand me?'

'I'm beginning to understand life,' he replied, 'but only

very slowly. I shall miss you when you go, Morgane. You've taught me a lot. This continent has taught me a lot.'

'Tomorrow we can visit the village, if you like. Now we must go in.'

The Gillespies lived in style. They were second generation Scots whose parents had fled the cold and damp of the east coast of Scotland before the First World War, when the Kenyan land was being seized for the white settler farmers while the natives were forced to provide free labour. But that was a long time ago and, in such cases, memories were short. Now the natives were paid for their labour, although the profits from their land went elsewhere, and the Gillespies, with their good Church of Scotland morality, could happily look upon the progress they had made in agricultural production, while ignoring the theft upon which it was built. They were kind, generous and charming, with the ease that is born of a life of comfort, if not plenty. Like most comfortable whites in colonial Kenya, they easily fell in with other comfortable whites, and that is how they had come to know the Owen family at the time when Morgane's mother was still alive. They had no understanding that Morgane held views they would regard as revolutionary, or that their position, to a newcomer to the continent like Freddie, could appear so untenable.

In the morning, Morgane took Freddie to visit the village below the house. They walked through the tea plantation in the bright sunshine. The fields were full of women and children, bags on shoulders, picking the tender shoots with skill and speed. Their white head-dresses flapped in the breeze.

'They get paid a pittance for each bag. Can you imagine the monotony and the exhaustion of the work, and for so little,' said Morgane.

Soon they reached the clearing where the village lay, a circle of straw houses, like low haystacks with holes neatly cut for windows. A corral of woven sticks held a few cattle and a herd of goats wandered freely among the huts, watched over by an old woman. It was a picture of the stone age.

'Where are the men?' asked Freddie.

'Some are away in the towns, working on construction sites. Others might be wage-labourers on other farms where there are cattle to look after.'

Freddie looked back up the hill they had descended. The white farmhouse looked majestically across the valley, like the Norman keep of a medieval baron, except that the power it wielded was not military, but economic, in a system that the oldest democracy in the world had instituted.

'The Gillespies are not bad people,' Morgane said as they walked back up to the house. 'They look after their families. But to return the land to the natives will be the end for them. They don't think about that because they are frightened to. I love them, but I pity them, and I can't help it.'

The next day they travelled back to Lodwar. Morgane spent the night at Freddie's house. Desmond looked after them both with quiet courtesy and after supper they sat on the verandah smoking and drinking until bedtime. Although they were not lovers in the true sense, they loved each other enough to feel the sadness of the moment. In two days Morgane would leave for Mombasa and the boat to Southampton. She would return a different woman and Freddie would become a different man. It was the last dance before the lights went down for ever.

'I have something for you, Morgane,' he said, rising to his feet and walking into his office. He returned with a cardboard tube and handed it to her. From inside she pulled out the rolled-up portrait Freddie had painted.

'I was a girl then,' she said. 'Thank you, Freddie. For the picture and for you.'

'For what? I was a fool when I came to Africa. Now I begin to understand how the world works, thanks to you. What a mystery it all is and each generation seems bound to make its own discovery, as if the world sprang new-born from its shell each time.'

'Come with me to Mombasa. See me off. We can drive to Nakuru in the Austin and take the train from there. It would make me so happy to have a friend with me.'

'Yes, we are friends, aren't we? Friends for ever.'

'But friends can still make love, can't they?' she added.

Freddie looked across the verandah at Morgane. The darkness was complete, save for the flickering lamp on the table. How far he had travelled since the day she had walked towards him and kissed him for the first time, not out of love, but out of her wish to challenge. She had taught him that; to challenge what he saw around him: Gordon's *status quo,* the deadly benevolence of the whites, the assumption of permanence in the affairs of man.

'Yes, of course we can still make love,' he replied.

Two days later they set off for Nakuru in the official car. Desmond was full of doubts. 'You should telegraph Hussain to come and fetch you, Bwana,' he had said, especially if Miss Morgane is travelling with you.'

'Nonsense, Desmond. This is an Austin of England. It can go anywhere.'

They left the car in the station yard at Nakuru and took the train to Mombasa. It was a long slow journey, each poignant moment stretched out, until at last Freddie found himself watching as the bows of the *SS Aurora* swung slowly away from the quayside, nudged and cajoled by the harbour tugboats. Morgane stood at the rail looking down. As the ship turned full circle she vanished from sight but not before she had made her final wave to Freddie. She was setting out on the voyage of her life and would never again be the girl that he had known. For her, the challenge of the new masked the pain of departing; for Freddie, returning to the strange new world he had by chance and ignorance adopted, there would always be the gap that Morgane had filled for those sweet first months in Africa. But he too was on a journey into a deeper understanding. Was this the real turning point of his life? How does one know such things until, in old age, the reel is rewound and the film stopped at the frame where it all began, in the knowledge of what the ending will be?

And so it was that Freddie embarked on the long lonely journey back home. He had telegraphed Gordon before he left

Lodwar to say he would be calling in to brief him on affairs in the north. He had no idea what he would report; and a strong suspicion that Gordon would not be interested. But it was a pretence he was happy to go along with.

The train to Nakuru was hopelessly delayed. For hour after hour, Freddie leaned his head on his hand, looking out of the window at the endless fields and dry plains, the infinite tiny villages with names known only to their inhabitants. He felt he had become invisible and anonymous in this vastness, as he counted in his imagination the millions of people in the world who did not, and never would, know he had existed. Unless, that is, he created something that expressed his being. 'Paint the beauty of the Africans,' Morgane had said, and he would try to do that, but he feared that his conscience might destroy him in the process.

It was not until late that night that the express pulled into the station. Freddie looked at his watch: it was ten-thirty, hours past the expected arrival time. He was exhausted and depressed. He could not face the prospect of talking to Gordon that evening so he found a telephone in the booking office and called the number of the Colonial Office. The stout housekeeper answered the phone.

'Ottaway, here. I'm afraid the train has been hopelessly delayed. Could you tell Mr Gordon I shall be arriving tomorrow morning.' He spoke quickly and put the phone down before she could even offer to pass him on to Gordon. A wave of relief surged over him. 'Now what?' he asked himself, wondering how he was indeed going to spend the night. Then he heard his name called.

'Freddie Ottaway! Good God, what are you doing here at this time of night?'

He turned to see the thin face and stooping figure of the Reverend Hugh Porter.

'Just got off the train,' he answered.

'And wondering what to do next,' added Porter. 'Just off the train myself. Come on home with me. There's a bed in the guest room. Don't want to be checking in to the local dosshouses here. Far too risky.' And so saying he grabbed

Freddie's bag and was about to summon a taxi when Freddie recalled he had left the official car in the station yard on his way to Mombasa.

'We can take the official car, Hugh. It's just over there,' he said pointing across the platform to the yard behind the low station building. 'You'd better show me the way.' Porter seemed to have the strange knack of appearing at moments of indecision.

The car bounced and veered its way through the pot-holed dirt streets of the town. There were no street lamps and the cones of white light from the car's headlamps picked out a strange slide show of the town's nocturnal existence: street dogs, wandering chickens and goats, sinister groups of men at street corners and passing glimpses of dark interiors lit only by a single lamp. Freddie had a vision of the man with the long knife on his first excursion in this country. Porter sensed his anxiety.

'Frightening, isn't it? Kenya at night time. And we think we have it under control, like Basingstoke. We only come out during daylight, metaphorically speaking.'

Freddie looked across at Porter. What did he mean? What was he trying to say? It was as if an idea were being pushed his way, for him to try for size.

The vicarage of St Andrew's Anglican church looked as if it had been lifted stone by stone from some English suburb and reassembled in the confused lanes of north Nakuru. It was a triumph of nineteenth century gothic, as anomalous in Africa as the religion it proclaimed. But it sat beside a comfortable-looking detached house, double-fronted, with a neat garden of shrubs and flowers set within English lawns. Freddie drew up the car at the gate and Porter showed him into a hall furnished with an Axminster carpet and a hatstand supporting a variety of knobbly walking sticks. There was a smell of floor polish, which seemed to have made it from Guildford to East Africa undiluted, taking Freddie back to his housemaster's study in the South Downs. The housekeeper closed the door behind them, bolting it top and bottom, and the peace of England was reinvented in the heart of Africa.

Despite the late hour, Porter seemed intent on conversation. They sat either side of a superfluous stone fireplace, furnished with brass fire irons. A framed photograph of a cricket team hung above the mantelpiece; no doubt Porter had been a tricky leg-spinner and useful lower order batsman.

'So, Freddie, and what do you make of Africa?' he asked, pouring out a pair of generous whiskies. 'Have you adjusted to the chaos of it all?'

'It seems to me a country that has lost its people. The real people, I mean, not the British. I feel as if they've moved aside to let us have the space. The country, I love. The wide open skies, the clear blue of it all, but there's something lurking, waiting to happen, as if a tiny corner of a beautiful painting is concealing a monster in the shadows while the central figures bask in the sunlight.'

'That's very profound,' said Porter after a moment's reflection. 'I suppose you mean nationalism?'

'Not nationalism exactly, more nationhood. I learned this from an eighteen-year-old girl, would you believe it.'

'I do believe it, Freddie, and I understand exactly what you mean. There are some people I think you should meet while you're here. Can you stay another night?'

'I'm due to meet the District Officer tomorrow but I guess I could escape after that.'

'Gordon, that buffoon, eh? Don't tell him what you have just told me.' Hugh Porter laughed. Freddie was beginning to see him in a different light; not the boring, lonely figure he had first encountered on the overnight train many months ago, but someone with a viewpoint that he might share. But it was getting late and the combined effects of tiredness and whisky were beginning to take over. 'Until tomorrow then,' said Porter, draining his glass in one go. 'By the way, you were at Clare weren't you? Read a thing in the papers about a don from Clare going to gaol for fraud. Something to do with a fake Shakespearean sonnet. Do you know anything about that?'

'No, I'm afraid not,' replied Freddie. 'Good night, Hugh.'

At nine o'clock the next morning Freddie drove to the Colonial Office. He found Gordon in his study, mounds of official-looking documents piled high all around him, many of them unopened. He was leafing through a large illustrated book of some sort, which he put down when his visitor entered the room. Freddie pieced together the title, reading upside-down: *The Hundred Best Golf Holes To Play Before You Die.* His heart sank.

'Ah, Ottaway. Good. Everything all right up there? You getting along alright with the locals. Owen tells me you've settled in well. Nothing to report, I trust.'

Freddie thought for a moment but decided it wasn't worth the effort. 'Fine thank you, sir. Nothing to report.'

'Excellent. Then we can get on. Good day for it.'

'For what exactly, sir?'

'Golf of course. You're making up a four with the captain and hon sec of the Royal Nakuru Golf Club, partnering me of course. Foursomes, so keep me on the fairway. Latimer was quite good at that, until he lost his leg.'

'But I don't have any clubs, sir,' said Freddie in the hope that this was a way out.

'No problem. You can borrow an old set of mine. Come on.'

Freddie was trapped. He knew he had to see this through. It was a true test of his manhood. Hussain was waiting outside with the District Officer's car. In ten minutes they had left the town behind and entered a green, tree-lined valley of gently rolling hills. The potholes turned to a fine gravel drive which curved through a copse to a red-brick late Victorian clubhouse with white-painted window frames. Beside the white doorpost a brass plaque proclaimed that HRH The Prince of Wales had played the first shot there in 1899. Although it was only ten in the morning, a steward attended them on the first tee with a tray, four liqueur glasses and a bottle of Kümmel. Four black caddies stood at a respectful distance observing the white men's ritual.

'Here's to a good game,' said the captain, raising his glass before emptying it in a single mouthful. The steward re-filled the glasses and Gordon said much the same, before emptying his glass. Freddie felt his cares drifting away behind his eyeballs as the alcohol took effect. After two holes of slicing, topping and shanking, Freddie's side were two down. Gordon's face was as deep a red as Freddie had seen and he knew he must redeem himself. At the third, Gordon placed him on the edge of the fairway, near a large walnut tree, one yard short of a creek full of water lilies. Freddie turned to his caddie for advice.

'One hundred and fifty yards to the pin, sir. Slight dog-leg right. Suggest you play a seven iron with a fade into the wind.'

'Do you play this damned game, Albert?'

'Oh, yes sir, but only when the gentlemen have gone. Handicap two.'

Albert handed him the club, Freddie took up his stance, swung the club and shanked the ball low into the trunk of the walnut tree. The ball rebounded like a shell from a howitzer, striking him full in the testicles, and he went down in a huddle, rolling slowly and gracefully into the creek as he lost consciousness with the pain. For a moment he was in a white tunnel, where he saw a vision of Morgane, smiling and walking towards him arms outstretched. Then he awoke at the sound of a loud crack. Albert had fired a hunting rifle two yards from Freddie's head and a large crocodile was rolling on to its back in the middle of the creek.

'For God's sake, Ottaway, I warned you to keep out of the water hazards,' shouted Gordon. But the match was abandoned. If Freddie had been able to foresee the future, he might have found the incident more intriguing, echoed as it was to be, in another time, another place. Instead, his balls just ached like hell.

103

Chapter 6

Amala Mohammed's first memory was of a donkey called Pedro. She had a memory of looking through bars towards a light and of an animal moving towards her. As with all childish memories, did she really remember, or had she been told? Whichever was the case, she carried with her a myth she was content to believe, that Pedro had looked through the fence posts at her when she was too young to remember a thing about her parents. Later, she absorbed the explanation that Pedro was too old to carry packs so was left to graze in the poor fields around the house in Lodwar. When she had passed the watershed of conscious memory, she knew for a fact that she had sat on his back, a feather compared with the load he was used to carrying, and Pedro was happy to take her wherever she steered him by gentle nudges in his ribs with her heels.

From the beginning of her conscious memory, she knew she was different. Her father had arrived in this alien country from West Pakistan before she was born. He was a trader who acquired a train of donkeys and, because he could transport goods to places where no roads existed, soon captured the market. He set up a general store in Lodwar, where he sold ironmongery from Birmingham and dry goods from wherever in the world. Slowly he established shabby little outposts throughout the north, which formed a ragged circle on the donkey route that he followed almost every week. He sold to the settler farmers, to the natives when they had money from their labours on the white farms and, in the absence of a viable competitor, soon had a contract to supply the needs of the colonial government itself. But despite his crucial role in the colonial system of the north, he was never accepted, never invited to join the club and drink gin at sunset with the Europeans of Lodwar, which was in the end an advantage, for the white population paid no heed and made no distinction when he took a Maasai woman to be his wife. Soon he became the richest man in Turkana County and bought his daughter a place in the Sacred Heart Convent School for Girls when she was eight.

Being an outsider seemed natural to Amala. The other girls regarded her with benign fascination. Her skin was darker than theirs, she spoke English with an Urdu accent, which was beautiful to the ear, and she was cleverer than almost all of them. The nuns taught her the catechism, the Hail Mary and the Our Father with total disregard for her Muslim faith; but that didn't matter, since it was social necessity, not religious fervour, which led the settler farmers to send their daughters to the convent. And so, with her differences clear to all, she blended in with complete success.

Outsidedness gave her independence and objectivity: she had no commitment to one side or another, to one religion or another, to one race or another. Her very existence was a muddle: Maasai women did not live in spacious houses as her mother did; Muslim men did not marry outside their faith as her father had done; and Muslim girls were never taught to be good Catholics in a white colonial boarding school. But breaking all the rules seemed to have worked. She grew up happy, free, unbiased, intelligent and beautiful. She found in Morgane a questioning, challenging sceptic from the colonial world and together they formed a perfect molecule, their contrasting atoms binding to each other with the force of material predestination.

Amala had heard all about Freddie from Morgane's long intimate letters. She knew that he was young, intelligent, handsome and talented. That he could paint and make love with equal verve. And, above all, that he was deeply suspicious of the claustrophobic despotism of British rule, despite the fact that it paid his wages. When Freddie waved goodbye to Morgane on the quayside at Mombasa he was not to know that she had already passed his case on to Amala, already handed him into her care, so to speak. His chance meeting with Hugh Porter at Nakuru station was therefore far from chance, for there was only one train back from

Mombasa on the day of Morgane's departure. So what seemed to Freddie just a coincidence was in truth a pattern of events some time in the making. Moreover, Amala and Hugh were well known to each other and shared the ambition of creating a new Kenya. They had discussed it many times, together with a growing band of Kenyan intellectuals, in one of those shadowy networks that hovered unnoticed beneath the surface of government in Africa at that time. It had not yet been compromised by the long knives of the armed bands that had begun to terrorise the loyalist natives in the towns and farms; its ideas were pure and unsullied by the demands of practicability. What they could not foresee with accuracy, although their fears had been aroused, was the wave of violence that before long would drown out its voice, never to be heard again in the age of *real politik* that ensued.

And so, when Hugh Porter telephoned to invite her to meet Freddie, Amala was only surprised by the suddenness of the contact, not the fact. She was already in Nakuru, staying with her older sister, as she often did during vacations from the university. The family had an apartment above the Mohammed depot by the station goods yard, where supplies for the north were assembled for transit. Her sister managed the business with all the acumen her father had shown in making his fortune. Amala looked upon it all from a distance; her business lay with ideals and aspirations, not dry goods and hardware. When she looked down upon the marshalling yard below her window, and the diesel locomotive shunting the wagons into the sidings for unloading, she could hear the long withdrawing roar of old Africa as it receded in the face of advancing western capitalism.

For his part, Freddie was glad to escape the clutches of Gordon as soon as possible and his superior had made no effort to dissuade him. The golf debacle had done little for his career and Gordon felt his own reputation had suffered. The story of Freddie's near-death experience in the creek at the third hole would be retold and embellished across gins-and-tonic in the club bar for many a year to come and Gordon would be a minor comic character in the sketch. As far as

Gordon knew, Freddie was setting off again to the north, and he knew nothing about the planned evening with Porter. Hussain, who had formed a sympathetic bond with Freddie owing to their unspoken shared dislike of the District Officer, had washed and polished his black Austin ready for the trip north. Freddie thanked him, giving him a knowing look before jumping in the car and setting off in the direction of St Andrew's Vicarage. He had no idea what the evening would hold for him.

He found Porter in his study, dispensing sherry to a black Kenyan wearing a well-cut western suit. 'Ah, Freddie, glad you could make it,' he announced enthusiastically. 'I would like you to meet Doctor Oduya.' Freddie held out his hand. 'Oduya is a professor of African history at the university. The professor was keen to meet you.'

Freddie was puzzled: why him? What did he have to offer such a distinguished person as a university professor? Porter could see the thought passing through Freddie's head and quickly moved the conversation on. 'We have another guest this evening,' he added, handing Freddie a sherry, 'but she's running a little late.' At that moment, they heard the sound of the doorbell and the heavy tread of the housekeeper on the Axminster carpet in the hall. A few seconds later, after an exchange of Swahili greetings, the study door opened and in walked Amala Mohammed. Porter stepped forward, as the other two men rose to their feet. 'Amala, my dear, how lovely to see you.'

Freddie felt as a minor noble in the court of King James might have felt on first setting eyes on Princess Pocahontas. Amala combined the exotic and the graceful to a degree that Freddie had never before seen. She had the slender limbs, long neck and high cheek bones of the Maasai, but the colouring of her Pakistani father. She had long black hair which her mother had always cut short in the Maasai fashion, until her daughter moved out of reach and adopted the western styles of the educated white girls among whom she moved. Amala greeted Porter and Oduya before holding out her hand to Freddie.

'This is Freddie Ottaway,' said Porter.

'I know,' said Amala. 'I've read all about him,' she added with a smile, as if she held some secret knowledge.

Freddie was even more puzzled until, half way through his second sherry, he suddenly remembered the connection: Morgane, the readings from the *Kama Sutra* in the dorm and Amala's diagrams. But he still could not quite understand what this evening was all about.

The party moved through to the dining room where an oval table had been set.

'I hope you have learned to like Kenyan food, Freddie,' said Porter. 'My housekeeper only cooks that way.'

There were four of them; Freddie sat opposite Amala. She was the most beautiful woman he had ever seen. It was not just her physical presence that struck him. Her self-possession was tangible. Professor Oduya sat at his right hand. He spoke perfect English and had impeccable manners. Porter sat at the head of the table, an embodiment of the fading westernism with which Freddie had become familiar since his arrival in the country, sloping shoulders, shabby jacket and a general air of slow decay. The flow of plates from the kitchen began until before them was arrayed a display of East African dishes that Desmond had never come near to serving at the little table in the window at Lodwar. First a plate of cornmeal made into balls; then a large dish of collard greens; a platter of grilled mutton, with green beans; and small bowls of aromatic and highly spiced sauces for dipping. The riches of the continent were there before him, as ancient and unsung as the culture of the tribes of Africa. A young boy waited by Porter's chair until the signal to pour the wine.

'My only gesture to the other world,' said Porter, as the boy filled the wine glasses with a burgundy. 'Let us drink to a new Kenya,' he said, raising his glass. And Freddie found himself happily joining in, the servant of the Crown, saluting the future and dismissing the present. At last, he began to understand the meaning of the gathering in this strange piece of English politeness in the heart of another continent.

But they were not revolutionaries. The talk was of

democratic institutions; of representation on the Legislative Council; of equal rights for all Kenyans, white and black; of freedom to own land; and above all, of opposition to violent protest. Freddie listened attentively to what was being said while the plates of *ugali*, *sukuma wiki* and *nyama choma* were passed around. Then Professor Oduya turned to him and looked over his spectacles, just as a stern tutor might have done in his Cambridge days. 'Do you have an idea what your role in all this might be, Freddie?' he asked. It was as if the question had been the whole point of the evening. There was a silence round the table while Freddie gathered himself. Finally, he spoke. 'I was told I should paint the African people and show them to the world. I'm an artist you see.' Amala looked at him as if she had heard the line before. 'But I think you want to hear more from me than that.' And for the first time in his life, he felt as if he were saying something that mattered, that he believed in, that other people would stop in their tracks and listen to. 'In fact, I have come to see the impossibility of Kenya, as it is; it has no way forward, as it is. It's like a wild animal that can no longer evolve unless the whole world changes around it. So I agree with you. Unless the country moves forward, the long knives will take it backwards.'

Freddie could almost feel the surge of goodwill towards him as he finished speaking; he felt among friends in a way that his shallow life of comfort and privilege had not so far offered him. Amala reached across the table, her long slender hand decked with bracelets grasping his as it lay on the cloth. 'Thank you,' she said. 'Morgane was right about you. You will help us.'

'You see Freddie,' said Porter, 'in two years Gordon will have retired and you most likely will become the District Officer. The Commissioner will listen to your reports from the regions and pass them on to London. There are several loud voices in Westminster already calling for modernisation in the colonies. The Colonial Office wants to avoid armed conflict at all costs. That's how you can play your part.'

Freddie was silent. A new feeling was upon him: he

realised he felt grown up, as if he had the power and the wisdom to change the world for the better. What an irony that he had discovered this truth while attempting to escape from his responsibilities in the old world of family and expectations.

'I'll do whatever I can,' he replied.

'But you must paint the people, whatever else you do,' added Amala.

The evening was over. Professor Oduya and Amala left together in a dusty taxi but, at the door, she held her face to Freddie's and he kissed her on both cheeks, as a host would kiss a guest goodbye at the end of a dinner party in Tonbridge. She looked him in the eyes: 'I'm coming to Lodwar next week,' she said, 'to visit my family. Perhaps we could meet again there.'

The next day, Freddie left the vicarage at first light, to drive the dusty road back to Lodwar. He stopped under the very epiyei tree where Hussain had brewed him tea a lifetime ago. But instead of journeying into the unknown, as he had done then, he now knew what he needed to do in Africa. Just before sunset he pulled up the old Austin before his house in Lodwar. Desmond came down the steps to meet him and brush the dust off his clothes. 'Welcome back, Bwana. All is well here,' he said.

'Desmond, do I have a typewriter in my office?'

'Mr Latimer put it away in the cupboard, Bwana. He said he had no use for it.'

'Fetch it down, would you. I need to start writing reports in the morning.'

Desmond looked at him, as if his master had caught a touch of the sun, but before morning the small Remington had been hauled down and dusted off, ready for action.

Freddie woke early to the sound of the cockerel's clarion call from the wood next to the house. He pulled back the mosquito net shrouding his bed and stepped across to the window to throw open the shutters. A bent eucalyptus tree drooped its swathes of silver-green leaves before his eyes, swaying gently in the dry breeze. A parakeet called from the tip of the tree and the sound of a dog barking drifted across the hill from the town. He threw on his dressing gown, lit a cigarette and stepped out on to the verandah. Desmond heard his step and brought him his morning tea. Freddie looked out across the green clearing to the dusty track leading down to the town; he listened to the taller branches of the tree hitting the corrugated tin roof; and he could hear the chatter of Desmond's little clan from their hut behind the house. It wasn't much, taken all in all, but it was everything he needed to make him content. His life had a purpose and a scope but it had taken the most bizarre avenue of misadventure for him to discover each. As he drank his tea, black and aromatic, fresh as the green hills of the Kenyan highlands, he thought of Porter, quietly plotting; of the eminent Oduya, placing trust in him; and above all of the enigma that was Amala, the fusion of cultures and religions that by chance he had discovered through the magical mediation of Morgane. And she had said she would come and visit him.

After breakfast he went into his office. Desmond had placed the typewriter on his desk as instructed. It was workable but stiff at first and a dead cockroach was jammed between the "a" and the "s". After much poking and shaking, the machine decided to cooperate and Freddie was faced with the most frightening moment of his brief reporting career − a blank page. It was so far from the literary essays he had been trained to write. It had to tell the truth, in a way that would convince. He gritted his teeth and began to write, first the date, then the place. Then what? He suddenly realised he knew very little about anything. He was gazing vacantly out of his open window when Desmond entered with coffee.

'Sit down, Desmond,' he said.

'Bwana?'

Desmond had never before sat in the presence of his master but he did as he was told, albeit reluctantly.

'I want you to tell me about your children, Desmond. Can they read and did they ever go to school?'

At first Desmond did not know how to respond. No white man before had ever shown interest in his private existence. He had come and gone as if he were invisible and had grown into the part. But he stumbled forward, with promptings, and as he spoke Freddie began to type. Later that morning he found an excuse to go into Lodwar and call on the little schoolmistress he had met at Owen's, to see the school in action. From that day he became a regular visitor to the simple building, a single classroom with rows of battered desks, taking with him his paints and brushes. The children painted their world in its priorities, a broad canvas of smiling faces set against a landscape where human and animal intertwined in a way lost to the west. That was the beginning of the Ottaway chronicle of life in Kenya and it grew, day by day. He decided to keep his typed sheets carefully under lock and key in the safe in his office. He realised what he was writing was not what Gordon expected him to do and they needed to be kept secret. He would keep them for the moment when they could be used, when he could exert his influence at some unknown point in the future, when the world might need to know.

That afternoon he assembled Desmond's two wives and three children on the front steps of the tin-roofed bungalow. Desmond looked on amused as the women giggled with embarrassment and the children wriggled like brown worms, all thin arms and legs. Freddie began to paint them. They were timeless: the women and children of the field, painted through every age, with their natural, unkempt beauty; their tragic poverty; their heart-rending mortality. They were the girls the Glasgow Boys had painted, working in the Scottish turnip fields between the wars, with the sun shining on their bending backs as they toiled; or the French peasants looking up from their harvesting to hear the Angelus bell ring from the nearby church tower. The group sat smiling on the steps of the house, not knowing that their shining faces would illuminate the ages, while the master worked ceaselessly behind his easel. It was the beginning of an obsession.

Several days later, a boy on a donkey arrived at the house. He dismounted, climbed the steps and knocked on the door. Freddie heard the gentle knock and looked up from his desk but Desmond had already intercepted the visitor, who had carried with him a message.

'Excuse, Bwana, the boy from Mohammed says Miss Amala is at home and you are invited to tea this afternoon.'

'Thank you, Desmond. Tell the boy I shall be happy to come.' Desmond looked concerned and stood rooted to the spot. 'Is there a problem Desmond?'

'Mr Latimer never went there, Bwana.'

'Well, I'm not Mr Latimer, and I shall go. Now go and tell the boy. That's an order.'

Desmond sidled away, still unhappy. Freddie realised he had broken another rule in the unwritten handbook of Kenyan life, but he was glad for that. Moreover, he looked forward to meeting Amala again, although he knew that the invitation would never have come from her father or mother, which added a certain tension to the event. And besides, he had a mission in mind.

It was the season of the short rains. Above the Mohammed general store at the crossroads in the centre of Lodwar, there was a dilapidated long upper floor, split into small rooms for passing travellers. A sign by the store entrance advertised their availability. And they were always available. Freddie had never known anyone to spend a night there in all the time he had been in the area and Desmond, whose extended family had links with everything that moved in the town, had never mentioned the fact. For a stranger to pass through Lodwar, other than the nomadic troops of casual farm workers, would have been an occasion of note. For a white man to rent a room there, one day in the short rains, was remarkable; for that white man to speak Russian was truly earth-shaking. The fact came to light when he was seen seated under the awning by the petrol pumps, waiting for the shop girl to serve him breakfast. A small black car, with a Nairobi number plate, was parked by the side of the building. Word spread like bushfire that Mr Antonov was here to do trade with Kenya, a suspicion that grew stronger when Knut Larsen, the fish canning man, was seen one day collecting him in his car, and was confirmed when the boss of the Italian geological survey team from the far north appeared in the town. It was not clear what kind of trade the Russian had in mind but it sat uncomfortably alongside the established order of things. Freddie sent Gordon a telegram asking what the protocol might be in these circumstances. The answer was short and to the point: 'Find out what the bugger's up to!' Tea with Shah Mohammed seemed a good opportunity.

The rain shower had finished its allotted span for the day, the sun burned off the water from the ground and steam rose gently in the warm air. The rain had cleared the dust and a brilliant blue sky appeared as the clouds evaporated. Desmond saddled Phoenix in the stable and led him out for Freddie to ride to Lodwar. His master had become a competent horseman, albeit on a beast as mellow as Phoenix whose greatest ambition was to eat leaves from the bushes by the roadside whenever he had the chance. Freddie was dressed in leather riding boots, jodhpurs, a thick cotton shirt with rolled-up sleeves and a wide-brimmed hat. He was tanned and fit; his body seemed to have thickened from the youth who had landed in Mombasa; and he had a new confidence, perhaps from his tutelage under Morgane, perhaps from the new purpose his life now possessed. At a glance, he could have been a young Hemingway, flourishing in the life of the outdoors, seeking the truth in life and the beauty that came with it.

Phoenix strolled sedately down the gentle sloping track to the crossroads in Lodwar, past the general store and the petrol pumps, to a large white bungalow on a rise in the ground. The house was encircled by a verandah and green lawns with, here and there, a scattering of flame trees resplendent in their vermilion blossom. As he approached the house, he became aware of its extent: it was truly vast. Beside it, two spacious garages with fine wooden doors stood open. In one, he saw the unmistakeable radiator of a Rolls-Royce; in another the huge round headlights of a Jaguar XK120. Shah Mohammed might not be able to drink at the club but he could certainly drive better cars than the Lodwar Europeans.

Freddie dismounted at the gate, tethered his horse, and walked up the path to the house. From the dark interior the tall figure of Amala emerged. She met him at the top of the verandah steps. Freddie held out his hand but she leaned forward and kissed him. Then taking his hand, she led him to the side of the house away from the road, where a cluster of chairs was arrayed around a garden table. A small dark man sat at one, smoking a cigar. He was dressed in western clothes with an open-neck shirt. A prominent gold watch with a gold strap sat on his heavy, short forearm. His hair was thinning and combed back. For all the world, he could have been a successful street trader in Peckham market, keen to show the world he had made it. Beside him sat his wife, ink black, short-haired, with only the tinge of grey appearing. She was festooned with jewellery, necklace and bracelets. She had translated her Maasai tradition into western decoration.

Shah Mohammed had the easy ways of a successful businessman. While his wife dispensed tea in silence, he engaged Freddie in conversation, about England and Cambridge, about Pakistan's first cricket tour to England, about the success of his business in Kenya. It was not long before Freddie began to feel uncomfortable, as if Mohammed actually looked up to him, not for anything he had achieved in his short life, for that amounted to very little, but for what he represented. He tried to change the subject but without success. He really wanted to talk to Mohammed about how it had been for him to struggle in the way he had; and how he felt about the way he was treated. But these topics were

115

buried deep below the ground, never to be exhumed. Amala was conscious of the tension and took the first opportunity to break up the party.

'Let's go for a ride,' she suggested. 'Come round to the stable Freddie.'

She took him across the large lawn at the back of the house, where two gardeners were working in the borders, to a wooden stable where a grey mare poked its head over the half-door and snorted as they approached.

'She makes Phoenix look like a gypsy's nag,' he said, as Amala led out her horse into the sunshine. 'Your father thinks too much of the British. He has achieved so much. He should be proud.' They walked round the house to where Phoenix was tethered. 'I'm nothing compared with him, just the average product of a few generations of money-makers.'

'Don't dismiss yourself like that,' she replied. 'That's the same mistake you criticise in my father. You must be what you want to be. He wanted to send me to boarding school in England, you know, but I wouldn't go. This is where I belong. Now let's ride.'

And she sent her mare into a trot. They circled the house and headed up the hill at the back, waving to her parents as they left. Freddie was saddened by it all; their isolation overwhelmed him and he was angry that the narrowness of his own tribe had forced such desperation on these people. He looked at Amala's parents, marooned amid a sea of English crockery, castaways on a colonial island, while their true reality withered away. He understood at once the root of Amala's determination to achieve change. It was about honesty.

They rode for an hour among the yellow dried grasses of the plain. It was just before sunset when they returned. Mohammed came to meet them at the gate. 'You must come again, Mr Ottaway,' he said, shaking Freddie's hand.

'Freddie – please,' he replied. 'I would like to.'

Amala walked with him a few yards up the road, the shadows slanting longer as the sudden fall to darkness approached.

'I've started painting,' he said. Her eyes lit up. 'Come tomorrow and I'll show you what I've done. I have a great idea I want to share with you. I might even start to paint you, if you'll let me.'

Chapter 8

Freddie realised he had done nothing to fulfil Gordon's orders to find out what Antonov was doing. The encounter with Amala's parents had not gone that way and he hadn't found the right moment to ask apparently harmless questions. But he did not have to wait long for an opportunity. Antonov paid Freddie a visit. It was in the middle of the following morning that the small black car with the Nairobi number plates drew up outside the Assistant District Officer's house. A tall, heavily built man got out of the driver's seat and stood looking at the house. He wore a baggy cream suit, full of creases, and a straw hat with a brown band round it. The sweat ran off his brow as if he were totally unused to living in a hot climate. Desmond was at the back of the house, with his family, so the visitor was at the open door before Freddie realised it.

'Hello,' he shouted through the opening. 'Do you mind if I come in?' Freddie looked up from his papers at the stranger in his doorway. 'Dimitri Antonov. I believe you are Mr Ottaway.'

Freddie's first impression was of a bald head, domed like an egg and too large for the body to which it was attached. Yet the man was not old, simply overweight, and heaving with the effort of moving. A pair of blue eyes, parked either side of a prominent nose, looked out from a piggy face, which was both chinless and hairless. He looked seedy, untrustworthy, and foreign. It was on such firm evidential grounds that Freddie came to the conclusion that he was dealing with a Moscow hood, whatever that might be. He recalled Gordon's order: *find out what the bugger's up to*!

'Good morning,' said Freddie, stepping forward and holding out his hand, which Antonov grasped in a soft yielding damp grip. 'Very good to meet you. Let's sit on the verandah. Freddie Ottaway, Assistant District Officer. Coffee?'

118

By this time Desmond had appeared and Freddie ordered coffee. They sat opposite each other in the basket chairs on the verandah. Freddie held out his silver case of Senior Service.

'Ah, English cigarettes, what a luxury,' said Antonov, gratefully taking one. Freddie lit it with his Ronson table lighter. 'You people have such style,' added his guest, much to Freddie's bewilderment. After the coffee arrived, Antonov spoke: 'I should explain my visit, perhaps. I am trade attaché third class, Dimitri Antonov, at your service. My Government has signed a bilateral agreement with your Government, as I am sure you know, to develop appropriate mutual trade exchanges.' At that moment a yellow-billed hornbill alighted on a branch before the verandah, its brilliant colours catching the sunlight and Freddie's attention; 'mutual trade exchanges.....' continued Antonov, then paused.

'Yes, of course, absolutely,' replied Freddie, wondering why the hell Gordon hadn't informed him. 'Do go on.'

'I am exploring the possibility of setting up a fish farming project here with your friend Kunt Larsen.'

'Ah, you mean Knut, I think, Kunt in English sounds like something else. Knut in English is pronounced "Canute", you know. He was a Danish king who tried to stop the tide coming in, apparently. Mind you, Knutsford in Cheshire is an exception to that rule.' Antonov looked at him blankly. 'Still, do go on,' said Freddie.

'You like caviar, Freddie?' asked Antonov, out of the blue.

'Well, yes, of course, with a little lemon juice. Very good.'

'There you are! We are proposing to set up a sturgeon farm here in Africa. This will be the first one in the southern hemisphere, using the cold waters from the highland rivers flowing into Lake Turkana. It will be a wonderful example of our two countries cooperating to our mutual advantage.'

His hand stretched out to take another Senior Service. 'Definitely a spy,' thought Freddie, 'with that cover story.' Then, out loud, 'Excellent,' he said, 'I'm sure we can work together closely on this. Our countries have not had easy relations of late but it is up to you and me to make things better, is it not.'

'I'm sure it is,' said Antonov, rising from his seat and holding out his hand. He grinned, revealing a gold filling in a front tooth. He had hairs on the back of his fingers, which resembled Richmond pork sausages. Freddie shook his hand, all the time wondering why bald men always seemed to be hairy elsewhere, as if it were a universal law of humanity. 'Until we meet again,' said Antonov, walking towards his car, which sank six inches nearer the ground as he lowered his body into the driver's seat.

Antonov's visit was brief and amiable but in retrospect strangely sinister. It was almost as if he were announcing his arrival in the area as the representative of some great power; that he would carry with him that power's protection; and that the world of Africa was no longer the preserve of the British. His admiration of their style was no more than a mocking; his ludicrous and unlikely cover story was intended to be instantly seen as a statement that he was here for something else entirely. This was how Freddie saw it and as soon as his visitor had bounced his way back down the track, he returned to his desk to draft a memo to Gordon on the Soviet-Norwegian fish farm project and Dimitri Antonov, KGB agent third class. He got an answer back very soon: *keep an eye on the bugger.*

Freddie could recite from his undergraduate days the whole of a poem by Andrew Marvell, a seventeenth century English poet. It was a plea to his coy mistress to give way to passion; but the most memorable bit for him in fact was the opposite: *our vegetable love should grow vaster than empires and more slow.* He had always found it remarkable that a poet could compare love with a cabbage or a parsnip and get away with it. But Marvell had and it worked. And strangely enough, that is how Freddie's relationship with Amala turned out to be. There was no love at first sight; no frantic ripping off of clothes; no energetic gymnastics of an afternoon, such as there had been with Morgane. Just a slow growing into each other. It was not something that could be traced to a single moment or word or gesture. Rather a slow, gradual recognition that they were part of each other's life; that nothing needed to be said or decided. But it was there and irrefutable. Neither had sought it; each had thought it unlikely; both realised it had happened. Their periods apart were frequent but this simply served to make the moment of return so much more poignant and reassuring, as if a part of the other had come home.

And when Amala arrived that afternoon, Freddie wondered what to expect from her. According to Morgane, she was the expert architect of sexual positions, but he was more in awe of her presence than her reputation. She was serious and analytical; reserved and sensitive, the opposite of Morgane. He showed her the half-finished painting of Desmond's family; he had also started sketches of Desmond and showed her these. She sat in the chair that Morgane had occupied the day she had offered herself to him and Freddie began to make rough sketches of her, with her graceful neck and shoulders and glistening black skin. And then she had to go and Freddie found himself longing for the next visit. But before she went that day she asked him about his great idea.

'It seems to me,' replied Freddie earnestly, 'that when a people can define itself, in images or in words, it becomes a nation.'

'But you are English, Freddie,' she replied. 'It is not for you to define a black nation.'

'Am I English, Amala? Am I still that? Or can a man define what he is by what he does and who he wants to be, just as you have decided who you want to be, instead of having his identity stamped on him at birth?'

'Is that your great idea?' she asked.

'Part of it, I suppose. Morgane told me to show the world the beauty of these people. I intend to do that through my paintings. And I don't think I can do that without losing something of myself, something of the outsider. And without someone else to help me.'

'They will destroy you, you know, your people. What you want to do is political. The last thing they want is to allow the Kenyans to celebrate their identity. With that comes purpose and determination.'

'Yes, I know all that but I'm still determined to do it.'

'Perhaps Oduya will help,' added Amala. 'It is a great idea.'

And the idea took root, slowly growing, spreading its branches and leaves, until it was if it had always been there, like an ancient oak. Freddie discharged his official duties adequately and without more embarrassment than the golfing incident had caused, determined not to draw attention to himself. But all the time he worked away at his idea. He travelled throughout the north, documenting what he saw. He began in earnest to record the events that he witnessed around him. He described the parlous state of the wandering families of Kikuyu, forced to eke out an existence in transitory camps while they moved from farm to farm to work in the fields. He noted the impossibility of any kind of education for the children, the lack of any consistent health care, high mortality rates and the rapid spread of diseases. Then there were the incidents: innocent native families attacked and murdered by gangs of armed insurgents on the assumption that they were loyal to colonial rule. He stored his typed sheets carefully under lock and key in the safe in his office; what he had written could have brought him down, it being so critical of the *status quo*, and for Gordon to catch sight of them would have resulted in their destruction. He was sure there would be a moment when they could be used, when he could exert his influence at some unknown point in the future.

But it was noticed in the community that he was seen more out and about, that he listened to the views of those he met, and was keen to loiter talking to the petrol pump man when he filled up his tank. He made friends with Mohammed, Amala was known to visit him in his tin-roofed house, and he insisted on learning Swahili from his houseboy Desmond. For the old guard this became a source of some concern: it was not done for the issues of the day to be discussed as if change was possible. Change after all meant the end. There were stirrings in the small group. Inspector Dalrymple began to take note: there was nothing more dangerous than a white man going native. Ottaway needed to be watched.

Meanwhile Freddie painted everything around him. From time to time he took the old Austin to Nakuru, packed with canvases, and stored them in a spare room at Porter's vicarage. These trips were secret odysseys, kept hidden from Gordon, but they were also opportunities for Freddie and Amala to meet in the upstairs flat overlooking the railway yard, on those occasions when she could escape from Nairobi on the overnight train. And that became their routine: Amala walking towards him on the misty station platform in the early hours while he waited for that moment of relief when she was in his arms; but embedded in it, the moment of pain, when he waved her goodbye and the clouds of steam engulfed her as the train slowly pulled away. It was a fragile way of life, clinging on against the hostile tidal wave of social convention.

Three months after the meeting with Antonov, Freddie received a visit from Inspector Dalrymple. 'Just thought I'd call in for a chat,' announced Dalrymple, although it was clear to Freddie that this was far from a casual visit. The police inspector was bristling with highly polished leather belts and boots. The dark blue, red and orange stripes of his Burma Star ribbon stood out boldly. A menacing holster stuck out from his side, with the butt of a Browning pistol just visible under the flap. Dalrymple had stepped from his jungle war against the Japanese straight into the Kenyan police and had brought with him the attitudes of a seasoned fighter. 'Wondered if you'd had any recent contact with Antonov,' was his opening line.

'Came to see me a while ago,' replied Freddie, showing Dalrymple to a chair on the verandah. 'Seemed to want to tell me about fish farming. We talked a bit about cooperation.'

'What did you make of him?'

'Tell you the truth, I didn't believe a word of it. Seemed an unlikely cover story to me. Telegraphed the District Officer to that effect.'

'Precisely,' said Dalrymple. 'You could say the sturgeon story is a complete red herring.' Freddie wondered if this was

123

a joke but didn't dare laugh as not a crease could be seen on Dalrymple's face. 'Thing is, he's completely disappeared. Must have gone up north, as we would have spotted him down here. Look out for him in your travels, would you Ottaway. If you hear anything from the natives, let me know.'

Freddie nodded. There was a pause. Something else was coming, even though Dalrymple had risen to his feet as if to leave.

'Actually, Ottaway, between you and me, we've heard from the intelligence people that's he's a Moscow man. Need to keep tabs on him. One other thing,' and he paused as if collecting his thoughts, 'are you still seeing the Mohammed girl?'

'What if I am?' Freddie bristled.

'Just this: she's on our books as well. And so is that fellow Porter. Just be careful what you say. It won't look too good for you when the shit hits the fan, mixing with that lot. Well, better be off. Remember what I said.'

Dalrymple strode over to his car where his driver opened the door for him. Freddie stood on the verandah, not knowing what to make of the visit, as the police car moved off in a cloud of dust. All he could work out was that this was a warning. Whoever "they" were, he was being watched, along with anyone else who had a vestige of liberalism in their bodies, and they were as suspicious to the authorities as a Moscow hood pretending to be a fish farmer. When Freddie recounted the conversation to Amala, a week later, she laughed.

'What's so funny?' he asked.

'The fact that you hadn't realised that already,' she replied.

Chapter 9

The High Commissioner strolled slowly from painting to painting, accompanied by Professor Oduya. The walls of the Senate House were lined with canvases of all sizes and in all styles. The unseen army of Kenyan artists who for decades had created their folk art in the faraway corners of the country, echoing motifs and methods passed down to them by their forebears, now had found an audience. Among them were sprinkled the Ottaways.

'Who is this Ottaway, Oduya?' asked the Commissioner.

'He's one of yours, actually,' he replied, 'based up in Lodwar.'

'Indeed. He's very good,' said the Commissioner, although he was deep in thought as he spoke.

The next day the Nairobi newspapers gave an account of the exhibition. One of them used the headline "Kenya Awakes".

Professor Oduya of the University of Nairobi was one of those Africans whose erudition and Oxford background had fooled the British into thinking he was one of them. He was regarded as safe which, of course, he was. He had won a Rhodes scholarship purely on the basis of his brilliance and he had charmed his way through the cocktail parties of Oxford as efficiently as he had stormed the heights of academic success. His return to Nairobi was therefore easily lauded as a triumph of British multi-culturalism. What no one seemed to have noticed was that the application of a brilliant and individual mind to the problem of Kenya was likely to produce a solution that might differ from the one propounded by the civil servants of Whitehall. If the Permanent Secretary at the Colonial Office had bothered to read the syllabus that Professor Oduya followed in his Department of African History, he would have regarded his appointment with as much relish as the Christian monks of Lindisfarne showed when the first Viking ship hove into view off the Northumberland coast. The High Commissioner, who saw in Oduya a jewel in the crown of British philanthropy, was equally unaware of the true significance of what he was seeing.

But a week later, after the surge of press interest, Freddie received a telephone call from Gordon. 'Ottaway. Get yourself down here day after tomorrow would you. The Provincial Inspector wants to meet you.'

'Can you tell me what it's about?' asked Freddie.

Gordon's voice was flat calm and very deliberate: 'That will be made clear.' And the telephone clicked down.

Freddie had never met the Provincial Inspector in the two years that he had spent in Kenya, which was in keeping with the ruling philosophy in the Service of leaving well alone. The fact that something was now happening suggested all was not well. As requested, he arrived at Gordon's office in the late afternoon. The District Inspector was not quite ready for him so he sat in the corridor on a straight-backed chair. He could hear the hum of voices from the office; it sounded as if there were three of them. After a few minutes, the door opened and Gordon stuck out his head: 'Come in.'

The room was thick with blue tobacco smoke. Gordon sat down behind his desk; to his right was a grey-haired clerical figure, with the look of the accountant about him, who turned out to be McLaren, the Provincial Inspector. He was thin, with a worn face, and wore heavy spectacles. He smoked incessantly and before him was a heaped-up ashtray of cigarette ends. In a corner of the room, as if there as an afterthought, sat another man, younger and totally impassive. He held a hand over his mouth, with his elbow rested on the arm of his chair, so that his face was always half-concealed. Freddie was offered a chair in front of the desk as if he were attending a job interview. The atmosphere was threatening. At last McLaren spoke in a quiet measured voice.

'Thank you for coming down Ottaway. I trust you had a reasonable trip. These roads are truly awful, are they not.' He picked up a manila file in front of him and began flipping

126

through the pages. Then he continued. 'You're quite a talented fellow aren't you. First class Cambridge degree. Settled in well enough here, I take it.' He looked across to Gordon, who nodded in agreement. There was a long pause before McLaren continued. 'The High Commissioner thinks highly of your paintings, by the way. Liked them a lot. Most unusual subject matter, he told me.' He stubbed out his cigarette and then lit another before continuing. 'But there's the thing, you see. Never had an officer painting out here before, most unusual. Few chaps doodled away with sketchbooks and so on, for when they go home, memento sort of thing you know. But never a real live artist who puts his paintings on display. In an exhibition.' He spelled out this last phrase deliberately and slowly. 'Created quite a stir in fact, newspapers and so on. Lot of stuff about rising tide of nationalism. I'm sure you read about it.'

'Yes sir,' said Freddie.

'The thing is, Ottaway, at this time I'm not sure that's a very helpful thing, what with the troubles in the country. Gives a mixed message.'

'About what exactly, sir?'

'About what side you're on,' came a voice from behind him, from the man with the hand over his face. McLaren looked up, slightly annoyed at the crude interruption to his flow. 'Precisely, thank you Crombie,' he said. McLaren put down the file and selected another from the pile in front of him. Reading upside-down, Freddie had noted that his own file had been marked "Personnel: Confidential". The next file was marked "Security: Secret" and he caught a glimpse of the name: Amala Mohammed. McLaren continued. 'You seem to be getting mixed up with a few people we're quite interested in. The young woman Mohammed, for example, very talented according to our sources at the university, but is she sound, would you say, Ottaway?'

'I don't think I quite understand the question, sir,' replied Freddie after a moment's thought.

'Let me put the question simply,' interrupted Crombie.'Would you say she wants the British out of Kenya?'

'I think she wants the people of Kenya to be free to run their own country,' said Freddie, 'a bit like the British do in their own country, really.'

The grilling went on, McLaren measured and polite, skating round points; Crombie blunt and aggressive. Gordon only spoke when invited and that only to confirm details about Hugh Porter's sermons from the St Andrew's pulpit. At last there seemed no more avenues to explore. McLaren lit a final cigarette, closed the file in his hands, and took off his glasses.

'We think it better for all concerned, Ottaway, that you should move on. New beginning, fresh start, chance to get it right this time. We're sending you to Brunei next week. Get back to Lodwar, pack up your things and be ready to sail from Mombasa to Bombay on the next boat out. Gordon, you will see to all that?'

McLaren was on his feet before he finished speaking, Crombie collected up the files and put them in his briefcase, while Gordon rang the bell for the housekeeper to clear away. Freddie felt as if he had committed a foul in a football match and the referee had sent him off. It was as sudden and final as that. It wasn't until later, when the brutal truth had set in, that he thought about Amala. He knew he could never leave her. He had just a week to come up with a plan.

He drove back to Lodwar with a heavy heart and, no matter how many times he shuffled the pieces, they always fell in the same pattern. By the time he had reached the outskirts of the town, he knew he had to resign. After that, he would stay in Kenya with Amala and continue to work for the cause of freedom. But events turned out quite differently. On the long drive home he had become aware of greater military activity. There were encampments of King's Africa Rifles along the road side and the occasional road block had been set up; army lorries trundled slowly northwards along the dusty road, visible for miles from the trailing clouds. When he reached his house, Desmond came to meet him, with an anxious look on his face. 'They are sweeping the area, Bwana,' he said.

'Who are?'

'The British, Bwana. They are rounding up the Mau-Mau and taking them north to the camps. If you have only taken the oath, you can stay in your village. There is a curfew after dark.'

'Have you taken the oath, Desmond?' asked Freddie looking him straight in the eye.

'No, Bwana,' he replied, 'but you must vouch for me, and for my family if they come here.'

'Don't worry, Desmond. I will do that.'

He did not have the heart to tell Desmond that in a week he would have left. As it turned out, he had less time than he thought.

Freddie slept little that night. Although he was exhausted from the journey, his mind seemed to carry an electrical charge, so that whenever he lay down his head to sleep, an overwhelming impulse prevented his rest. He rose early the next morning and wandered through to the verandah to smoke a cigarette. A few minutes later Desmond appeared with his tea. 'You are awake early Bwana,' he said.

'Yes, Desmond. I have much to think about.' He knew that Desmond had all the answers. 'Do you know if Miss Amala is in town?' he asked.

'She is, Bwana. Do you want me to take a message for you?'

'Tell her I will drive across this afternoon to see her.'

Freddie had known Amala for two years or so. When they were apart he could feel the tension in his shoulders as if the world were a frightening insecure place full of demons; when they were together, his body felt light and carefree. It was strange, as if their love were a kind of spiritual communion, and he could not explain it. That afternoon at five o'clock, his duties over for the day, he drove across to the Mohammed house. Amala sat alone on the verandah and, when she saw the car pull up, ran across the lawn to meet him. Freddie got out of the car and held her in his arms. He kissed her gently on the forehead and she held her face to his so that he could smell the scent of her hair.

'I have something to tell you,' he said. 'But let's drive back to my place. We can have dinner alone.'

She looked up, sensing it would be something serious, but did not ask. That evening Desmond served them at the little table in the window. After the meal, Amala reminded Freddie of what he had said. 'You have been distracted all evening, Freddie. What is it you have to tell me?' she asked.

'I have to resign from the service. It's no good any longer. I can't go on with this charade. You were right, Amala. They mean to destroy me. You were right about my great idea. They saw it as political and I suppose they were right. They're booting me out. The only thing I can do is resign and carry on here. I won't run away, as they want, to fester in some far distant posting where I can't do any damage.'

For a moment or two she said nothing. Then, lifting her eyes she said: 'This is my fault, isn't it. What you did was beautiful. But it was foolhardy. And I shouldn't have encouraged you. I remember our first meeting at Hugh's house. You were so innocent. I think we all took you in. We should have protected you but we led you into this.'

'Don't think like that, Amala. This is the first time in my life I've stood on my own two feet. I'm happy about that. The only trouble is, where do I go from here? I'll have no job, no income, nowhere to live. Nothing to fight with except my art.'

'Take me home, Freddie. I have an idea. I must talk to my father,' she replied.

It was late. The sun had set and a full orange moon hung low in the sky. They had meant to spend the night together under the tin roof of Freddie's house. But things had changed. Although there were check points on all the roads and armed patrols of KARs and Kenya Police passed regularly through the town, Freddie decided to take a risk and break the curfew. He started up the car and they drove slowly down the track to the road.

It was no more than a twenty minute drive to the Mohammed house but the route took them for a half mile through a dense wood where the trees closed over them, shutting out the moonlight. Freddie drove slowly, with only side lights showing, for fear of attracting attention. They rounded a bend and found themselves face to face with an army truck parked sideways across the road. Freddie slammed on the brakes and the car slid to a halt. Two soldiers stepped forward, one with a rifle held across his body, the other a corporal with an electric torch. The corporal knocked on the driver's window and shone the torch into the car. Freddie wound down the window.

'Out of the car,' he shouted. 'Don't you know there's a curfew?'

Freddie and Amala got out of the car while the corporal searched inside. He opened the glove compartment. As he did so Freddie realised with horror what he would find. He had kept the office pistol there ever since his first night in Lodwar, in case he encountered more trouble on the road. The soldier held up the pistol, shouted in Swahili, and suddenly Freddie and Amala were pinned against the side of the car, the barrel of the rifle pushed hard against them. Amala protested in Swahili and pushed the soldier away but in an instant felt the butt of a rifle struck hard against her shoulder. The pain must have been excruciating for she fell to her knees on the ground. Freddie turned in anger, swung a fist and caught the soldier with the torch hard on the chin. The pistol fell from his hand on to the driver's seat and, before he knew what he was doing, Freddie had grabbed the gun and was pointing it at the soldier with the rifle. He had never fired a gun in his life but the sight of the advancing soldier ready to shoot set off an instant response. He squeezed the trigger, pointing only generally in the direction of the man, but the effect was staggering. Almost without audible sound, it seemed, the gun went off and the soldier fell to the ground. Then he pointed the gun at the corporal who raised his hands.

'Get in the car,' he shouted to Amala, who struggled to her feet. Then Freddie jumped in, all the while pointing the pistol at the corporal. He started the engine, rammed the car into reverse and spun it round in the opposite direction. By the time the army truck became mobile, the Austin had disappeared into the black night.

131

'Did you kill him?' whispered Amala, clutching her shoulder.

'I think so,' said Freddie, shaking and white.

'Take me home,' said Amala. 'I'll show you another way.'

They drove on in silence, Amala pointing out directions at road junctions. Then she passed out with the pain.

Freddie's mind was racing. He was confident that the soldiers could not identify Amala and in any case she was an innocent bystander. But *he* was a different matter. He had shot a soldier; and he was a white man driving a black car. It would not take long for Dalrymple to put two and two together. Freddie had never killed a living thing but now he would be hunted down as a murderer. His days in Kenya were over. As for Amala, she had to be kept out of it until the dust had settled and she could return to Nairobi.

It was not a long drive but it seemed that time had slowed to a crawl. At last, Freddie pulled up before the Mohammed house. The lights from the windows shone down in wide swathes across the manicured lawns. At the sound of the car pulling up, a servant appeared at the door.

'Come and help me,' shouted Freddie, as he opened the passenger door. Amala lay unconscious in the front seat. Her face was pale, with a reddening bruise across her temple, where the butt of the rifle had glanced against her head before impacting on her shoulder. She lay so slender and so vulnerable, to be hacked down so brutally. Freddie felt no remorse that he had shot the soldier. Gently he placed an arm under her body while the servant, who had rushed to the car, lifted her legs out of the foot well. Then Freddie took her full weight and carried her across the lawn to the house.

Mohammed too had heard the car and stood in the doorway, trying to make sense of the figure walking towards him with what seemed like a corpse in his arms. Then he realised it was Amala. 'What happened?' he shouted, rushing forward.

'A soldier attacked her, at a road block. I shot him,' replied Freddie, in a cold matter-of-fact voice. He carried Amala into the drawing room and laid her on a sofa.

Mohammed shouted for his wife to bring water and they bathed her temples while she slowly regained consciousness. For a while she did not speak, then she looked around her and saw her father. They spoke briefly in Urdu, which Freddie did not understand and then she fell asleep. Together they carried her to a simple bedroom at the back of the house where she slept, her mother looking on.

'You must stay here tonight, Freddie,' said Mohammed. 'Hide the car in the back behind the stable. Then tomorrow I will show you where you can dispose of it. That will give you time. Amala told me it was a mistake. Is that true?'

'It's true that I have never intentionally killed anything in my life,' answered Freddie, 'but I pointed the gun at the soldier and pulled the trigger. I make no excuses. Amala must be kept safe. She is innocent of everything.'

'I will protect her, don't worry,' said her father. 'When she is a little better I will drive her to Nairobi. It will be as if she had never been here.'

'But there are road blocks everywhere,' said Freddie.

Mohammed smiled. 'You had a gun in your glove compartment. I have a more powerful weapon than that. I can buy the silence of every KAR soldier between here and the capital with a single roll of bank notes. Now you must sleep too, dear boy, and in the morning we can talk further.'

He spoke in Urdu to the houseboy, who scuttled off towards the car. Freddie heard the sound of the engine turning over and saw it move behind the house and out of sight. Mohammed put his arm round Freddie's shoulders as if he were his only son.

Chapter 10

It was by chance that Freddie had already packed the two most important things in his world in the boot of the car: his journal and his sketches of Amala. These he stowed in a loose canvas bag, together with the Browning pistol. He looked at the ugly metal barrel which had fired the dreadful shot and felt utter disgust. He drove the car to the top of the slope leading down to the cliff edge and pulled on the handbrake. Then he got out, took his bag, released the brake and stood back. At first there was no movement; then the wheels began to turn inch by inch and the empty car slowly gathered momentum until it was racing across the green sward. As the ground disappeared beneath the front wheels the car seemed to leap like a living creature into the air, somersaulted, then dived front first into the white swirling water a hundred feet below. Freddie rushed to the edge to watch. The car floated for a while, turning in the violent currents, before sinking out of sight into the black depths of the river. He had a sudden memory then of Desmond, his faithful houseboy, cheering when his strange new master had brought the car to life those years ago. He wished him well and hoped he would be safe. Then he turned and trudged back up the hill to where Ahmed, Mohammed's packman, waited for him with his borrowed horse. He turned his face to the north and they set off, never to return to the land he had learned to love.

It was a day's ride to the edge of the lake and Freddie was glad of Ahmed's company, although they spoke little. Mohammed had given Freddie a packman's coat and headgear so that he very quickly looked the part: an ordinary train of packhorses following the well-trodden route to the northern villages, with two Indian packmen in charge. Nothing could be more natural. And as he rode he tried not to think of the future; if his past had been labyrinthine, the future might be even more so. But the face of Amala drifted in and out of his mind as he half-slept in the saddle with the heat of the sun beating down on his shoulders. In the late afternoon they reached a small knoll and looked down upon the lake. In the distance, they could see Larsen's canning factory, a wisp of smoke spiraling into the still air above a circle of native huts, and beyond them the ugly corrugated iron shed that housed the machinery.

It had been a long day. It had started at first light when Mohammed had come to Freddie's room to wake him. He felt like a man dreading the sound of the bolt sliding back on his cell door, on the final morning of his life, with the gallows awaiting him. What would life be without her? He could not bear to think of it. But Mohammed filled the space with his clear instructions as to what must happen. Differences between man and man are but the trappings of society; when what really joins us is the shared humanity that flows in our veins, regardless of our origins. Freddie felt a bond of trust with Amala's father that he could not have believed possible.

'There is no need to panic, Freddie,' Mohammed had said. 'What happened last night involved the army and they know nothing of you or Amala. It will take time for the civil authorities to become involved. Then Dalrymple will work out what happened. So we have a few days yet. But you must leave now. Ahmed will take you to the lake. I have given him a message for Larsen. You will find help there. In the meantime, you must take the car to the river and sink it. Not far from here there is a deep gorge where it will disappear, probably for ever, but certainly until the next dry season, and by then you will be long gone.'

'I must say goodbye to Amala,' said Freddie. 'How is she?'

'Well enough. You will find her on the verandah. She slept a little. Her mother has been with her all night.'

It was the misty first hours of the day. The sun had scarcely shown itself and the world was steeped in a grey half-light. Freddie found Amala alone, sitting on a woven chair on the verandah, a Maasai shawl around her shoulders. She looked more beautiful and fragile than seemed possible, and he knew he was forced to leave this other-self, perhaps for ever. It was the hardest, most cruel moment of his short life.

What was there to say? What possible combinations of words could capture the emotions that overwhelmed these two young lovers. They were wrenched apart by the act of a moment, as a Montague from a Capulet, by a simple sudden impulse, a muscle driven by the brain driven by the heart. But it was now too late. The world had turned a notch on its axis and could not be reversed in its ceaseless grind of time. Freddie, dreaming in his saddle, could not remember what he had said, if indeed he had said anything. But he remembered Amala saying that she would come to him and the final soft touch of her lips against his. And this is what filled his mind on the journey that day.

At dusk they entered the village and Ahmed led the packhorses to the well to water them while the men of the village unloaded their burdens and carried them to the store. The two men walked through the straw huts towards a low building in stone standing on its own on a slope overlooking the lake. In the background they could hear the diesel engine that drove the generator. A light shone in the window and a tall figure stood on the steps, smoking a curved white pipe. It was Larsen. He looked up as they approached and knocked out his pipe on the door post. 'Ottaway, you? What brings you here?' he asked.

'I have a message from Mohammed,' said Ahmed, handing over the envelope he had been given that morning. 'It explains a little.'

'You'd better come in, both of you,' replied Larsen.

They followed him into the dark interior of the building. It was a bachelor's quarters, a single living room with a small bedroom at the back, Larsen's place to spend a night when he visited the plant. It smelled of tobacco and had the careless untidiness of a single man's pad. One clear light bulb hung from an electric wire in the centre of the ceiling, the only acknowledgement of the electricity supply, apart from Larsen's refrigerator. They sat down round an iron stove on a dusty hearth and Larsen lit a lamp to read by. He scrutinised

Mohammed's note carefully before looking up and speaking. The African night had descended fully by this time and the oil lamp threw flickering shadows of the three men on the walls.

'News travels here in the north only at the speed of a walking horse. You are safe here, Freddie, for the time being. No one yet knows what has happened. I see you are wondering why Mohammed trusted me with this news. A fair question. There is a lot you don't know. Ahmed, I think it better you leave now for your quarters in the village. Ottaway and I need to be alone.' Ahmed did as he was asked. 'You must be hungry after your long trip, Freddie. Let's eat while we talk.' Larsen shouted through to the back room and there was a shout in Swahili and a clatter of dishes in response. A few minutes later two army mess tins appeared with what looked like a kind of kedgeree dumped in them, with a hunk of corn bread. Larsen produced a bottle of aquavit and two bottles of beer from his fridge, plonking them down on the camp table. 'Basic, but good,' he said. 'What did you expect to eat in a fish cannery?'

'It's fine,' said Freddie. Larsen poured out two glasses of aquavit and handed one to his guest, together with a bottle of ice cold beer. He raised his glass to Freddie.

'Skol! This is quite a mess Freddie. Let's drink to that! Then you can tell me about it.'

They settled down to eat their humble supper, enhanced by the beer and aquavit chasers, while Freddie slowly reassembled his memory of the events of last night. It was a painful process. When he had finished speaking, Larsen picked up the bottle of aquavit and topped up the two glasses. 'Mohammed is right,' he said. 'You need to leave as soon as possible. You realise it could have been different, don't you,' he added.

'How could it?' asked Freddie. 'I killed a man.'

Larsen laughed and then continued: 'Do you think the life of a black soldier counts for much here, Freddie? Let's say you had Gordon on your side; let's say you had toed the line the British have drawn in the sand; let's imagine you hadn't painted those pictures; and let's imagine your girlfriend was the daughter of the Provincial Officer, instead of someone like Mohammed. Don't you think a chance shot in the dark could have been passed over, as it always has? Buried under a layer of bureaucracy. The fact is, Freddie, they wanted you out anyway, and you've given them their chance. This is how it works. You don't belong here. I knew as soon as I met you that things would end in tears. It's not enough to love a country, the trees and the skies and the people; there's more to a country than that. You forgot the generations of expectations that a nation carries with it.'

'So what do I do,' asked Freddie, 'and why did Mohammed know you would help me?'

'Mohammed and I are outsiders, Freddie. We haven't joined the club, you see. Sure, we make money out of it all. But we don't believe. We don't have that extra little dimension that makes us want to be like them. I'm not against them; I just don't care, and they know that. They couldn't rely on me when the chips are down. Mohammed thinks like me. It's understood. Do you get it?'

'I'm beginning to. So what do I do?'

Throughout the conversation, Larsen had been filling his pipe. Now he lit it with a match and a halo of sweet blue smoke surrounded him. Then he stood up, crossed the room, and pulled out a rolled-up sheet of paper from a drawer in his desk. 'Look at this,' he said, spreading the map on the table. 'I'll put you in a boat tomorrow. One of my men will take you.' He pointed to Lake Turkana, a long blue splodge stretching to the far north of the country. 'At this point here the lake crosses into Ethiopia. There is no border guard and no questions, simply an imaginary line in the water. My man will drop you on the shore near a small town called Dande. The area is deserted. Follow this stream inland and you will reach it in a half-day's walk.' Freddie followed Larsen's finger as he traced the thin blue line of the stream on the map. 'When you get to Dande, ask for Antonov.'

' You mean Antonov, the Russian spy?' said Freddie.

'If you say so,' replied Larsen, giving him a long-suffering look. 'You may call him a spy if you like but I would call him a businessman looking for new partners, except the business is on behalf of the Soviet state. I ask you, Freddie, what happens when the British leave Africa? Who's going to fill the hole, do you think? Democrats or communists? The Soviets are waiting to move in the moment your lot move out.'

'And you'll do business with anyone,' said Freddie, suddenly realising why Larsen's meeting with Antonov had taken place. Maybe Antonov really was a fish farmer, but with a little communist garnish to add to his caviar harvest. 'And when I meet Antonov, what then?'

'I'll write him a note. Believe me, he'll be delighted to see you! Do you have money?'

'Fifty quid. That's all.'

Larsen crossed to his desk and took out a bundle of notes. He counted out a hundred pounds and handed them to Freddie. 'That's enough to see you through.'

'How shall I pay you back?'

'Pay me back? We can find a way, some day.'

Freddie gave it no further thought. They drank the bottle dry that night. For Freddie it was anaesthetic against the pain of losing Amala and he drifted into his alcoholic dreamstate grateful for the escape from reality. But it was not real sleep, just a suspension from thinking, from which he awoke frequently during the night. In his dark loneliness he could see no way forward; but when the daylight broke through the gaps in the shutters, and he crawled out of his camp bed in the livingroom, he felt a spark of hope that things would come right.

His boatman was a strongly-built Kikuyu called Joshua. Larsen walked down to the wooden jetty next to the canning plant to see them off. It was early morning and a ten-foot layer of fog, like a thick woollen blanket, lay over the water. The lake was silent and smooth, only the occasional voice of the fishermen returning from a night's work could be heard along the shore. Sometimes the black silhouette of a boat drifted into view as the fog momentarily cleared, with a man standing in the bows casting a circular net into the water. Freddie threw his canvas bag into the boat, shook Larsen's hand, stepped down and Joshua cast off. The inboard diesel spluttered into life and the wooden launch set off into the unknown. Freddie was adrift in an alien world, with a set of memories, a gun and a hundred and fifty quid. He looked back towards the jetty where Larsen stood, waving his hand before disappearing into the bank of fog. Mohammed, Larsen, Antonov – what a strange collection of friends he had acquired, he thought, and yet they seemed to want to look after him. But for the time being he did not question their motives.

After an hour, the fog lifted as the sun burned through. They were travelling in the shallow fringes of the lake, sometimes cutting through banks of sedge where flights of duck rose slowly into the sky at their approach. Or past long shining mud flats, turning pink when the grazing flamingo opened their wings to fly. It was another world, as if the boat were carrying him away into a fourth dimension, and all the time his memories dragged him back to a cold reality. Joshua stood at the tiller resolute, hour after hour, while the relentless sun beat down. He did not speak. The lake narrowed as they travelled north until, having passed a strange white marker post on the shore, Joshua pulled on the tiller and steered east to the opposite shore, aiming for a wooden jetty.

'We are in Ethiopia now, Mr Ottaway,' he said. 'We have crossed the border.'

Freddie had no idea what to expect. He peered into the distance and slowly the wooden jetty began to take shape in more detail. Heavy black stakes rose from the water, criss-crossed with beams, and along the top he thought he could make out a rail track with an ancient wagon parked there. A ramshackle wooden building stood behind it, sun-bleached wooden boards hanging loose. It was a scene of dereliction and decay. Joshua steered the boat alongside a rickety ladder leading to the top of the jetty and passed the bag to Freddie, who began to climb the rungs.

'Follow the stream, Mr Ottaway, and you will be in Dande by nightfall.'

And with that he pushed off from the jetty and turned the

boat round to the south. Freddie heard the slow beat of the marine diesel fade as Joshua disappeared into the haze over the water. He felt utterly desolate and alone in the world. As far as the eye could see he was the only living creature in this lonely place; not a bird sang nor a lizard scuttled; nor a blade of grass grew in the red shale. Only the trickle of the tiny stream could be heard as it fell into the lake. Freddie picked up his bag and set off, following the winding channel as it disappeared inland between encroaching rocks.

It was a hard slog of four hours before he reached Dande. He was exhausted and parched, his feet were blistered and his eyes encrusted with red dust. The village announced itself before he arrived. He was resting by the stream, which had narrowed to a rivulet, when he heard the clank of a bell and, looking up, he saw the head of a goat looking at him, then another, and another until finally a boy appeared holding a stick. Freddie looked at him and said 'Antonov', not expecting a response. But the boy waved his arm and set off, with Freddie following amid the herd of African goats. A quarter of a mile further, they reached Dande, no more than a dozen native huts around a muddy pond from which the stream flowed, shaded by a clump of trees. A small crowd had gathered out of curiosity and Freddie saw the distinctive shape of the Russian stepping forward to greet him, and the shining bald head as he took off his hat.

'Mr Ottaway, I did not expect to meet you here. Come to my house. Larsen sent you, I suppose?'

'He sent you a message.' As he handed it over, Freddie suddenly realised his folly, to have trusted Larsen, who could have delivered him to an unknown fate, as Hamlet with Rosencrantz and Guildenstern. But it was too late now; he would have to trust himself to Antonov, the very man he had decided was untrustworthy. But as he walked he felt the canvas of his bag to make sure he could lay hands on his Browning pistol if the need arose.

Chapter 11

Morgane Owen had become acclimatised to life in Edinburgh where the cold east winds blowing off the North Sea chilled her to the bone, or the south westerlies racing across from the Atlantic brought soaking showers. Unlike Africa, change was ever-present and unpredictable, which was invigorating. She had learned to appreciate the cold wet streets in the autumn, the hard frosts of winter, the sudden burst of green leaves in Charlotte Square in the spring, and the fresh clear skies of summer with their billowing white clouds. She had completed three years of her turgid, grinding medical degree in London and now she was embarking on the exhausting clinical work which would convert her from a repository of medical information into a woman who could really heal the sick. For a year she was learning paediatrics at the best children's hospital in Scotland, under the eagle eyes of Professor MacKendrick. Each morning she set out early from her tiny flat in Glen Street, where she lived cheek-by-jowl with the working people of Edinburgh and the transient medical students of the world, in the flat-faced stone tenements that had stood for a hundred years gathering grime in the smoky air of the city. Her walk took her through a narrow close past the gaunt Scottish church at the end of the street, and across the Meadows to Marchmont. This she did at all hours of the day and night, in all weathers. She had become serious and dedicated, as befitted someone who had seen the miseries and joys of life in all their sharp relief. She returned to Kenya once a year to spend time in her father's clinic in Lodwar, where her paediatrics were in great demand for the myriad native mothers and children who, without her knowledge, would be lost. On her first return she had heard with dismay of the disappearance of Freddie Ottaway, who had vanished into nothing, leaving not a trace. He had simply disappeared one night in his car and neither he nor the car were seen again.

Dalrymple had suggested to her father that Freddie might be mixed up with a shooting at a roadblock but the details never emerged. It therefore came as a surprise when months later she received a letter from Freddie from an address in Camberwell. It had travelled by a circuitous route, beginning with the office of the medical faculty at London University, then to Guy's and from there forwarded to Miss Morgane Owen, c/o The Royal Hospital for Sick Children, Sciennes Road, Edinburgh. It was a month in the journey. It was a simple enough letter but it raised more questions than it answered:

My dear Morgane,

I am in London and I hoped we could meet. I have written to the only address I thought might find you. If you reply to this letter, please address it to Hugh Montague, by which name I am now known.

with every good wish
Freddie Ottaway

She knew he must be in trouble. So she scribbled a reply in her coffee break that morning, to Hugh Montague at 35 Camberwell Grove, London SE5, telling him she was in Edinburgh until July but that she would love to see him anytime, and where he could find her during the daytime. She posted her letter at the sub-post office in Marchmont on a Tuesday. On Saturday morning she picked up a letter from her doormat in Glen Street. It simply said: *Arriving Waverley Station, Monday three o'clock. Will call into the hospital, Freddie.*

In truth, Freddie was desolate. He slept little and when he did, he dreamed of Amala and their final parting, kissing him and saying she would come to him. But he had written to her and there was no reply. He had written again, and again no reply. What was he to do? He had a tiny cold top-floor flat in a tall dilapidated house in Camberwell, with brown lino on the staircase and creaking bare boards on the floor. For a man so peaceful as Freddie, it was strange that he had carried the Browning pistol all the way to London, and kept it at the back of a kitchen cupboard. It was also strange that he thought very little about the mysterious forces that had managed his escape from Kenya, or what the consequences might be. He had little money, only the remnants of a long-forgotten post office account from which he could withdraw small amounts of cash on presentation of his pass book. So far, the name Ottaway had not triggered a response from the authorities but he was not sure how long this would last. And above it all, was the burning sense of loss he felt, which the passing of time did little to cool.

He took the train north from King's Cross at nine-thirty that Monday morning. He had bought a third class ticket and sat in the corner of the carriage. He had lived six months in England in the shadow of his past, with a name he had assumed, since his own name was a passport to arrest and condemnation. He had thought of contacting his father but had rejected the notion; he had made a break with his comfortable childhood past and would not return to that thraldom. But, as the train slowly pulled out of King's Cross, winding between the sooty walls of railway cuttings, over viaducts with bleak vistas of city wastes, he thought of the strange sequence of events that had brought him to London as Hugh Montague, aged twenty-five, born in Birmingham, according to his passport.

Antonov had read the note that Larsen had sent him but said nothing about it. He had merely offered Freddie a bed for the night in the wooden villa at Dande. In the morning, over a simple breakfast, Antonov had explained the plan. 'There is a truck leaving here today for Addis Ababa. You can leave with it. You will not be stopped. The driver carries a pass from the government to say that he is on approved commercial business, so you will be safe. When you reach the city, go to this address.' And he had handed him a slip of paper with a few words on it. 'You can buy a new British passport there. With that you can take the train to Djibouti and a merchant ship to England. They stop at Djibouti for refuelling. You can forget about Freddie Ottaway. You must become someone else.'

'I don't understand. Why should you help me?' Freddie

had asked, bewildered.

Antonov had wiped his bald head with his handkerchief and poured out another vodka for himself, even though it was only ten in the morning. 'Help you?' he had said. 'One day you may be able to help us. If you need to contact my friends in London, phone this number.'

That was all he had said but he looked long and hard at Freddie as he spoke, as if the sparse words had deeper unspoken meaning. An hour later Freddie had found himself sitting in the passenger seat of the driver's cab of a Bedford truck, beside the native driver. The heat in the cab was overpowering and the red dust of the road insufferable. The lorry carried no load which suggested it was fetching something from the north but what it might be was by no means clear.

'Why are you going to Addis Ababa?' Freddie had asked the driver out of the blue. The man was unprepared for the question, a native with little interest in anything except his wage, and answered more fully than was sensible. 'I collect machinery from the airport,' he had replied. 'They land it there in big planes.'

He had said no more but, as they drove north, a lorry had passed them travelling south with an unseen load under a canvas cover flapping in the wind. Antonov's purpose was much more than fish farming.

The road to Addis Ababa seemed interminable and the truck had travelled at a snail's speed through the winding undulating dust plains of Ethiopia. Occasionally they had pulled up at a truck stop, no more than a tin hut by the roadside, with a man selling tea in small cups, and piles of tiny sticky cakes, around which the flies buzzed. It had seemed a journey into nowhere, from nowhere, but for some reason Freddie had trusted Antonov to get him to safety.

At evening they reached the city. Freddie looked at the piece of paper Antonov had given him.

'Do you know where this place is?' he had asked the driver, as they drove slowly through the wretched suburbs on the edge of town. The driver took the paper, glanced at it briefly, and then answered. 'It is behind the railway station. I take you there.'

The buildings had became more cluttered as they neared the centre of town but there was no beauty, no symmetry, merely a piling up of haphazard shapes and structures as if no one had had the time to think where to place them. Then strangely they had glanced across the end of a wide road and, turning right, the driver swept past the most beautiful railway station Freddie had ever seen. It had a wide frontage of white stucco, with a dozen romanesque arches leading into station offices. On the first floor, painted in deep blue, a row of tall windows stood within the walls, as beautiful as might have graced a Parisian boulevard. Under the eves of the roof, Freddie read the words *Chemin de Fer Djibouto Ethiopien* in black elegant lettering. The driver continued a hundred yards or so then stopped, pointing to a side street leading off into a warren of tiny alleys. Freddie got down, grabbed his bag and, before he could wave goodbye, the truck roared off into the night.

The name on the paper was Wasim Sadiq. At the corner of the street was a shop with a bare electric light bulb hanging from a hook over the trestle tables covered in boxes of vegetables and spices. A man sat on a stool in the corner. Freddie said the name and the shopkeeper pointed up the street and, surprisingly, added in English 'three houses along'. A few yards further Freddie stood before a white painted wall eight feet high, with a wrought iron gate in the centre, through which he could see a paved courtyard and a fig tree. A bell pull protruded above a brass name plate that read *Wasim Sadiq*. Away in a distant recess of the house Freddie heard the ringing of the bell; then a dog barked, an outside light switched on, and a dark figure moved across the courtyard to the gate. All Freddie saw was a small dark face peering through the grill.

'Wasim Sadiq? Antonov sent me. My name is Ottaway,' Freddie had said, and the man slowly drew back the bolt and the gate creaked open. Without speaking he led Freddie indoors to a cool, marble-floored room, with low chairs and a coffee table. A hookah stood on the table with a small white cup of Turkish coffee beside it.

'Have you eaten?' asked Sadiq.

'No', answered Freddie.

Sadiq clapped his hands and a black Ethiopian woman appeared. There was a brief conversation in one of the languages of the country, Freddie knew not which, and after a few minutes a large round plate appeared with splodges of what looked like a meat stew with vegetables. Sadiq tore off a piece of sourdough flat bread, scooped up some stew and vegetables with it, and handed it to Freddie.

'It is the custom of our country to hand our guests their food,' said Sadiq. His half-moon reading glasses glinted in the light from a table lamp. He was a silver-haired Asian, small and neat. 'Please eat, Mr Ottaway. Tomorrow we can talk business.'

Freddie had slept soundly that night, he remembered, waking only to the musical sound of a small fountain in the courtyard below his window. As light broke, a cockerel called from somewhere across the roof tops, a dog barked and the sound of a cartwheel echoed from the street. That was his distant memory.

The Edinburgh train slowed before crossing the long winding viaduct across the Tweed. In an hour he would be at Waverley. In his inside pocket he carried the passport which Sadiq had carefully assembled for him, complete with black and white photograph developed in the cellar of the house in Addis Ababa. Hugh Montague was already a well-travelled man, for several pages were haphazardly filled with forged entry and exit visas, but the latest were genuine, showing he had departed from Djibouti three weeks before disembarking at the Port of London. The line curved round across the estuary, shallow and wide, with the ramparts of the border town running down to the water's edge. It was a fine spring day and the rolling breakers threw up white spray over the shallow waters of the sand banks. Freddie caught a glimpse of the engine as it slowed before the station. 'How English, how far from Africa,' he thought. How unlikely it seemed that

Amala could ever reach him here in this alien cold land. He heard the station master shout 'Berwick' and the brakes squealed as the train drew to a halt. In the silence that followed, Freddie felt the weight of his loneliness.

Morgane was there to meet him at Waverley. The train arrived in a cloud of smoke under the glass dome of the station. She stood behind the barrier and waved when he walked down the platform. She kissed him on the cheek and smiled. Freddie looked at her. She had left Kenya a girl; now she was a beautiful woman in full flight, looking down upon the world, her wings outstretched.

'How are you Freddie?' she asked. 'You look tired. Has it been a long journey?'

'I feel as if I've been travelling for ever,' he replied. 'That's why I've come to find you. You're the only person in this country I really know.'

That night, in her flat in Glen Street, Freddie told her everything that had happened to him and she listened patiently to his story.

'And you have heard nothing from Amala?' she asked at last.

'Not a word,' he replied.

'I travel back to Kenya in two months and stay for a month,' she said. 'I'll try to find out what has happened. Will you be at the same address in London when I get back?' Freddie nodded. 'Well, then, I'll visit you there.'

They slept apart that night. Freddie's prediction made when Morgane left Kenya for the first time had been right: she was a different person now and they inhabited different worlds. But they were connected by that mysterious thread of human friendship that can stretch across continents and ages.

It was a long hard summer of emptiness and waiting. On fine days he took his sketch book and his easel to Ruskin Park, a short walk away, and began to paint a series of portraits based on the sketches he had drawn in Africa. And so the muse that was Amala began the process of migration to an English park in south London, where the beauty of Africa took shape against an herbaceous border in full bloom.

Passers-by would stop and gaze but no one found it unusual. He wore a wide-brimmed straw hat to keep off the sun and became a familiar figure, the eccentric young artist from Camberwell Grove who painted pictures of a black girl in an English summer garden.

When September came the leaves on the trees in Ruskin Park began to turn yellow. The end of summer was near and the flower borders grew old and tangled. Morgane had not contacted him and he began to think he would have to endure another English winter with no news of Amala. It was almost a year without word. He had moments of panic, when he feared he could not remember what she looked like, as if her presence were slowly draining from him. At these times he went to his sketches and his pictures but these proved brief respite and his loneliness grew worse. His funds were running low and he could see no way forward in his life. He began to wonder if it were worth living at all. One morning he received a letter, with a London postmark. It was from Morgane, back in England, and living across the river in Clapton, doing a year in Bart's, she had said. 'I'm in every evening after six. Come when you can. Love, Morgane.'

He was filled with fear. There was no other word for it. He wanted to pretend it wasn't happening, as if a fatal illness might go away if the letter carrying the test result were simply thrown on the fire. But he knew he had to find out. He carried still a slender hope that all would be well. That same day in late afternoon he walked to the Oval tube station and took the Northern Line, changed at Moorgate for Liverpool Street and then caught the suburban train to Clapton. The trains were crowded and stuffy but he passed through the jostling travellers without noticing them. At Clapton he emerged into a wave of sound and fumes from the rush hour traffic on Lower Clapton Road. Morgane's flat was in a heavy Victorian semi, next to a World War II bomb site overgrown with weeds, with front steps up to a large front door. To the side, steps led down to a gloomy basement flat with a door in the area. There were six name plates on the front door, Owen being the first. He rang the bell and after a while the door swung open. He tried to read Morgane's face but she simply smiled at him and put her arms round his shoulders and kissed him. They sat at her small kitchen table while she boiled a kettle on a single gas ring to make tea. Freddie could not begin to ask but inside he knew what the answer would be.

'I have news,' said Morgane, 'but it is the worst. Amala is dead.'

At first, he felt only numbness. His eyes focused on a corner of the room, staring vacantly. It was as if his brain refused to accept the meaning of what he had heard and there was some process of mental deletion going on. He wanted to feel something but he could not. He felt guilty that he could not. He ought to be screaming, shouting, anything except this blankness. The spell was broken when Morgane reached out her hand to grasp his across the table. He looked up and at last spoke. 'Tell me,' said Freddie. 'What happened?'

'When I got back to Lodwar, I saw that the Mohammed house was empty and locked. My father told me they had moved to Nairobi but he didn't know why. So I travelled to Nakuru. I knew that Amala often stayed there with her sister in the flat by the railway station. She told me what had happened. The British had declared a state of emergency in October last year and shipped in KAR troops from Uganda and all over the place. Kenya was swarming with them. They screened the whole of the native population for anyone who had taken the Mau-Mau oath. The men were shipped off to detention camps in the north while the women were sent to holding reservations. Most of them had never lived outside the cities and the towns so it was a nonsense for them to live in native settlements.'

'But Amala was an educated woman, for God's sake. She was finishing her law degree. She had nothing to do with Mau-Mau. She was only interested in the democratic rights of all Kenyans. Surely they didn't round her up.'

'Apparently they did. They ignored Professor Oduya, who was obviously too prominent a figure to arrest, but they had a list of black students with liberal attitudes, and she was rounded up and held in a reservation. Can you imagine it,

Freddie? Of course, the worst happened. Typhoid broke out and many of the women and children died. Oduya made an appeal to the Commissioner and Amala was released and taken home. But it was too late. She died in her parent's house in Nairobi. It was November 1952.'

'So that's why I never received a reply to my letters. She was already dying.'

There was a silence. Morgane could say no more. The plain facts spoke for themselves. As for Freddie he could only think of the brief years he had spent with Amala and an overwhelming sense of emptiness crept over him like a cold creeping illness. His life had suddenly become meaningless, with no purpose, no escape route into those brief interludes of happiness when the pain of human life is suspended. Why go on; why bother to live; why drag himself each day into the bitter light for this suffering, this emptiness? These were the thoughts that raced through his head. They lasted only a second but it felt like hours. Morgane stood up and walked round the bare kitchen table and put her arms round Freddie's shoulders. He buried his head in her breast and wept.

'Do you want to stay here tonight, Freddie?' she asked.

He thought for a while and then said: 'No, thanks, Morgane. Thank you for what you have told me. She was your friend, I know. I'll go home. I need to think.'

'Call me,' she said, 'you can get me at Bart's.'

'One thing, did you hear anything of Desmond, when you were at Lodwar?'

Morgane hesitated before she answered. 'Father told me he had died.'

'How?'

'The Mau-Mau murdered him one night. He was a loyal Kikuyu, you see. They burned your house down afterwards.'

'And his women and children?'

'All dead, Freddie. I'm sorry. Their hut was burned to the ground. They all died.'

'My God! Poor Desmond. I promised to take care of him.'

What could she say in his despair? She kissed him goodbye at the front door. Freddie walked slowly down

Clapton Road. It was dark and cold. The traffic had subsided. He had no purpose in his mind but to walk, which he did without thinking. He kept no track of time and the minutes rolled by unheeded. Before he knew it, he had reached the river. By instinct he turned right and walked on, oblivious of the occasional passer-by. The cold night wind blew the river smells into his face, the smell of mud and water and chimney smoke, and the bleakness of life smothered his spirits. Before long he reached Tower Bridge and began to cross it. In the middle he stopped and looked down into the dark, swirling waters of the Thames as they flowed towards the sea. So easy, he thought, to escape from this pain. He stood, unaware of time, looking down into the water. He saw the faces of Amala and Desmond, and the giggling wives and children sitting on the steps of his house. And then he heard a voice at his elbow. 'Don't worry, Bwana. We are all well.' He turned to see who was speaking but he saw nothing, only the darkness of the city reflected in the dark waters below.

It was the early hours before he stumbled up the stairs to his top floor flat in Camberwell Grove. He collapsed on to his bed, fully dressed, and slept a kind of half-sleep. The morning light woke him through the open curtains. But as he came to his senses, he realised he had come to a decision. His sense of loss had become anger and indignation. He stretched out for his jacket which lay crumpled on the floor by his bed where he had flung it the night before. In the pocket he found the piece of paper that Antonov had given to him all those months earlier and which had travelled with him from Dande. He waited until the parish church clock struck nine before he walked to the telephone box at the corner of the street. He took out the small piece of paper and dialled the number. He heard the receiver lifted and he pressed the button. The coins fell and a voice answered. Then Freddie spoke: 'Antonov gave me this number. I want to come onboard,' he said. A shiver passed through his whole body, not from the cold of the morning, but from the first moment of betrayal. He loved his country but it had destroyed him.

The voice on the telephone did not sound surprised. It

was as if it were a commonplace occurrence to receive such a call. The voice did not hesitate: 'Meet me tomorrow at three o'clock by the Peter Pan fountain in Kensington Gardens. You know it?'

'I know it.'

'I shall have a dog with me.' Freddie half expected it to be called Nanny but the voice continued: 'It's a rough-haired dachshund.' The line went dead. As he walked back to his flat he thought of the irony of it all, to betray one's country to a man with a dog, by the statue of a boy who refused to grow up.

But the reality did not feel so dramatic. The process of betrayal turned out to be no more than one small step followed by another. Freddie arrived in the vicinity of the Peter Pan statue five minutes early. A ring of park benches stood around it, with the usual collection of people using them; a mother with a pushchair, a couple of tourists studying a map, a man eating a sandwich, but no sign of the dog. The whole thing began to feel like a hoax: Antonov's practical joke. Then, at a minute to three, from nowhere as it seemed, a man with a dachshund appeared, sat down nearest the statue and began to read a newspaper. Freddie strolled towards the bench and sat down. He had been given no introductory line but he did not need one.

'Mr Montague, I presume. My name is Fowler. How nice to meet you.' He was English, respectable and utterly nondescript. 'Now, tell me, what do you think you can do for us?' He offered Freddie a cigarette from a Craven A packet and took one himself.

'What do you want me to do?' asked Freddie. 'I have no special skills.'

The man drew on his cigarette and looked at Freddie long and hard. Then he smiled. 'That's not what Dimitri told us. But don't worry, you don't need any special skills, Mr Montague. You have everything you need. You are English. You have a British passport. You can wear a club tie and not look out of place anywhere the British are in charge. What more do you need?'

'I'm still not sure what this means,' said Freddie.

'Be patient. Go on with your life....and wait. Oh, and by the way, get yourself a better place to live and some, shall we say, business clothes. I know you must be short of cash. Let me know how much it costs. We can meet again here next week. Look out for Percy and you'll find me.'

That was how it began. Freddie found a new flat north of the river and Fowler paid the deposit. He opened an account with a tailor in Soho and gave the statement to Fowler at one of their meetings. And very soon he was given a cheque book with an account at Barclays in the Strand, into which a reasonable monthly sum was paid. But nobody asked him to do anything. If this was the life of a traitor, it was a very comfortable one. He would have welcomed pain, fear, discomfort, if only to chase away the misery of his thoughts of Amala. They coloured every moment of his life; they were the backdrop against which he played out each daily act.

It was six months before he was called upon. A letter arrived at his new flat in Millbank. It contained two keys, one with a plastic fob imprinted with a number; the other, small and light, as if it might open a box or a case. The instructions were to take a train to Crewe, open the left luggage locker, retrieve the contents and deliver them to an address in Camden. The next day he took a train from Euston. 'Why Crewe?' he asked himself. The answer was simple: Crewe was the crossing point of six railway routes to all directions in the north of the country. Whatever he was to collect could have come from anywhere. The operation went smoothly. Inside the left luggage locker was a slim leather briefcase which was locked. As the locker key could not be removed from the lock without further payment, it was obvious that the small key in Freddie's possession must open the briefcase. He travelled back to London without delay, opened the briefcase at Euston, took out the large envelope inside and dumped the case in a rubbish bin. That evening he walked from his flat to St James's tube station and took the Circle Line to Embankment and from there the Northern Line to Camden Town. He wore an overcoat and inside the lining he could feel the envelope rubbing against his shirt. He felt as if all eyes were upon him as the silent fellow travellers swayed with the movements of the train. At Camden, he walked for ten minutes along quiet streets to a semi-detached house, rang the bell and handed the envelope to a housekeeper. There were no words exchanged; no acknowledgements; the business was done. It was simple; it was meaningless. Freddie could not understand what he had done or why he had done it. Was this a way to revenge the murder of Amala? If so, it was a mundane and slightly squalid affair. But, as he realised with a cold chill that evening, he was a condemned man now, in the hands of whoever controlled this secret world he had entered. He had no way back. In his Millbank flat, with a view of the river, he picked up his brush and painted, and a tear formed at the corner of his young eye.

PART THREE

Chapter 1

Whitby, North Yorkshire, August 2005

It was high summer and the cliff-top pastures were rich in meadow grass, buttercups, daisies and clover. The lazy cattle grazed contentedly in the warm sunshine. Edward and Julie lay on their backs gazing up at the blue sky, watching the skylarks, with the tang of the salt sea blowing in on a gentle breeze.

'You know, Julie, every time I come here, my mind turns to Freddie,' said Edward.

'How do you mean?' she asked.

'I mean, how he died. By my calculations he was only in his late seventies. OK, old, but not decrepit. He had enough strength to climb one hundred and ninety-nine steps, and then walk a mile to this point. No, I don't buy the idea that he slipped.'

'So what *are* you saying? That he was pushed?' she replied, threading the last daisy into the daisy chain she was making.

'Pushed, possibly. But unlikely. Why would anyone want to push an old man over a cliff? This is quiet little Whitby remember, not Los Angeles. People don't push each other off cliffs here. That's far too sinister an idea.'

'So you think he jumped? That's just too depressing to contemplate,' said Julie.

'If you look at it the conventional way, yes, it is depressing. If you always regard suicide as an escape from misery, it must be. But what about people who *want* to depart this world because it is the right moment to do it, their work is done, their task completed, they are happy to go?'

'There is someone on the other side, you mean, waiting

for them?' said Julie.

'Yes, maybe,' said Edward. 'It makes sense that way. I can't get away from the idea that Freddie deliberately engineered a situation to get me here. I can't think of any other explanation, can you?'

'He probably wanted you to fall into my arms, Edward,' she said with a smile.

'You know, Julie, I think he may well have. You may laugh, but I've often thought that. But I still wonder why he would want it.'

Both fell into silence but neither had dismissed the thought entirely. For Edward, the desire to find out more about his uncle's missing years became ever stronger and the only lead he had was Viktor Malinov, the sad little Russian billionaire who wanted to be an Englishman, who had loved Freddie as a brother in some dark forgotten life. But Viktor had drawn a veil over this intrigue when Edward had last spoken to him, amidst the Royal Worcester tea service on the lawn at Ponsonby Hall. If he were to get Viktor to tell more, he needed a lever to do so.

Later that week a letter arrived with a York postmark. It was from Scrivener, Freddie's solicitor, and was addressed to Edward in most apologetic terms, enclosing a safe deposit key for a numbered box in the York branch of Barclays Bank. 'I most sincerely apologise for this oversight in forwarding the key to you,' the letter had said. 'I trust the delay has not inconvenienced you.'

'How could it?' thought Edward. 'I didn't know it existed until now.'

He put the key in his pocket, took the solicitor's letter, and walked up Henrietta Street to Julie's shop. She was in the backroom, blowtorch in hand, bent over her silverwork. A blue scarf held back her long black hair and her brown eyes peered through a pair of work goggles. She wore blue workman's overalls with the trousers rolled up over the ankles. He stood and watched her for a while, lost in his thoughts. Then she looked up, smiled and pushed her goggles on to her forehead. 'Was it love, or just a thing about women in overalls?' Edward thought.

'Haven't you got anything better to do than stare at me?' she said.

'Probably not,' said Edward. 'On second thoughts, I'm taking you out for lunch,' he said. 'Come on.'

'Sounds good. Are we celebrating?'

'No, but I have the key to a mystery box, which no doubt will be full of gold bars.'

'What on earth are you talking about, Edward?' she said, but she put down her torch, turned the shop sign to closed, and locked the door. He handed her the letter as they walked down the street to his house. 'We're going to York, I suppose.'

Jim was standing in his open doorway, smoking his pipe, as they passed. 'Fine day,' said Edward.

'Aye, right,' replied Jim.

A few minutes later they were driving up the hill out of town on to the Scarborough road. It was a brilliant day and the moors stretched away into the distance beyond the fields of yellow rape along the roadside. They turned inland towards Malton along a flat green valley bottom where the cattle grazed in the clearings among the gorse. The sweet scent of the blossom hung on the air. In the distance the tall spire of Ganton church reached upwards out of a clump of trees.

'There's a half-decent pub here, called *The Greyhound*,' said Julie. 'It's midday. We can sit out in the garden.'

Edward pulled the car off the road into the pub car park. The garden was a square of well-kept lawn, sheltered by stone walls on three sides, with clematis, wisteria and ceanothus climbing magnificently upwards. There were a few people about but plenty of spare tables to choose from. They drank their beer and wine in the shade of a parasol and ordered something with chips from the bar menu. They had reached that stage when it was no longer necessary to talk; they were just happy in each other's company, as long as they were holding hands. Half way through the scampi, Julie said: 'Why are you so dreamy today Edward?'

'Dreamy? Am I? I suppose I am. Funnily enough, I do a lot of thinking these days. Maybe if I had done more thinking in London, I might have made a go of it. But then, I wouldn't be here, would I?'

'You're very other-worldly,' she remarked, 'a bit like Freddie in that respect.'

'The thing is, Julie, when I washed up in Whitby a few months ago, I thought I'd ended up in a stage play. Everyone knew their lines, except me. Take this morning, for example. Jim's out there, doing his "aye rights" but really keeping tabs on everything that moves. And as for Ruby, how come she took over my welfare when I fell down the steps? She didn't even know me. They're all keeping an eye on me, or that's how it feels. I do a lot of thinking about that.'

'Is that so bad, Edward? Surely it's better than battling with the nameless crowds on the tube every day.' Julie was beginning to get quite angry, and Edward noticed it.

'Of course, you're right,' he said.

'I'll tell you something, Edward. Jim's no mug. He lost his job as a policeman. Drank too much. Something bad happened, not sure what, and he blamed himself for it. Took to the bottle. Freddie kept bailing him out so Ruby feels she owes you something. But Jim's still a copper at heart. As for Ruby, she had to give up her job to look after Jim. She was a midwife at the Royal. I guess when she saw you needed help, her instincts kicked in. I don't think it's any more suspicious than that.'

Edward was silent for a while. 'Sorry,' he said, 'I'm behaving like a shit again.'

Julie laughed out loud. 'We've finished. Come on! Let's go and see what's in this box!'

The main branch of Barclays Bank stood at the corner of Parliament Street and Ousegate. It was a fine red sandstone building, rich in Victorian heaviness, with a neo-gothic archway over the main entrance and rows of large windows on all three floors. An attendant sat at a desk in the entrance lobby and directed Edward to the customer service desk in the large open tellers' hall. After a few minutes, during which he presented his numbered key, the probate document he had received from Scrivener months before, and his driving

159

licence as additional ID, another member of bank staff appeared, a young man in a suit. He opened a flap in the desk, and led Edward down a flight of stone steps to a heavy locked door, which he opened with much ceremony to reveal a large windowless vault lined with numbered boxes. The young man placed the box on the table in the centre of the room and left Edward alone, saying 'Ring the bell on the wall when you are ready, sir.'

Edward opened the steel bank box. Inside he saw a cardboard box which, when opened, revealed a maroon velvet bag with a pullcord. He opened the bag and looked inside. To his amazement it was a pistol, the kind that British officers going over the top in war films always seemed to be pointing at the enemy. He looked around nervously but quickly realised there were no CCTV cameras in the room: privacy was, after all, the key point. But if anyone saw him with a gun in a bank he would no doubt be quickly flattened by a burly security guard. He put the gun carefully back in the bag and the bag in the cardboard box. There was one other item, a slim leather-bound book, the kind that Victorian ladies might use to keep a journal. He picked up the cardboard box, stuck the book under his arm, and rang the bell for the attendant. Somewhat nervously he walked back up the steps, across the tellers' hall and into the street. Julie was waiting in the sunshine. 'You look a bit shaken,' she said. 'Is anything wrong?'

'I've got a bloody big pistol in the box, that's all. God knows if it's legal. Probably not.'

'Why on earth would Freddie keep a gun? He couldn't hurt a fly.'

'There may be more to Freddie than meets the eye. I'll feel a lot safer when I get back home and lock this away,' said Edward. 'Oh, and the other thing is some kind of journal I think.'

It was late afternoon by the time they got back to Henrietta street. Julie was keen to examine the journal and settled down on the sofa alongside Monty to spend an hour or so reading it. Edward sat at the table examining the gun. It was a brutal looking thing, heavy and unbeautiful. He didn't know what make it was or what harm it could do. Then he had an idea. He remembered what he had learned that day about Jim. He put the gun in the box and went and knocked on Jim's door. It was too early for him to have started what seemed to be his regular evening drinking session so he opened the door promptly.

'Jim, can I come in?' said Edward. 'I need your advice on something.'

'Aye right,' said Jim, turning and heading into the living room. Edward could hear Ruby in the kitchen.

'Do you mind if we close the kitchen door, Jim.'

Jim pulled the door closed and they both sat down. 'Sounds mysterious,' said Jim.

Edward opened the box and pulled out the gun. 'What do you make of this?' he said.

Jim took the gun and checked it wasn't loaded. Then he broke it and looked into the chambers. He spun the barrel and felt it in his hand. 'Haven't seen one of these for years,' he said. 'But when I first started, we did firearms training with something similar. Standard army issue the Browning pistol and all the security people used them. Where did you get it?'

'It belonged to Freddie,' Edward replied.

'Freddie never said 'owt about the army. He didn't look army either.'

'But he might have been in some other service, might he not?' asked Edward.

'That he might. It was always a mystery where he came from,' said Jim, lighting his pipe.

'Could you kill a man with this?'

Jim looked askance. 'Kill a man? You could blow his bloody head off, if you could hit him, that is. Brownings were notoriously inaccurate.'

'You sound as if you know a lot about it, Jim.'

'I should do. Served ten years with the Met before I joined the Cleveland force. I wasn't always like this you know. Had to get out at the end. Family problems.'

'I'm sorry. I didn't mean to pry,' said Edward.

'No harm done, son. Put this gun away somewhere safe when you get home. You could get done for possession.' Then he looked at his watch. 'You'll have a whisky?' he said.

So Edward and Jim sat and talked over their whiskies. They had never exchanged more than the briefest of words in the past but Jim was far more than the sum of his words. Edward had never really studied his face before but now, in the fading light of the evening, he could recognise in the lines and the furrows the deepest sorrows, even under the anaesthetic of the whisky. When at last he staggered home, he found Julie stretched out on the sofa with Freddie's journal lying closed on the floor. She opened her eyes as he entered. 'You've been ages. What have you been doing?'

'Getting to know Jim and learning a bit about this lethal weapon. I need to lock it away somewhere. Whatever was Freddie doing with it?'

'I think I know the answer to that,' said Julie gravely. 'He mentions it in his journal. But what about Jim? Tell me.'

'Just that you were right. Something big went wrong in the family but I'm not sure it was all Jim's fault. He simply called it family problems. I don't think he has ever recovered.' Edward paused for a moment. 'But tell me about the gun.'

'Freddie shot a man with it. A soldier in Africa. Killed him. He mentions it just before the last entry. I couldn't believe what I was reading. Freddie so kind and gentle, killing somebody. Don't know why. He doesn't make that clear. And there's more. He tells how he met Amala, the girl in the pictures. You'd better read it for yourself. It's really very moving. The puzzling thing is that there's nothing after October 1952.'

Edward was struck dumb by what Julie had said and had no reply. But Julie continued. 'And the other thing is, why did he bring the gun with him to England?'

'Maybe he was on the run with it. If he really did kill someone he must have had to get out pretty quickly. And maybe that's why the journal and the gun were under lock and key all these years. It was the evidence. Freddie must have forgotten all about them and they've only come to light now because Scrivener finally remembered the bank box key.'

That night Edward read the journal for himself. At two in the morning he found himself lying in bed staring at the ceiling, Juliana sleeping quietly beside him. His mind was racing. He couldn't sleep and had walked to the window overlooking the harbour. It was a windless night with a clear sky and a full moon. The still water reflected the silver light and a lump formed in his throat at the realisation of the torment that Freddie must have endured. To kill a man, to lose the dearest person in the world, to live out your years in this pain, never ceasing, never receding, day in, day out. Then he thought of the clifftop: could it be what he suspected? To be pursued to the end and to find no release. He covered his face with his hands. Then he felt a gentle touch on his arm: Juliana had padded quietly across the room to him.

'What is it Edward? Tell me.'

'I never knew him, Julie, but I feel for him. What must he have suffered? There's only one person I know who can shed any light on this and that's Viktor. I've got to get to the bottom of it.'

'Talk to George in the morning. Come back to bed now.'

Morning brought with it a greater sense of clarity. Edward knew the questions he needed to ask. It was strange: he remembered saying to Juliana months before that it was time he grew up. Now he found himself in a world that was evolving around him, that he didn't really understand, but was dragging him screaming into the light, inch by inch. The simple clear happiness of his brave new world was becoming complex and clouded the further he dug into it. He took the car across to Ruswarp to seek out George. He found him varnishing a boat which was standing on trestles on the river bank, in his familiar empire shorts and floppy hat, sticky paintbrush in one hand and dripping varnish tin in the other. Edward had become very fond of Uncle George in the few months that he had known him; he had that indefinable talent of bringing honour to the most mundane of tasks. In London Edward had mistaken pretence and pretentiousness for values. George had taught him genuineness.

163

'Edward,' he shouted with enthusiasm on seeing him step out of the car. 'How good to see you!' He put down his tin and brush on the grass and wiped his hands on a rag. 'Come and have some coffee. No Juliana this morning?'

'Working away, George,' he replied. 'Actually, I wanted to try out some ideas on you.'

'Sounds alarming,' George replied with a raised eyebrow as they walked along the road to the white cottage, 'but happy to help, if I can.'

They sat drinking their coffee in the back garden running down to the river.

'What's on your mind?' asked George. 'I presume it's more about Freddie.'

'Right. Julie and I went to York last week. Freddie's solicitor sent me a bank box key, which everybody seems to have forgotten about. When I opened the box I found a service pistol, which was a shock in itself. But there was also a kind of journal of his couple of years in Kenya. The awful thing is....he appears to have killed a man, shot a soldier with the gun.'

'Good God!' exclaimed George. 'I find that difficult to believe.'

'It seems to be true. Which explains why he left Africa so soon. And why the gun and the journal have been locked away from sight. The last entry in the journal is autumn 1952. When do you reckon he arrived at Angelus House?'

George thought for a long while before answering. 'That's a difficult one, but it must have been in the seventies I reckon. Possibly around '73. Yes, that's when I first met him. I was working on a barn conversion in Egton that year. Kept having power cuts so the work kept stopping. You know, three-day-week and all that stuff. I'm pretty sure that's when I first came across him.'

'That's more than twenty years since he seems to have disappeared from Africa. What was he doing all that time? There's only one man who can fill the gap and that's Malinov, isn't it.'

'He's up next weekend,' said George. 'First match of the

season. He'll be at Ponsonby Hall no doubt. Do you want me to contact his London office?'

'Would you? See if Sunday would be OK.'

As it turned out, Sunday was fine. Edward had worked out that the only lever he had to get Malinov to tell more was the gun and the journal. He took both with him in the cardboard box. Viktor was in fine form; his team had won their first game of the season and he was happy to see Edward. It was a repeat of the Royal Worcester and the cucumber sandwiches. But the atmosphere turned chilly when Edward produced the Browning pistol. The gentle conversation over the tea things stopped abruptly.

'What do you mean to do with that?' asked Viktor at last, eyeing the hard metal barrel of the gun.

'I don't mean to do anything with it Viktor but let me just say that I know Freddie killed a man in Africa, almost certainly with this gun, and had to get out. You told us yourself about Amala and her death. You said your organisation gave him a job. You owe it to me to tell me what you know.'

'I don't owe you anything, Edward, as it happens. But you are my friend, and Freddie was my oldest friend, and so for that reason I will tell you what I remember.'

165

It was mid-afternoon when Viktor began his account. By the time he had finished the sun had sunk over the ornamental pond at the end of the lawn and the moonlit shadows of the cypress trees stretched across the grass.

'I first met Freddie in London in 1970. I was 30 years old. I was sitting in a bar somewhere, maybe Soho. My boss had told me to meet a man and give him a package. To tell you the truth, I had no idea what I was doing at the Soviet Embassy. OK, I had a title, so-called trade attaché, but what the hell did that mean? I was a kind of office boy. Anyway, I was to meet this chap, Montague. We were not supposed to talk, just do the business. So I sit and wait, drinking some flat English beer. The bar is full of smoke and it's dingy, down below street level. What you might call a dive.' Malinov was warming to his task, showing his command of colloquial language. 'Then I look up and this real Englishman is standing in front of me. I say real Englishman because I had learned to spot the signs: proper leather shoes, you know, brown brogues, and a pair of flannel trousers, a checked shirt and a striped tie, and his jacket just a bit crumpled but tailor-made. Greying hair just over the collar but everything about him said breeding. You don't find them anywhere else in the world. He made my shiny suit and sharply pressed trousers look cheap crap. I was a second-hand car salesman and he was a country gent. You know what I mean Edward?'

'So you liked him?'

'Liked him? I loved him from the start. I was just an uncouth Cossack lost in a big western city. He was what I wanted to be.'

'What happened?'

'I gave him the package and we had a drink. Then he said he was going out to eat. Did I want to join him? Against the rules, but I said yes. So he took me to Simpson's and we had roast beef. We ended up in a club in St James's. Told me he had a few old acquaintances who were members there so if he ducked behind a chair, not to worry. We drank a couple of malt whiskies, smoked cigars and then disappeared our different ways into the London night.'

'What did you make of him?'

Malinov was silent, thinking. Then he said: 'I thought he was lonely. And there was something else. I thought I saw something in his eyes, a kind of sadness. Later on I learned he had been working for us for nearly twenty years. I told you he loved his country but the weird thing was he had been betraying it all that time. But then I worked it out; betrayal, that is. He loved his country for what it was for him and he never betrayed that. But he saw how the shits who ran the country had cocked it up, for their own stupid selfish political ends. That's what he hated. There's a big difference, Edward.'

'Yes, I can see that,' replied Edward, and inside he was thinking that Malinov was a lot more intelligent than he had given him credit for. 'So what happened next?'

'I guess you could say we became friends. It wasn't supposed to be like that. Not good for security. But when Freddie, or Hugh as I knew him then, came back from a trip abroad as a phoney British businessman, he would get in touch and we would explore London together. Once he took me to St Paul's for evensong. I began to understand what it meant to be English. At home in Russia, before the clampdown, I remembered how we would stand, separated from the altar by a golden screen, while the priest declared the mysteries of the faith, in a swirling cloud of incense, invoking an invisible all-powerful God. Divinity was a secret from which the peasant believers had to be kept away. Messages from above only came down through an interpreter. But I remember sitting under the great dome of the cathedral listening to the simple repetitive plainsong. In England evensong was just music and poetry, a background to whatever you wanted to say to your God in private. The atmosphere was the magic. And everybody seemed to have a different idea of God, which was OK because the English always agreed to differ, then made a joke about it.

'I remember one weekend we travelled somewhere,

Oxfordshire or Gloucestershire, I can't remember which. Freddie had a little black English car. The countryside was all tiny square fields, separated by high hedgerows, and secret copses with church spires standing above the tops of sycamore trees. All the villages had names, even if they were only a mile apart, and everybody knew the differences and fought to keep them. Where I was born, if there had been a hill to stand on above the plain, and the earth had no curve, I imagine I could have seen all the way to Vladivostock, uninterrupted, all the same. And that is why we Russians, when the change came, all swept along together in one direction, a tidal wave; and when the next change came, we all swept back together in another. What I learned from Freddie was that the world lives inside you, not the other way round. That's freedom, Edward. Politicians don't understand that.'

'That doesn't sound like a communist speaking, Viktor. It's the cult of the individual. You would have gone to the gulag for thinking that.'

'Edward, I tell you, I didn't know what the hell I believed in then. To me it was just a job.'

Edward sat in silence. He had never thought that Viktor could be a philosopher but it was so. And, from what he had learned of his uncle, he was not surprised that Viktor and he grew close.

'What did Freddie say about Amala?'

'He said nothing except the bare facts. Remember it had happened eighteen years before I met him. In truth, he didn't need to say anything because it could all be seen. He didn't need words.'

'I don't understand,' said Edward.

Viktor stood up and stretched. The sun was falling in the sky. From beyond the shrubbery the strange plaintive call of a peacock could be heard. 'Let's walk, Edward. I have something I would like you to see.' Edward followed Viktor into the house. They crossed the chessboard hall, climbed one of the staircases to the first floor, making two right-angled turns as they rose, until they stood in the middle of a long gallery running the length of the whole front elevation of the house. Viktor half-turned in each direction, pointing with his head. 'You see why Freddie didn't need to speak to me about Amala. He spoke about her every day of his life, but not in words.'

Edward looked in each direction. On the outside wall the tall Georgian sash windows stood in rows, looking out over the gravel drive and the front lawns. On the inside wall of the corridor in each direction he saw a gallery of paintings. Edward and Viktor walked slowly in one direction and then back in the other.

'Is this love, or is it madness, or are they the same?' asked Malinov.

Edward looked at the first painting. He saw a smiling African face. Behind the face stood two native women in white clothes, with three children smiling on the steps of a small pavilion with a corrugated tin roof. A eucalyptus tree leaned over the verandah, its grey-green leaves shading the group.

'Who are these people?' asked Edward.

'Freddie told me the man was called Desmond. He was his house boy in Kenya. The women are his wives with their children. He said they were murdered by the Mau-Mau.'

They walked further. In a gilt frame a tall girl stood in jodhpurs and sun hat, jet black hair and dark eyes, holding a chestnut mare. In the distance flat-topped trees rose from a golden plain.

'Morgane Owen,' said Viktor unprompted, 'later an eminent doctor with UNHCR, as I understand. And this is Shah Mohammed and his Maasai wife, standing before their house somewhere in northern Kenya. He was the richest man in the country, according to Freddie.'

'And the rest of the paintings?'

'All Amala,' replied Viktor. 'I wept for him, Edward. He told me that she promised to come to him. But he never saw her again. The British killed her, in effect. And that is what made his life what it was.'

Edward recognised the girl in the picture whom Juliana

and he had identified from the small collection in the Henrietta Street loft; the slender figure, the dark hair and the eyes that seemed as deep as the African continent, that had followed Freddie through his life.

'How did you get all these paintings, Viktor? There must be at least forty here.'

'When I became rich, by accident, I bought them from him, one by one. I paid him a so-called market price. You see, he was obsessed and I made his obsession a living for him.'

'So that's how he made his money. You must have paid him well.'

Viktor looked at his feet, as if he were shy of the truth. 'I paid him what I owed him, Edward. He saved my life.'

'Viktor, may I ask you one thing? Why are you telling me all this? Won't it compromise your position in this country, if the owner of an English football club, and the boss of an international company based in London turned out to have been a Russian spy?'

Viktor laughed out loud. 'Do you think all this has any credit worthiness now? We're all money-makers. Nobody believes in anything any more and because of that nobody can be bothered to shop anybody either. Life, Edward, it's just an international trading floor. Wave your arms about, bet on this going up and that going down, make your money. Isn't that the case?'

'I used to think so Viktor,' replied Edward, 'but I don't think that anymore. And from what I've learned of Freddie, he didn't think so either. What's more, I've got Julie.'

'You're a lucky man, Edward, a lucky man. You're richer than I am by a mile.'

The conversation had drifted into choppy waters and neither man knew quite how to steer into the calm. Then Viktor looked at his watch. It was five-thirty.

'White Russian time!' he announced, seizing Edward by the arm and leading him the length of the gallery to a small oak-panelled library at the end. Leather- bound volumes filled the shelves, the characteristic authors of the nineteenth century English country gentleman's library: Voltaire, Pascal,

Locke and Hume, together with Burke's *Peerage*, according to Oscar Wilde the best work of fiction in the English language. A yard of shelf-space was given over to *The Waverley Novels;* more unlikely still, a full shelf of *Wisden*. Like Ponsonby Hall itself, the library was no more than a part of Malinov's fantasy of what it was to be British. They sat in easy chairs either side of a marble fireplace and Viktor rang a bell which sounded faintly somewhere in a distant quarter. After a minute or so a servant appeared with a tray of cocktails, mixed a couple of drinks, handed them round and disappeared, all without speaking a word. Malinov downed his drink at breakneck speed and mixed himself another. His mood had become serious. He turned to Edward, the low rays of the declining sun catching the lines and furrows of his face, and said slowly: 'If you want to hear a story of real betrayal, Edward, I can tell you one.' Edward said nothing but sipped his drink. Malinov seemed to drift off into a distant dream for a few moments before continuing. 'It must have been in 1973. Freddie and I had known each other some years and were close friends. Remember, he was still living his shadow life as Montague, the well-travelled businessman. But he was tired. It was twenty years of deception and pretence and it had worn him down. Sure, he had all the papers and the phoney identity sorted out but living a lie seems to sap the soul of something, despite all the perfect arrangements in the world. There was an undeniable voice inside him that wouldn't go away. He said he wanted back his own identity.'

'But wouldn't people remember him if he became Freddie Ottaway again?'

'It was a risk, I suppose. But he told me his father had died and he had lost contact with his only relative, a brother. And then he showed me a newspaper clipping from 1952. He said it was the only mention in the British papers. It was the story of a colonial officer in Kenya wanted in connection with a shooting, but that it was assumed the officer had killed himself by driving his car over a cliff into a river. A body had never been recovered. It was a very short item but it gave his name. Freddie thought anybody who cared about him would have thought him dead for over twenty years, so he would be pretty safe in returning, as far as they were concerned. But the authorities were a different proposition. He was afraid his name still lurked in some prosecutor's pending tray in a dusty government department. He said he needed a guarantee, an amnesty from prosecution, and a real passport again in his own name. And to get out of London to somewhere remote. All he wanted was to paint. I said I would see what I could do.'

'What did he think you could do for him?'

'He knew I dealt with people who traded in identities, fake or genuine, whatever. You see, Edward, my world was one of shadows and half-truths, suggestions and ambiguities, so it was not unlikely that I could find a way to spirit him away to start life afresh.'

'How did you do it?'

'I did a deal, Edward. It was the greatest betrayal of my life. But I did it, unflinchingly, with no regrets. You see, I needed to offer the British something in return for what I was asking of them, something very big. It was the moment when I ceased to be a nobody and became a somebody and when you are somebody, Edward, you can take history by the scruff of the neck and shake it. That's how I became rich when the Soviet roof caved in. I had no more conscience than a wild animal stalking its prey.'

'So why help Freddie if your sole motive was your own ambition?'

Malinov drained his glass and thought. Then a smile crossed his lips as if he were finding Edward's naïve honesty faintly amusing. 'It occurred to me that I could use Freddie's desire to return to the real world to advance my own career. You see, if Freddie could become the channel for crucial information about Soviet intelligence in Britain, revelations that would break the reputations of my colleagues and ensure their deportation back to Moscow, but at the same time keeping my hand out of things, I might emerge with reputation enhanced. I would be the only experienced operator in Britain. It would be highly likely that Moscow would keep me in place and at a senior level.

'So I created a phoney history for Freddie which placed him at the centre of Soviet intelligence in London. To ensure that the British would find his information credible, I gave him a biography, assignments, contacts, networks. We spent weeks rehearsing the story. And then I set the trap. A simple message through the channels: *a senior figure wants to do a deal*. It was not that uncommon from either side. The British went for it. In a very short time Freddie was reborn, fresh and innocent, with the slate wiped clean. I rose inexorably to the top, while the senior people in the Soviet networks were rounded up, bargained for, and shipped back to Moscow with the label of failure round their necks. They would never be able to work again. They were blown. And Moscow had an uncanny habit of disposing of those it found to be an embarrassment. It's an unlikely story, don't you think, but the least likely tales are often true.'

Edward was silent, trying to take in what Viktor had told him, but he struggled to make sense of it all. Malinov the sad lonely billionaire, regretting his lost childhood, overcome with kitsch sentimentality, seeking a new identity as a kind of British *grotesque*; then Malinov the arch schemer, the ruthless operator, the smiler with a dagger beneath his cloak, climbing to the top over the bodies of his betrayed comrades; and over and above all of it, Freddie's friend, loyal and genuine, weeping at his sense of loss. How could such a being exist? It was as if Malinov could read Edward's thoughts.

'You simplify life Edward. Loyalties and betrayals are complex. We are human. We can hold two different sets of values or beliefs if you like, simultaneously, without destroying ourselves. Didn't somebody say that was the definition of an artist?'

'Do you really believe that?'

'Perhaps I do. But it was never a position I arrived at by logic or choice. What life does to you is wear you down, drip after drip, until you make the best you can of the disappointments, failures and compromises it forces on you. Sometimes it squeezes the conscience out of you until you can't tell right from wrong. That's probably how I live with myself.'

It was getting dark. From the window on the first floor the lawns ran down to the edge of the estate and, between the green hills beyond, a small triangle of sea was visible. Lights from a fishing boat flashed and faded, as if they were signals from another world.

'I got Freddie out of London. We had a safe house in north Yorkshire, Angelus House. It was set up as a bolt hole together with some kind of communications base but never used as one. He went there to live. It was about 1973 or 74, I can't quite remember. I was the only person in Soviet intelligence who knew he was the source of the information. The irony is we kept him on the payroll but, since I was the boss, no one except me knew he did nothing for us. I put him there and authorised the payments. He painted in peace and I thrived. It was a good deal for us both.'

'But you didn't do all that just to get on.'

'No. I did it because I loved Freddie. You see, we Russians can say that!'

'Did you see him again?'

'Oh, yes,' Malinov drawled, the effects of the alcohol beginning to show. 'I used to visit him in Yorkshire sometimes. It was an escape. Nothing seemed to happen to disturb the peace, not like my life in London. And I could talk to someone who shared my recent past, so it was not a strain. I could look at the sea and walk on the cliff tops. I said to myself I would go back there one day when all this was over. You see Edward, I was really a prisoner of the way I had chosen to live my life.'

'You said he saved your life?'

Malinov rose slowly from his chair. The room was in semi-darkness now and he switched on a lamp on the Sheraton table in the corner. The cone of light shooting upwards illuminated an oil painting of a race horse against the setting of an eighteenth century English landscape. It could have been a Stubbs which Malinov had procured from some over-priced agent in London to add to his country house collection; or it could have been nothing at all for all he knew. 'It was years later. I had progressed to the top in the London operation and Freddie had been in Yorkshire for years. It must have been around 1987. Yes, the Iron Lady was still in power. There was a bar we used to go to in Paddington. We would take a taxi from our office just down from the embassy in Kensington Palace Gardens, two or three of us, when the day was over. We drank a lot, sometimes we got girls. There was a fellow there who arranged that. He was discreet. Said nothing. Then one day it started to go wrong. At first I thought I could contain it but then things started really to get out of hand. I had a flat in Holland Park provided by the service, where I lived under another name. I knew something was up when a letter arrived addressed to Viktor. There was nothing inside except a small black and white photograph and a telephone number. There was no message but there didn't need to be. The photo said it all. Straightaway I recognised the girl in bed. I knew I was about to be blackmailed. She must have found my address from something in my jacket pocket when I was sleeping that night in the hotel.'

'Was that so disastrous, Viktor? Indiscretions often happen, don't they, in your line of work?'

'If this got out, the least that would happen would be an instant recall to Moscow and an assignment to some mundane job in a cellar in the censor's department steaming open letters. I had become a liability. I was used to the lights of the big city in a rich western democracy remember.'

'So what did you do?'

Malinov stared blankly out of the window for a few moments before replying. 'I thought I could buy my way out of it. I called the number from a telephone box. I didn't want any calls on record. The voice of a young man answered in a strong London accent. He asked who was speaking and when I said who it was I could hear a sharp intake of breath. We arranged to meet the following night in a cafe somewhere south of the river. It was a seedy little place in Battersea called *Pacitto's*. The moment I saw him I knew he was an amateur. He was no more than a twenty-year-old with a crewcut and spots. I bought him a coffee and he started to tell me about himself. He was nervous. It was like a scene from a comedy sketch. His name was Terry. He was a porter in the Paddington hotel the girl and I had used that night. He told me she was his sister. It was not just a lucky chance that he saw us checking in that night. I reckon the girl called him to set it up. I seem to remember she had said she knew a good place to go. But I have no idea how he got the pictures. He wanted five grand for the negatives. He was just a petty criminal; if he was anything bigger he would have asked for much more and I would never have even seen him, let alone know his name and where he worked. I was relieved. I could easily pay him off from operational funds, put it down to some surveillance exercise. It was definitely not an MI5 effort to pull me in. We even shook hands, can you believe it, and we agreed to meet again the next day at the same place to finish the deal.

'He'd obviously done his homework overnight, probably talked to some mate in the pub. He was cocky and much more confident. He said the price had gone up. He claimed she was underage and that was a criminal offence. I said I needed to see proof so he pulled out a green plastic card with a passport photo on it. I couldn't believe it. It was a Lambeth Borough bus pass for schoolchildren. The name on it was Tracy something, her date of birth was sometime in 1972 and the photo proved she was the girl. That was a game changer alright. He said he knew someone in the Met, which I never believed, but the point was made nevertheless. This had suddenly got serious. If it got out, my people would have had me back in Moscow on the next flight. The trouble was that the welcome home party would be a bullet in the back of the head in some damp cell in the Lubyanka.

'I decided to play for time. I suggested we took a walk down to the river where we could talk in private. Like a fool, he agreed. It was a fine night, I remember. Strange isn't it, a night so fateful and I can remember the stars and the moon glinting on the Thames. Lights from the buildings on the Embankment shone out across the water. We reached a kind of boardwalk running along the front of a block of flats. I thought I would test him out. I told him I wouldn't pay any more than five grand. He said if I didn't pay, he would send the stuff to *The News of the World.* I could see immediately that he just wanted the money; sending the stuff to the papers didn't appeal to him. He had no reason to expose me other than cash and he didn't have the sense to sell the stuff to the paper. I sensed he felt cornered. I knew I was right when he pulled a knife on me.

'I didn't mean to shoot him. But the instinct of a lifetime kicked in. Before I knew it my hand was on the Makarov pistol in my pocket, the barrel was pointing at his head, and two muffled raps translated into neat holes between his eyes. He slumped to the ground, face down on the boardwalk, dead. I searched his pockets but found no negatives. Then in an inside pocket I found his wallet and in it an address. There was nothing else on him. I knew what I had to do. I could see the tide was ebbing and the river was beginning to run fast. I grabbed his legs and levered him up and over the rail. His body splashed down into the water and disappeared. Then I watched it slowly return to the surface, roll over like a dying whale turning its belly to the sky and then turn and head downstream with the current. There were at least three hours before the tide would turn and I calculated that the body would be miles downstream by then. In fact, they never found it, as far as I know. They tell me a body leaving the Thames is likely to be brought ashore in Belgium. Do you think that can be true?'

Edward could find no words to answer. Throughout, he had sat motionless in his chair while Viktor related his story.

'You are shocked Edward. Is that not so? Don't be. It's what I was trained to do.'

'Did you kill others too?'

'That was my first and last time.' He paused. 'You are wondering what kind of a man I am.'

'And the girl? What about her?' asked Edward, fearful of the answer.

Malinov resumed his seat on the other side of the

fireplace. Dispensing with the complexities of mixing a cocktail, he simply seized the vodka bottle and poured himself a good shot. 'That is the strangest thing of all. It was not what I expected. The address I had found in Terry's pocket turned out to be a block of council flats in Charlton. It reminded me of the outskirts of Moscow, a great concrete block with a filthy staircase rising up floor after floor, galleries stretching off in each direction at every landing and row after row of numbered doors behind which invisible occupants seemed to be cowering. Groups of youths hung around corners. I found the flat and knocked. After a while the door opened. It was Tracy. She recognised me instantly. From inside I could smell stale tobacco smoke and heard the mindless drone of a TV programme. She asked me what I wanted and then where Terry was. I said he wasn't coming back. She opened the door wider and I followed her in. It was obvious she knew what was going on. I told her the blackmail was off. Then I told her Terry was dead. She was silent for a while and then she laughed. "Thank God for that. I suppose you want the pictures. They're in there," she said, pointing to a sideboard drawer. I slid it open, took out a yellow Kodak envelope, checked the contents and put it in my pocket. "You gonna kill *me* now?" she said.

'I looked at her standing helplessly in the shabby room of the council flat. She was just the age to be my daughter. She was pretty, blonde haired and blue-eyed. What the hell was she doing getting paid for sex with older men? I looked around the room. There was nothing but the flickering TV screen, heaped ashtrays and empty beer cans. In the kitchen I could see a pile of dirty plates and empty tins. The alienation and the squalor were overwhelming. And then I thought: if your brother is your pimp you probably don't have high expectations of life. Maybe she thought this was all there was. I wanted to enclose her in my arms to protect her but then I had already done that in another squalid shameful way. I felt sick inside.

'When I had told her her brother was dead she had showed no reaction. It was as if violent death was simply routine. "There'll be another guy along to take his place," she said, adding "There's plenty of them at it." I asked her if she wanted to get out of this. "Sure, wouldn't you? But why would you want to help me?" I said she could have been my daughter. I don't know why, after what I had done, but she seemed to trust me. "Do you have a daughter?" she asked. "No, but I wish I had," I said.'

Edward stared across the fireplace at Viktor who had slouched in his chair, his face in his hands, before looking up, drawn and gaunt. 'I just felt sorry for her, as well as every other feeling that passed through my mind. I asked her again if she really wanted to get out of this shit-hole and go somewhere nice and be looked after. Amazingly, she said yes. I asked her where her mother was. She gave a sneering laugh. "Prison," she replied. "Never knew my Dad. I was in care until I moved in with Terry."

'I called Freddie in Yorkshire that night to say I was motoring up the next day to Angelus House, with a girl. He had a housekeeper. I told him to tell her to get a room ready and keep her mouth shut. She would be paid to look after the girl.'

'And did you see her again,' asked Edward.

'Never. Shortly afterwards I was called back to Moscow and promoted. Then the Soviet Union began to crumble and the senior officers in KGB were the only fixed points in a world in turmoil. We took over the national assets when the empire finally collapsed in 1993 and I found myself with a nickel mine in Siberia. Ten years later I was a Russian billionaire in London and the rest is history. I never heard of Freddie again until a short while ago. After I bought the football club I had the directors over for drinks when I set up in Ponsonby Hall. George Allington recognised the name on the paintings in the gallery and told me Freddie Ottaway was dead.'

'Did he tell you how?'

'He told me how, but not why. Was there a *why*?'

'That's what I'm trying to find out,' said Edward.

Viktor fell into silence. He had no more to tell.

'I should go, Viktor,' Edward said.

The day was over, the sky black and the only lights visible the occasional lamp from a passing fishing boat far out in the distance.

'Before you go, Edward, I want you to tell me something, please,' said Viktor. Both men were on their feet and Viktor grasped Edward's hands in his. 'What kind of a man do you really think I am?'

'The truth is Viktor, I don't know what you are or what made you the way you are. I know that sounds harsh and cold.'

'No, no, I understand. You see Edward, all my life, I've just been adrift. I have nothing to hold on to and nothing to believe in. Don't ever get that way. Hold on to what you have. There's nothing else out there. Believe me, I know.'

The two men walked back along the gallery, down the stairs and across the chessboard hall to the front door. No word was spoken. Edward started his car and drove away. In his rear-view mirror he saw the receding figure of Malinov, statuesque between the pillars of the front door, alone in the world but owning half of it, adrift without a friend.

Edward drove slowly back to Henrietta Street. Juliana met him at the door. 'Good God, Edward, you look ill! Whatever's the matter?' she asked.

'I've just spent an evening with a hollow man, Julie. Come here, let me hold you. I need the feel of a living person.' He took her in his arms and buried his head in her soft dark hair, breathing in her familiar scent. 'Never let you go. I'll never let you go,' he said to himself.

That night he told her everything he had learned from Malinov. She listened without speaking. Later, as they lay together in their tiny bedroom, Julie said: I met Molly today. 'Jane's coming back tomorrow. She has a fortnight before she goes to Cambridge.'

'That's great,' said Edward. 'It'll be good to see her again. It's her fault I fell in love with you.'

'Fell into my shop, more likely.'

'Same thing.'

When Jane stepped off the plane from Heathrow at Leeds/Bradford airport, on a wet windy Thursday in September, she carried in her hand a piece of cabin baggage and in her head the meaning of life. The latter she had learned from a diminutive shaven-headed monk in a ramshackle monastery in the foothills of the Himalayas. Incense sticks, wind chimes and little copper bells provided the special effects. She had saved her wages from part-time jobs for over a year to cover her trip to explore the roof of the world, with a party of strapping Brits from *Trek Nepal*, and had returned to sea level in wind-swept Yorkshire as a Buddhist. She watched the grey clouds thin and disperse as the aircraft descended over Lincolnshire. It was quite a shock, after the towering grey pinnacles of the Himalayas, snow-covered, brilliant and severe against a powder-blue sky, to sink down towards the mud flats of the Humber where the silver ribbons of quiet waterways wandered through black wet fields of vegetables, scattered here and there with red-roofed clusters of houses. A slight doubt entered her mind that the spiritual calm she had aspired to in the thin air of Nepal might be harder to attain in the heavy damp atmosphere of these dull flat lands. The bump of the undercarriage on the runway jolted her back into reality, the engines reversed thrust and the process of disembarkation took over from the search for inner peace. She was in Leeds/Bradford airport and her feet were firmly back on the ground in the land of Yorkshire bitter and the golden rhubarb triangle. By the time she had collected her rucksack from the carousel, she was having difficulty remembering the *Four Noble Truths* let alone the complicated bits of the *Eightfold Path*. She could recall the symbol of the wheel, which looked very like the wheel on a boat, and the basic message that you should do right and stay calm. 'Christ,' she muttered to herself as she followed the winding route towards the exit, 'why can't I remember anything?' Then she thought about the Sunday school stories she had learned and the primary school nativity plays in which she had performed; Good Friday when Jesus was nailed to the cross to save the world; and Easter Sunday after church when Lent was over and she could eat chocolate again. She was beginning to realise that nothing could live out of the water in which it was born to swim. What the hell, *Love Thy Neighbour* was as good as any of the *Noble Truths* wasn't it? As long as she had something to live by, she thought, did it really matter what colour and shape it was? Then she saw her Dad standing at the barrier waiting for her to come through and she knew she was home again, just the same, but with an overtone or two of Buddhism attached. The concatenation of spiritualities was all part of growing-up, although she didn't think this thought at the time.

They drove back to Whitby in the dark. Jane told her Dad all about her great trek, the mountain tracks they had followed, the peaks they had climbed, the native Nepalese she had befriended and the hairy-legged British Mountaineering Club chaps who had chatted her up.

'I bet you've become a Buddhist, our Jane,' he said with a laugh.

'Only a bit,' she replied. 'I lit a few incense sticks and learned a few names. Not very different from what we believe really.'

'Is that so?' said Dad.

The car headlights shone out through the black autumn night as they drove across the moors to the coast. Nepal suddenly seemed a million miles away. Jane's mind had already turned in a different direction called the future, which would begin in two weeks. She put *Nirvana* on a mental shelf, to be thought about later, while she imagined what it was going to be like walking down Trinity Street with her own money to spend, inviting her new friends back to her own room after hall to drink coffee from her new John Lewis coffee-maker. Buddhism might come in handy then. What she didn't realise was that her past would always travel with her,

182

lighting the way towards the future and sometimes getting bent in the prism of the present. Dad pulled up before the *Caedmon* and she was back home where people lived their lives under the grey clouds, sometimes glimpsed the sunlit uplands on a clear day, but never knew the sacred snowfields that lie nearest to God. But that didn't mean they hadn't worked out the meaning of life.

The next morning Edward woke late. When he went downstairs he found the house empty, apart from Monty curled up asleep in the middle of the dining table. He made tea, ate a slice of toast and marmalade, and strolled up the street to see what Juliana was up to. He opened the shop door quietly. The front shop was empty but from the workshop beyond he heard a low droning incantation, a tuneless monotone. He peered through the connecting door and saw two women sitting cross-legged on the floor, praying hands joined beneath their chins, in a fog of incense from a pair of joss-sticks stuck in tea cups on either side.

'Does it take long to reach *Nirvana*?' he heard Julie ask.

'Most of one's life, I gather,' replied Jane.

'What are you two playing at?' he interrupted.

'Oh, just seeking the inner peace that comes when you know what life is all about,' said Julie.

'Ed, great to see you,' shouted Jane, jumping to her feet, crossing the room and planting a kiss on his cheek.

'Great to see you too Jane,' and he cast his eyes over her sun-tanned face. 'Good to have you back. You look well.'

'I am Ed, thanks. Well, I'd best be off,' she added. 'Promised to give Mum a hand this morning.'

'I hope we'll see you again before you head off to Cambridge,' said Julie.

'You will,' and with that Jane disappeared through the shop doorway and headed down the street.

'She seems to know what she's about,' commented Edward, a little listlessly, 'more than can be said of everybody.'

Julie looked at him carefully. 'I suppose you mean Viktor.'

'I do. What did you tell Jane?'

'Nothing at all. She has no idea what happened the other night.'

'Good. We'd better keep it that way. The fewer people who know about his past the better.'

'I agree,' said Julie. 'You know what stuck in my mind from the story Viktor told you? It's the girl, Tracy. Where did she go to? She can't have been at Angelus House for more than a few months. Viktor never saw her again. Freddie moved down here shortly after that and Angelus House was closed up. But what happened to Tracy? A fifteen-year-old with no money and no home, being looked after by someone as caring as Freddie, and never heard of again? Doesn't that really sound odd to you Edward?'

Edward had sat in the swivel chair at Julie's work bench. He swung round to face her. 'Yes, exactly. You know I've been so occupied with thinking about Viktor's meaningless existence I had completely ignored the other people in this mystery. I'm sure Viktor couldn't remember her surname or he would have mentioned it. But you're right, her disappearance must tell us more about what happened to Freddie. If she went missing, why wasn't it reported and in the news; if she didn't go missing, where is she now?'

Just then the shop doorbell jangled and Julie went through to deal with the customer. Edward followed her, saying in passing: 'I'll see you later, Julie. I've just had an idea.' He walked down the street to where his car was parked, got in and drove off up the hill out of town on his way to Egton. He wanted to take a closer look at Angelus House. It was early autumn and the hedgerows lining the the narrow road were heavy with brambles, rose hips and clusters of rich purple elderberries. Flights of dunnocks, wrens and finches fluttered in small dark clouds from bush to bush. As the road gained height, the vegetation thinned to sparse cotton grass and springy heather; in the peaty hollows by the road ewes slept with their lambs, plump from a summer's feeding. Edward drew up before the locked gate of Angelus House, unsure of what he was seeking. He clambered over the gate and walked up the track to the house. He remembered the open back door from his previous visit. Nothing had changed; it still swung to and fro on its hinges. He passed through the scullery and kitchen and climbed up the bare wooden staircase to the first floor. His shoes clunked heavily on the treads and the empty house echoed back the noise from its bare walls as he passed from room to room. He was looking for the most obvious place where a young girl might have lived all those years ago. Was there any scrap of evidence that might give a clue as to her identity? He knew that the house had stood empty since 1987, the year that Tracy had been taken there. Perhaps there would be a scrawl of a name on the wall where a bed had stood; or a scrap of paper wedged in a gap between floorboard and skirting. But there was nothing at all. The empty shell of walls and ceilings gave up nothing. It was a while before Edward realised that he had drawn a blank; and when he did his spirits sank. Would he ever solve the puzzle of Freddie's death and the strange events that his link with Malinov seemed to have triggered? And then he knew that it had been a stupid idea all along, the idea that he would find a clue at Angelus House.

He found his way to the back door and squatted on the ground in the autumn sunshine, his back leaning against the scullery wall. What now? Across the rough grass the copse of conifers waved in the wind. Between him and the screen of trees he saw the remains of a vegetable garden, overgrown and wild, but with a vague pattern of beds and footpaths, albeit mostly under the invading moorland. And then he remembered. Jane's father had said he had worked here before moving to Whitby. Perhaps he had met the lost girl from south London. It was time to talk to Dan again. The trip to Angelus House had not been pointless after all.

It was late afternoon before Edward returned home. He found Julie sitting at the table in the window, pencil in hand and sketching pad before her. The outline of an ornate floral cluster was taking shape. 'So what was your great idea, Edward?' she asked without looking up.

'My great idea was a great stupidity,' he replied. 'I went to Angelus House to see if I could find a clue to Tracy's identity.

I'm convinced her story will throw light on Freddie's death.'

'And did you find anything?'

'Bugger all. But it did remind me of something. You remember telling me a while ago to go and talk to Dan, Jane's father. Well, I was sitting there on the back step, having failed to find anything of course, when I remembered he had worked there up until Freddie left.'

'Well?'

'So I went to see him, Julie. Strangest thing. You know Dan is the gentlest of souls. I asked him if he had met a girl called Tracy at Angelus House. He just clammed up. Not a word. Then I asked if he knew her surname, and what happened to her, and he got quite irritable. Asked me why I was so interested in the past.'

'What did you say?'

'Nothing. But I'm sure he knows something. His reaction convinced me. Finding out about Tracy is the way forward.'

'And how do you propose to do that?'

'I don't know yet, but I'm going to think about it.'

A week later Edward and Julie held a going-away party for Jane before she left for Cambridge. Their tiny house was cramped but it managed to accommodate the residents of the top end of Henrietta Street without too much difficulty. Dan and Molly were there, of course, together with Jim and Ruby. Uncle George rolled up to complete the gathering. Edward looked at the faces that were gathered there that day. He constantly marvelled at the closeness of the little world of Henrietta Street, how the inhabitants seemed to know each other inside out, and seemed to cast a protective circle around each other. It was the strangest of feelings for a man who had lived in the faceless city and travelled each day among the careless crowds. What held these people together? Was it shared love or was it a shared secret knowledge, the kind that passes down from generation to generation among the lost tribes, unspoken and unrecorded but real and binding for all that? It was a little world made cunningly and above it stood the shadow of Freddie, his kindness living on, like a guardian angel with ah! bright wings outstretched.

As the evening drew to a close Edward summoned the group together, placed his camera on a table and pressed the time delay button. He sprinted back to the group. In the middle, radiant and happy, Jane stood beaming at the camera, surrounded by the inhabitants of the little world of Henrietta Street, as if she were the tiny thing they had planted in the oyster shell and nurtured for so long into a pearl they were now about to release into the wide world. 'Five, four, three, two, one, smile,' shouted Edward and the light flashed.

Edward had only been to Middlesbrough once before, for the memorable first encounter with Viktor Malinov at the Riverside Stadium, and had since felt no burning need to revisit it. And that could be understood on the part of a southerner with Edward's background. This was not the silver Thames, flowing gently through the shires of the mellow south, past the centuries of royal palaces. This was the Tees, which had suffered the ravages of industry for two hundred years; and this was the north where the iron dust and the chemicals and the smoke from blast furnaces had smeared generations and was only now casting off its grime. His journey to the Riverside had taken him along a busy road, rising at times on flyovers, from which he caught a glimpse of towering cranes and bridges and mile after mile of complex industrial chimneys and pipes, like a steel jungle throbbing with the heat of its activity. And scattered among it all were swathes of red brick houses which seemed from above to follow no particular pattern but were littered here and there. The slow sliding river wound its way between mud flats to a wide estuary a mile or two east of the town, where the derricks of the port reached up into the sky.

The offices of *The Evening Gazette* were in Borough Road in Middlesbrough. Edward had decided that the best way to investigate the fate of Tracy would be through the annals of the local newspaper. If she had simply gone missing, it might well be reported. If she had died it could be a headline story. And the story must have been enacted in 1987 or 1988, if Malinov's account were to be relied upon. After a couple of diversions in the town centre, he finally found his way to Borough Road and parked his car in a visitors parking space in the asphalt area to the rear. The building was a plain office block, dull and ordinary, with square flat windows rising in columns for six floors. At the reception desk he asked where he could view past editions of the paper and the bright-eyed young receptionist directed him to the lower ground floor, which was down one flight of stairs. There he found a small lobby with a counter, beyond which he could see row after row of sliding file shelves at right angles to the wall. He rang the bell on the counter and after a while a young man appeared from a door at the far end of the room. Edward asked if he could consult the issues for 1987 and 1988. The young man walked down the central aisle, turned the wheel at the end of a wall of shelves and the structure magically slid into the open. Edward watched as several cloth-bound volumes the size of a newspaper page began to pile up on a trolley. He counted eight in all, four for each year. He realised this was going to take some time.

'Where can I read them?' he asked.

'There's a reading room on the ground floor. If you take a desk in there I'll bring these up to you in the lift,' the young man replied.

At first the task seemed daunting: page after page to be turned, six issues each week, acres of turgid local news. Neon strip lights overhead shone down harshly and the black printed pages often seemed to blur before him as his eyes lost focus. He stuck at it for an hour, until his head seemed to burst. But at last he began to discover a pattern repeating itself in the newspaper and he became adept at skimming the issues. He had reached a week in November 1987 when he found it. There, on an inside page, was a short item. A girl from Egton near Whitby was missing. She had not been seen for two days and the police were becoming concerned for her safety. She had last been seen getting off a bus in Saltburn. Anyone with information about her whereabouts should call the Cleveland police and a telephone number was given. Her name was Tracy Woodford. Edward looked at the photograph in the paper. It had been taken in a passport photo booth and the police had blown it up in size, for the detail was grainy. Half-smiling out at him was a young blonde-haired girl with blue eyes. This had to be her: Tracy from Egton; there could be no other. He was on the trail. He skimmed through the next few issues but could find no further news. Then, five issues later, on the front page he saw again Tracy Woodford's half-smiling face. The headline was bleak; it hit Edward like a hammer blow. A girl's body had been found on the rocks at low tide near Saltwick Bay, twenty miles south of Saltburn where the last sighting of her was made. The report carried a quotation from a police inspector: the body was believed to be that of Tracy Woodford but a formal identification had not yet been made. Police were attempting to locate the next of kin. But these were not the details that most caught Edward's attention. It was the name of the policeman – Inspector Jim Moxon. He left the volumes of issues on the desk and walked out into the entrance foyer. He dialled Julie's number on his mobile and heard her voice answer after a few seconds.

'Julie. I've just found something. Tell me, what's Jim's surname? For some odd reason I've never heard it.'

'Jim next door? He's a Moxon,' she replied. 'Why do you want to know?'

'Tracy died, drowned in the sea and he was the officer investigating the case.'

There was a long silence on the end of the phone. 'Christ', he heard her say.

'Christ indeed! And who else was involved? That's what I'm asking myself. Do you think Jim will talk to me about this?'

'Edward, I've no idea. You can only try, I guess.'

'I have to try. I need to tackle him when he's sober.' He went back into the reading room. There was a bell on the main desk to ring for an attendant. He pressed the button and waited. After a couple of minutes the young man appeared, looking at his watch. 'Just about to close up,' he said. 'You finished?'

'I'd like a couple of items copied, if that's OK,' Edward replied. He could feel the annoyance on the part of the young man.

'Which bits? It'll be £5 per item.'

Edward pointed to the two items, the young man took the volume over to a large copier and slowly copied the two separate pages, folded them, put them in a brown envelope and handed them to Edward, together with a receipt for £10.

Edward walked slowly back to his car in the fading light. He had never heard of Saltburn until he read the name in the newspaper reports. When he got to the car he took out the road atlas and searched for Saltburn. There was a coast road out of Middlesbrough which passed through Redcar. He had heard of that from the racing results, but that was all he knew.

It took him half an hour to reach his destination which turned out to be a faded seaside town. He turned left down one of the streets leading off the main thoroughfare and reached a long seafront parade with tall Victorian yellow-brick houses on one side and the North Sea on the other. He could imagine that summer might bring warmth to this place but now the cold wind off the sea made it dark and grim. At the end of the clifftop road a sharp left turn led down a steep winding descent to the sea itself. He parked the car and rolled down his window, smelling the sharp salt air. A hundred yards away a string of lights stretched out to sea, looping from post to post, the length of an ornate iron pier. Could this be where it really happened, whatever it was that befell Tracy the night she went missing? He looked out into the cold grey breaking waves and his body shivered at the thought of it all. And who was responsible for this: Viktor, with his squalid amorality and disregard; or was Freddie in some way to blame, despite his mythological reputation for kindness in the little world of Henrietta Street? And Jim Moxon, perhaps shrouding a painful memory in the haze of the whisky bottle, what would he be prepared to reveal? But Jim would have to say something; his name was in the paper after all. Edward had never sought to become involved in this macabre mystery but he was in it up to his neck and he would not be able to rest until he knew the full story. The body of a young girl washed up at the very place where years later his uncle had mysteriously died; a Russian ex-spy embroiled in it all; and the investigating police officer living next door. This was all too unlikely for words and all too unlikely to have occurred by chance. Someone somewhere knew how all these pieces fitted together, like some grotesque jigsaw where only the final piece revealed the complex pattern of it all.

These were his thoughts as he headed back to Whitby. He drove up Church Street towards Henrietta Street and parked his car in the gap between the houses. For the first time in his brief sojourn he felt something was not quite right about this place. But when he opened the door to the cottage and found Julie half asleep on the sofa, with a fire burning in the grate and a half empty bottle of wine on the table, his fears seemed to evaporate. He told Julie what had happened and showed her the newspaper reports. 'I'm not looking forward to confronting Jim with all this,' he said. 'It might be something to do with whatever happened to him and Ruby those years ago and he won't want to dig it all up again.' And when the cold light of the morning broke over the winter horizon, his feelings were no less apprehensive.

When Edward had first encountered Jim, he had thought him a harmless old eccentric too fond of the bottle and with very little to say. He now knew he had been mistaken. So that morning he armed himself with his newspaper cuttings as evidence and knocked on Jim's door. When he told him what he wanted to ask, and mentioned Tracy by name, Jim looked coldly at him before retreating into his hallway, grabbing his coat, and pointing down the street. Edward could hear Ruby at work in the kitchen.

'We can talk better out of the house,' said Jim, nodding towards the sound from the kitchen. It was eleven o'clock and the pubs were just opening and Jim clearly knew what he needed. Edward simply followed in his wake. Without speaking they crossed the swing bridge over the harbour and headed for *The Smugglers* by the fish quay. The bar was empty. A stale smell of beer still hung in the air although the floor had been washed and the tables wiped from the night before. The landlord nodded when Jim walked in and, without speaking, pulled him a pint of beer and poured a measure of whisky into a small glass. Then he looked at Edward who ordered a pint without the chaser. The bar was divided into alcoves enclosed by dark wooden panels and the two men took the corner one furthest away. Jim sat down, drank an inch of beer from his glass then sank the whisky glass in it, before drinking again. It was the start of the day for him; the start of another deadly odyssey into forgetfulness.

'I saw your name in the paper, Jim, in your policeman days. I'd like you to tell me what you know about Tracy Woodford,' Edward began, pushing the newspaper cuttings across the table. Jim looked at the papers and then at the photograph of Tracy.

'What I know? What I can remember more likely. That was years ago. Why do you want to know anyway? There was nothing strange about it, as far as I recall.' He took another drink.

'Tracy lived with Freddie at Angelus House before she died. Viktor Malinov told me.'

'Malinov? What's he got to do with it? How do you know him?

'Through George Allington, Julie's uncle from Ruswarp. He's a director at the Riverside. We met Malinov there.'

'You seem to move in rich circles,' said Jim, with a barely disguised sneer.

'It doesn't matter about Malinov,' said Edward. 'He wasn't here in 1987 when Tracy died. But Freddie was here and knew her. Then eighteen years later there's another body on the rocks at Saltwick – Freddie's. Doesn't that strike you as strange?'

There was a long pause while Jim considered the facts. Edward sat in silence. He had never before really looked closely at Jim but now that he was seated opposite him he was able to study his face. It was worn and blotched, with all the signs of a heavy drinker. Edward guessed that 1987 might have been his last working year as a policeman and the years since had been filled with boredom, that numbing sense of aimlessness as one empty day followed another. And now he was asking him to dredge his memory for something that happened a long long time ago.

At last Jim spoke, after another long drink. 'Yes, I remember the girl,' he said, 'but as for Freddie Ottaway and

Angelus House, I knew nothing of them at the time. Whoever reported her missing didn't use that address. It's an unusual name. I would have remembered that.'

'Tell me what you know, Jim.'

'It's not a lot. A couple of days after she was reported missing we put a notice in the local paper. This one here.' He pointed to the newspaper cuttings on the table. 'We'd had no information from the public up till then, nothing at all. No possible sightings. Nothing. It looked like one of those cases when people, especially kids, just melt away. Then we got a call from a bus driver on the Middlesbrough to Saltburn route. He was pretty certain he'd dropped her off from the last bus that night at the end of the line. Said he'd even asked her if she was alright. So we did a house-to-house in the streets around the bus station. Nobody could remember seeing her that night. Except for one guy. He was a Pakistani shopkeeper. Said he'd sold her something but told us it was sweets. Like hell! More likely booze or fags but that would have put him in trouble of course. She was underage.'

'Was that the only evidence you had for thinking she entered the water at Saltburn?'

'No, it wasn't. We searched the seafront for a day and found a girl's coat under the pier. Would have fitted Tracy. The woman who reported her missing identified it as Tracy's. It was a sad case. Not unusual of course. We were always fishing bodies out of the sea or the docks. You get used to it.' He stopped, lifted his glass and drained it. 'She probably just couldn't take any more, life that is. I can understand that.' Then he looked across the table at Edward and said no more. Edward went across to the bar and ordered another pair of drinks for Jim and set them down in front of him.

'Tell me Jim. Who was the woman who reported her missing?'

'Can't tell you that, lad. Didn't meet her. One of our uniformed people would have spoken to her. The address was somewhere in Egton. Don't ask me where. Same woman would have identified the body. We never did trace any relatives as far as I can remember.' He repeated the same

194

procedure with the beer and the whisky.

'You remember quite a lot for eighteen years ago,' said Edward, hoping to inspire more information.

Jim looked as him wistfully. 'I should do, lad. It was my last case. I was finished after that. Dead and buried and still am for that matter.'

There was no more to be learned. Edward left Jim in the pub and walked out along the west pier for some air. He felt deflated and a little light-headed from his pint before midday. He was filled with a burning sense of the unkindness of life, life the juggernaut crushing people under its wheels as it careered aimlessly, unpredictably along. Innocent bystanders caught up in its wheeling carnage. The eighteenth century jetty, solidly built from Yorkshire stone, was connected to a later iron and oak construction which had extended the harbour further out into the sea. A narrow gangway spanned the gap and beneath it Edward watched the endless rise and fall of the waves breaking with a cruel inevitability over the rocks beneath the pier. He saw the face of Tracy, golden hair floating and blue eyes open, as she might have drifted, five days alone, a cold lonely journey to the rocks at Saltwick. Not her fault, innocent and a victim, but someone must take the blame. He had hoped for a line from Jim to draw under it all. But there was nothing to add. When he had asked Jim about the coroner's inquest he had simply said: 'Open verdict. The coroner couldn't say it was suicide or death by misadventure. Five days in the water doesn't help the post mortem. Who knows what happened.' But Edward knew better; there was more to say than this. He pulled up his coat collar and turned back into town, past the fish market and *The Smugglers*, where he fancied he caught a glimpse of the back of Jim's head, silently drinking his day away.

That evening they drove to Ruswarp. George had invited them to dinner.

'No idea why,' said Julie as they drove across. 'Not like George. I don't think I've ever had dinner there. There must be some new development.'

When they got there they found they were four. It was

195

indeed a new development.

'I thought I should tell you both,' said George in the entrance hall to the riverside cottage. He was holding the hand of his erstwhile housekeeper. 'Patsy and I are getting married.'

Julie looked at Edward and he returned the glance, despite his best efforts not to look amazed. What could one say? It was thirty years in the making.

'We are very happy for you,' said Julie, kissing them both, while Edward shook George's hand and planted a kiss on the cheek of the housekeeper. Edward had a distant memory of his first meeting with George's housekeeper, serving tea in the cottage garden one fine summer's day, and this had done nothing to prepare him for Patsy's new persona. She had stepped into the light of recognition and her vivid lipstick and perfect hair-do guaranteed a star entrance. This she confirmed during the evening, as the perfect hostess, while George luxuriated in his new-found grandeur. They were perfect together in a kind of Saga advertisement way: well-preserved and turned out, just off to pack a suitcase for a river cruise down the Danube or a golfing holiday in Florida, with complimentary drinks included in the ticket price. At various points in the evening Julie and Edward had to work hard to avoid each other's eye as Uncle George gazed longingly at Patsy over the beef Wellington.

After dinner, Edward told George what Jim Moxon had said to him that day. 'What strikes me as strange about it all is why Jim thought Ruby shouldn't hear anything we discussed. He was so keen to get me away from his house. It was as if it would have caused Ruby pain to hear our conversation. The other thing is that it was clearly his last case before he left the police, or got kicked out. Why? Was there something dodgy about what happened? And why wasn't Tracy reported as missing from Angelus House? I know for a fact she had been living there for a few months, if Malinov is telling the truth. And who was the woman who identified the body?'

'I think I might know the answer to that,' said Patsy. All eyes turned to her. They were sitting in the bay window overlooking the river. It was dark outside but the lights from the house reflected on the still water and a glittering track reached across the river. On the opposite bank aspen and elder rustled in the night breeze. 'There was a woman in the village who worked at Angelus House as a housekeeper years ago.'

'Patsy was born in Egton, you understand,' added George.

'Do you remember her name?' asked Julie.

'I've no idea I'm afraid. It's a long time ago and I moved away from Egton years back.'

As Edward drove back that night, Julie suddenly spoke. She had been thinking. 'It's plain to me that Jim is only telling you the bits he's happy for you to know.'

'What else do you think he should tell us?'

'Well, the results of the post-mortem for a start. Surely that would be on the police file.'

'You're right,' said Edward. 'But how would we get to see that? I don't think anybody can demand to see a post mortem report or, for that matter, a police file.'

As it happened he was right. Edward and Julie had joined the modern age at last and the next morning Edward opened up his laptop and logged on to the Internet to find the government information website for the Coroner Service. It was pretty clear that neither he nor Julie qualified as an "interested person" as far as access to post mortem reports was concerned. 'Damn,' he said out loud. 'What do we do now?'

'Do what we usually do,' replied Julie from the breakfast table. 'Ask George.'

George was a kind of catch-all in the sphere of worldy-wisdom. He might look like a retired colonel in the members' seats at Lords but he knew how things worked and, above all, he knew people who made them work. 'Leave it with me,' he had said over the phone. 'I'll get back to you.' He was becoming more and more interested in the case as he learned more about it.

A week later the phone rang. It was George. 'I was playing golf at Ganton earlier this week and mentioned the Tracy Woodford business to an old contact of mine. He owed me a favour for a slightly dubious planning application I got past the planning department a few years back. The amazing thing is he runs a business storing records for large companies. Used to be a farmer but found it earned him more money to use his buildings for secure storage. He does regular collections, boxes the documents up, locks them away until they are needed or destroyed.'

'That's very interesting, George,' Edward said, wondering where the conversation was going.

'The thing is, Edward, he has a contract with the Coroner Service. He told me they keep hard copies for thirty years.'

'OK?'

'Don't you see? He has the coroner's reports for 1987.'

'But how does that help us? They're in secure storage.'

'I told him it was for reasons of compassion.' There was a long pause from Edward. George continued: 'OK, I bent the rules a bit. But it's true – you only want to know the truth about Freddie.'

'So what you're saying is that we can take a look at Tracy Woodford's file?'

Edward heard George clear his throat. 'Yes,' he replied.

'You crafty old bugger,' Edward thought. 'So what do we do now?' he asked.

'You don't have to do anything, Edward. He took me for a guided tour of his operation after the game, company called Boxit, lots of little white vans going back and forwards. And I saw Tracy Woodford's report. She'd had a child, it seems, not long before she died. That's all I can add to the story. Moxon's already told you what the coroner's verdict was.'

'Thanks,' said Edward, 'so why didn't Jim Moxon tell me that?'

'Why should he, if he didn't want you to get any further? A teenage girl goes missing, she's depressed, no one to turn to, walks into the sea and drowns. That's a simple story with an end to it. Now it's a story that asks a question.'

'A number of questions actually, like who was the father and where did the child go and what's it all got to do with Freddie?'

'Precisely.'

Chapter 5

At the time, Tracy could never have imagined that anyone would have bothered to find out about her eighteen years in the future. She thought that nobody cared about her now, let alone later. She looked at herself in the mirror. She couldn't see how pretty she was, with her blue eyes and blonde hair. All she saw was another day of emptiness ahead. She didn't miss Terry. She had always hated him. She was glad he was dead. As for her parents, who were they, and where were they now? She had no memory of her father. Her mother had been a dark shadow in her childhood, drifting in and out of reality, before disappearing entirely to leave Tracy in a twilight world of foster parents and council homes. When Terry became eighteen and got a council flat she moved in with him and nobody seemed to bother to track her down. But her life was on the brink of a dark chasm. A steady stream of drug addicts flowed through the flat, paying Terry in bundles of notes for small packets, and Terry would often disappear for days, leaving her with no money for food or the electric meter. Then one night he had got her drunk on vodka and a mate of his had raped her on the living room sofa. She had tried to blank it out but all she could remember was seeing a few five pound notes change hands as she lay in a semi-sleep.

She brushed her blonde hair mindlessly as she sat staring into her own eyes in the mirror. She was fifteen years old or probably sixteen now. She once remembered celebrating a birthday but she had forgotten the date. And what was there to celebrate but the years of loneliness and fear? She was numb and did not feel pain any longer. And that was why, when the Russian called Viktor asked her if she wanted to get away from the dark little flat in Charlton, she could think of no reason to say no.

She had never been out of London before. The road north had passed in a blur as she sat in the front seat of the car, head leaning on the window, mile after mile of cars and lorries left behind in the slow lane, blue motorway signs flashing by. Then a dual carriageway narrowing to a simple road, winding, rising and falling in a green hilly country; sandstone cottages in village streets and painted pub signs depicting the sun, a ram, a bull; a rough track winding up to a plain stone house on a rise, with a view of the blue sea between two hills; then a friendly woman's face at the door, showing her a clean little bedroom with a window overlooking the moors and the grazing sheep. Then, next day, a man called Freddie, with a flop of grey-blonde hair, a paint-splashed shirt, saying very little, but with a kindly look that she felt safe with. But she had not left London alone. She carried inside her another life and it was three months before she knew it and another two before she said anything. In the meantime, the strange, remote artist had asked her to sit for him, which she did, and he painted her as any older man would paint his daughter, with the kindness of real love. So they had become close, without speaking about it, finding a common humanity that sometimes brings together disparate generations, spinning into each other from colliding universes.

When she knew her time was coming she had set off on her own to walk to the town where she thought she could find a hospital. She wanted to keep it as her secret. She was young and had concealed the fact easily. She was a girl with a name but no history; she had a child with no father; and when they told her it was dead she didn't really understand the words. But she had no idea what she had done to bring a dead child into the world, or what she wanted to do now that she had done it, but it was over, just as her life was over, empty and pointless. She had not lived long enough to suspect that there could be another land over the horizon. So she sat at the mirror contemplating another day in her empty world and it did not seem to be worth the effort.

One day she put on her coat and walked down the hill from Angelus House into Egton Bridge. It was the middle of the afternoon and the quiet village streets were deserted. She had no plan; she simply followed the road, which took a couple of turns before reaching an automatic crossing over the railway line. The barrier was already raised and she crossed into the station yard and walked on to the platform. There was a bench in front of the stone-built station house and four tall lampposts along the platform with a single rail track leading east and west. No one else was around. The crossing light began to flash and the warning bell sounded. A train was coming and when its two diesel carriages arrived, she got on. It was the train to Middlesbrough. She told no one that she was leaving or where she was going. The journey lasted over an hour, the train stopping every few minutes at tiny country stations, with strange north country names – Battersby, Lealholm, Glaisdale – not like the stops on the District Line. The odd passenger got on here and there but she spoke to no one. At Middlesbrough the station was half a mile from the town centre. She was surprised by the size of the place. It was cold and a slight rain fell on to the pavements as she walked. She was used to walking hard pavements. It reminded her of south London. It was as if she had returned to her point of origin, the hard urban world where it was easy for a person to become invisible.

The decision to end her life was never formulated, never that clear-cut. It came from weariness, just a wearing down, the steady drip of hopelessness, nothing dramatic, just gradual. She had never asked for an explanation of life; it wasn't that kind of problem.

She had a little money in her coat pocket. There had always been money, where it came from she was never sure. She had walked for an hour and the town centre had changed into the suburbs and then a country road with light traffic. Darkness was falling and an evening chill set in. She felt tired. A little way ahead she saw a bus shelter with a bench and she sat down, not waiting for a bus but simply waiting. Then out of the twilight she saw the lights of a single decker approaching. It pulled up, the automatic doors opened and a woman got out. The doors stayed open and the driver looked across to Tracy, sitting in the bus stop.

'You getting on, love?' he asked.

'Where you going?'

'Saltburn's the end of the line.'

Tracy stood up, climbed the steps and paid for a ticket to Saltburn. The doors swung closed and the bus set off with a lurch. Tracy was alone in the bus. She had no idea where Saltburn was but it was just the next thing to do. She looked out into the dark night, the fine rain running in streaks on the windows, and through that she could see the reflection of her face in the window. The bus stopped once, to pick up a single traveller. At nine o'clock the outlying houses of the town appeared and the bus drew up in a square by the railway station. The driver turned off the engine and opened the doors. The other passenger was off in a moment but Tracy remained seated, her head resting on the window. After a moment the driver walked down the gangway of the bus. 'This is Saltburn, pet. This is the terminus. You getting off?'

'Yeah, sure,' she replied.

'You alright? Do you live in Saltburn? I only ask 'cos this is the last bus back to Middlesbrough tonight, if you want to get back.'

'No, I'm OK, thanks,' she said, rising to her feet. She got off the bus into the dark cold night, with no idea where she was or what she was going to do. So she walked. The main street was closed up and deserted except for a corner shop, an open-all-hours general store. She stopped and bought a half bottle of vodka and twenty Embassy. The shopkeeper looked at her but took her money without question, handing over the cigarettes and the bottle in a plastic carrier bag. The street led downhill towards the sea. She walked on, reaching a junction with a long sweeping promenade, lined on one side by substantial brick houses, mostly flats interspersed with bed and breakfast places. On the other lay the black empty North Sea, and a cold wind tugged at her coat collar. She could hear the rolling breakers a hundred feet below her as she walked down a flight of steps to the beach. A row of white lights stretched out to sea on a pier but there was no sign of life when she got there, only the boarded-up seaside shops, and a flight of concrete steps leading down to the sand. The tide was half out and she walked down on to the dry soft sand under the pier, sat down leaning against an iron pillar, unscrewed the top of the bottle, took a mouthful and lit a cigarette. In a minute her head felt light and a warm feeling began to spread through her body. Smoking and drinking seemed to shrink her loneliness, as if a bottle and a packet of cigarettes were her friends.

She must have fallen asleep leaning against the iron pillar of the pier for when she next looked around she could see moonlight on the water and the tide had risen. When she walked into the water, it was not to kill herself. She simply wanted to know if she could do it, if life became too bad. For her logic was that life might be easier if she knew she could escape it if she needed to. It was just a test run.

She felt the cold water round her knees and went further out. The waves began to break over her thighs but the vodka had numbed her senses. A little further out and she would turn knowing she could do it if she wanted to. But as she turned a wave swept in higher than the others and the undertow seized her legs and she fell deep into the dark cold sea. But it was strange. There was no panic but the simple thought: well, so this is how it is.

A mile to the south of the town the bay swept round under the base of high cliffs and the circulation of the sea caused a fast cross-current that ran away from the shore and carried flotsam far out. One week later the body of a young girl was washed up on the rocks at Saltwick Bay, twenty miles south, where cocklers found it at low tide. Around its slender wrist was a gold bracelet with the name *Tracy* engraved on it. She had lived her life without being noticed, until she was dead.

Chapter 6

When Dan Martin heard Edward mention the name Tracy he froze inside. It was his worst nightmare returning. He had said nothing at the time but, in the early hours of most mornings, he pondered over his abrupt conversation with Edward. And he had no one to talk to, least of all Molly. Under no circumstances must she know. His life ground on day after day; he woke to black thoughts and spent the waking hours turning things over in his mind, again and again. He could live with the truth, he knew that, but for Molly it would be the end. Dan was a simple man. His life had passed doing simple things and he had reached that point when he knew that nothing more ambitious was possible, that his life had taken its course, and that he had no value except what those nearest to him accorded him. It was a precious little circle that must not be broken: Dan, Molly and Jane.

When Edward asked about Tracy, Dan had given the wrong answer. He should have said: 'Yes, I knew her. She lived at Angelus House for a while, years ago. She was a nice girl. But there was a tragedy and she died. No one knows why.' Instead, his reply to Edward had just said, in not so many words: 'There's something to hide. I know what it is but I'm not going to tell you.' But it was only a year ago that he had discovered there really was something to hide. He could either bluff it out and hope that Edward did not come back to ask more questions; or share his secret with him, trusting Edward to keep it to himself.

And now he rested on a Victorian tomb in St Mary's churchyard, taking breath after climbing the steps that led out of Henrietta Street to the cliff top overlooking the town. He needed space to clear his head, to think through what he was going to do, away from the business of the *Caedmon*. To the east the sea stretched its grey expanse to a disappearing horizon where sky and water were inseparable. In the distance an empty tanker ploughed northwards to the oil terminal in the Forth; closer to the cliffs an inshore fisherman dropped his lobster pots one by one in a line a quarter of a mile from the rocks; and in the harbour town below he could see people going about their business as if they had intent and purpose enough to get them through another day. For this was his thought: if the magic circle of those he loved and who loved him were to be broken, what was the point of it all, dragging hopelessly onwards? All around him the world seemed to have purpose and he dreaded the moment, if it ever came, when he lost his. Dan was not clever or educated; his only talent was to be honest. And yet for a year he had sheltered a dark secret he had not dared share with anyone. He felt that he had been stretched upon a wheel of fire and he longed for the escape that sharing the secret might bring. And that is why he decided to tell Edward. How strange it might appear to the outside world for an odd-job man turned fish frier, to share his secret with an Old Etonian futures dealer who had parachuted into the little world of Henrietta Street only a few months before. But Edward had inherited the legacy of kindness that Freddie had left to him. This was Dan's thinking. He knew he could trust Edward.

The herring gulls wheeled and screeched overhead as he descended the abbey steps, past the closed door of Juliana's little shop, where the artist's hand moved silently in the back workshop. A little further down the street he found Edward at home, sitting at his easel by the closed french windows, working up another generation of seascapes. Edward seemed at peace with himself since he had come to share his life with Julie; Dan was not to know that in sharing his dark secret with Edward, he might offer a glimpse into another older mystery that had created a different kind of torment.

Edward opened the street door in response to the knock. He was surprised to see Dan standing there.

'Hope I'm not interrupting you,' Dan said. 'I was just passing.'

Edward knew this to be no reason at all; Dan had never before called by uninvited. But he covered up well. 'Of course not, Dan. Come in. I'll make some coffee. Have a seat.' Dan looked around, ill at ease, before settling on the sofa, while Edward put on the kettle, spooned Nescafe into two mugs, and took a carton of milk out of the fridge. 'What can I do for you?'

There was a long pause before Dan spoke. 'Actually, Edward, I just wanted to apologise. I was rude the other day. I'm sorry.'

'Sorry for what, Dan?'

'When you asked me about the Tracy girl from Angelus House, I more or less told you to get lost.'

'Oh that. Well, I suppose you did give me the cold shoulder,' said Edward, 'but no hard feelings. Here, have your coffee,' he added, handing him a mug and turning his kitchen chair round to face Dan.

'The thing is, I've been pretty worried recently, Edward, and things had got on top of me.' He took a sip of his coffee. 'You've never had kids, have you? You spend all your time bringing them up and then when they grow up, you're afraid of losing them.'

'You're not talking about Jane, are you? Jane loves you and Molly, I know that. Don't worry about her, Dan, she's just setting out in life. You haven't lost her at all; you never will.' Edward wondered what was coming next; why would Dan talk to him, of all people, a newcomer to the street, about his private affairs?

'I know what you're thinking, Edward. Why the hell am I telling you all this? Right?' Edward nodded. 'Well, it's Freddie's fault really. We owe him so much, me and Molly and Jane. You've kind of stepped into his shoes, I suppose. You're outside it all, you see. You're not one of us. So you can see us for what we are.'

'Dan. Stop there. I don't get any of this,' interrupted Edward. 'Just tell me what's on your mind, from the start.'

Dan nervously fingered the handle of his mug.

'It's about Jane. When you have a child, you see them every day. You watch them grow up. You help them with homework, as long as you can understand it, which in my case wasn't not very long.' Dan laughed. 'You see, Edward, I'm not a clever fellow like you.'

'Never thought of myself as clever, Dan. Not even street-wise as it turns out. I've learned more since I moved to Henrietta Street than in all my years of posh schooling. So don't do yourself down!'

Dan laughed reluctantly. 'But you know what I mean. Jane soon left me behind, she was so clever. I used to think I could check out her boyfriends, but she had them sussed long before me. So what did I have to offer her really?' Dan held his head in his hands as if he were in despair. He did not know how to put his feelings into words. The years had flashed by and Jane had grown up and left home to head for a glittering career. But he was left on the shore, washed up, with nothing but his memories and his silly sentimental emotions which he thought were too childish for a man to share with anyone. What was he to do then? Worse, what was a man to do if it had all been a lie and the emotions had been drained out of him only to find it all a falsehood?

'Dan, listen to me. You don't have to offer her anything but yourself. That's all she wants. You're her father for God's sake!'

Dan looked up, his face showing real pain. 'That's the bloody point, Edward. I'm not her Dad. It's not possible! All these years I've been living a lie.' Silence fell and held them both in its sway for a long time.

'I'm sorry, Dan. I don't understand you. What the hell has happened? You *are* her father and you have been for at least eighteen years as far as I can see.'

'Look at this,' said Dan, drawing a folded sheet of paper from his pocket. 'I printed this off the computer. Our Jane taught me how to access the Internet last year.' He passed the paper to Edward who unfolded it carefully. It was a chart in four columns, each column showing in capitals the letters A, AB, B and O.

'OK, blood types, so what?' asked Edward.

'Look at the bottom row. O plus O equals O. Do you understand it?'

'I understand it but I'm not sure what it means.'

'It's obvious. Molly and I are both type O. It's the only combination that produces only type O in a child. But Jane is type AB.'

Edward took a while to register the import of Dan's statement. At last, he spoke. 'Good God, I see. You're sure about this?'

'I only found out when I came across Jane's blood donor card lying about the house a while back. She's not our kid Edward. She can't be. I only looked it up for interest sake. I never thought I'd discover this. I wish to God I hadn't!' Dan broke down. He put his head in his hands and wept.

Edward had no idea what to do. He was not used to comforting crying men. 'Who else knows about this, Molly or Jane?'

'No, they must never know, and nobody else,' snapped Dan. 'It would kill Molly and God knows how Jane would react.'

'So you're saying Molly couldn't have got pregnant with another man?'

'Edward, I know so, for a fact.'

'That's a big claim – for a fact. How can you be so sure?'

'Because I know what happened. I've heard the true story and I believe it.'

Edward looked at his watch. It was eleven o'clock in the morning. He knew that Julie would be home any minute for a coffee break and a chat. Dan sat crumpled on the sofa, in no state to encounter her. 'Dan, get your coat on. We're going to walk the cliffs to Hawsker and back. You can tell me your story. The fresh air will help.' Edward heard himself saying these words as if he were outside of his own body, looking on. How could he be so wise now and such a fool before? But Dan had put his trust in him and he had grown into it and he had surprised himself.

It was a cold morning. The wind whipped round their legs as they climbed the abbey steps and blew their breath away when they passed the parish church. The clifftop path stretched ahead of them, winding precariously in and out of bays and over headlands, with the white-topped waves breaking and sounding below them on the rocks. What Dan told Edward was the perfect balance of kindness and cruelty, both existing in equal measure in the one act, inseparable, and irredeemable in their finality. His story was not new. It had blown down the windswept alleyways of time, ever since man and woman stumbled into this failing flawed world, after the fall. And Dan shouted it across the buffeting wind that day as he and Edward walked the cliffs, a testament to the raging skies that humankind can mingle kindness and cruelty, love and loss, fellowship and disregard, in equal measure, all encompassed in a single unthinking act.

'I asked Ruby to tell me what happened,' he said.

'Why Ruby, of all people?'

'Because she had to be there at the beginning. She had to know what had happened,' Dan replied.

'Sorry, Dan. You've lost me.'

'She worked at the Royal – maternity wing. She was there when Jane was born. She had to know!'

And then Edward remembered Julie telling him that. He had just not made the connection.

They had reached a stretch of the cliff route where the path descended steeply down to a shingle beach in a small bay sheltered by rising headlands on each side. The descent gradually protected them from the wind but a fierce shower suddenly doused them. They were like characters from *King Lear,* seeking shelter from the storm, which they found in a shallow cave wedged between high rocks, a foaming ocean rising and falling with a roar on the shelf of pebbles. They shook their coats dry as they entered the recess into the cliff face and squatted on the damp cave floor.

'I suppose you told Ruby about the blood types?' began Edward.

'Yes, I did. Then I asked her what she knew. I asked her just to tell me what happened and that I needed to know. I must have shouted at her, I was so worked up. She started to cry. But I think she must have understood alright why I needed to know. All she said at first was: "Molly must never know".'

'I suppose she knew Molly pretty well?'

Dan looked at Edward in disbelief. 'Course, man. They were sisters! Didn't you know that?'

'No, I didn't,' replied Edward sheepishly, inwardly noting another example of his failure to understand what really moved in Henrietta Street. 'I'm sorry, Dan. Go on. What did she say?'

Dan pulled his coat collar up against the cold sea air and lit himself a cigarette, cupping the flame of the lighter in his hands. He laughed. 'Started smoking again, didn't I. Stupid bugger.'

'I know exactly how you feel, Dan,' said Edward. 'It hits you when life is shit.'

'Aye, well. It took her a while to get settled, she were that upset I guess. Then I remember she wiped the tears from her eyes and took a deep breath. She told me it was years ago but she could remember the night quite clearly.' And Dan recounted slowly what Ruby had said. He told it in his own way, which was stumbling and clumsy, but in his head he could still hear the pain in Ruby's voice as she related her story. She had started:

'It had been raining hard all day and the night was freezing cold. It was one of those days when it never seemed to get light, as if the grey morning and the gloom of dusk could find nothing to come between them. I was on night duty alone, apart from a junior nurse and the night security people. We didn't expect anything to happen but I could always call in the emergency cover if I needed to. We only had one bed occupied. And you know who that was, don't you?

'Don't ask me why I did it. I've asked myself that a million times over and over again. It was a kind of madness I suppose. I'd always done everything just as it should be. Never got anything wrong. The funny thing is I can never decide whether I regretted it or not. It comes and goes. Finished me, of course, inside my head, that is. I was never found out at all. But I lost faith in myself. It's like pinching stuff, I suppose. You take something from a shop once and after that you never quite know if you won't do it again. I couldn't trust myself, you see. I said it was a kind of madness but at the time it seemed to be the opposite to madness; it was an act of the greatest kindness, it seemed to me. Kindness and cruelty; two sides of the coin. I see that now.

'It must have been two in the morning when the porter on the front door brought the young girl to the unit. She was soaking wet and frozen, hypothermic, and in the later stages of labour. I can see her face now, her wet blonde hair hanging limply down. But the baby was born quickly and safely; it's often the way with young girls. She said her name was Tracy Woodford. She looked to be no more than sixteen. She said she'd walked from Egton that day but I didn't believe that could be possible. We put her on a drip and gave her a sedative. She slept for eighteen hours in a recovery room. When she came to I don't think she understood she had given birth. If she did, she never showed signs of remembering her baby. It was a girl. She never held it. It was as if she had blanked it all out. Maybe later, when she went missing, the memory came back to her. I think it must have, to have done what she did.'

Dan stopped when he could no longer translate Ruby's narrative into his own words. He put his head in his hands, seeming unable to carry on. Then he took another cigarette from the packet and lit it.

'Do you mind if I have one?' asked Edward out of the blue. Dan looked up and reached out his hand with the packet. 'Solidarity – and old time's sake,' said Edward. Dan smiled as if he understood the message. 'Two men in a cave by the North Sea smoking fags and both non-smokers! How about that? Don't worry Dan, it'll be alright,' added Edward.

This seemed to give Dan a breather, enabling him to continue his tale. 'Ruby told me it was a simple enough thing to do. The doctor wasn't present at the birth of either child. When he signed the death certificate he had no idea that the identities had been swapped.'

'Either child?'

'Of course. The other one was Molly's – and mine. Are

211

you getting it Edward? Ruby stole Tracy Woodford's baby and gave it to Molly. And gave our dead baby to Tracy.'

There was a long silence in the cave. Edward took a draw on his cigarette and felt the tobacco smoke burn the back of his throat. 'Yes, I'm getting it Dan. I get it. But how did it all end up?'

'You mean for Tracy?'

'For both of you.'

'Ruby told me they had kept her in for a few days. And then they found out where she had come from. They called Freddie Ottaway to tell him what had happened and he came down from Angelus House to take her back. He was badly shaken, as far as I know. The next thing Ruby heard was that Tracy was missing and a week later her body was found at Saltwick. But that's not the end of the story. You know Jim Moxon used to be a copper. Turns out he was investigating the case. When Ruby heard that, she told him everything. She couldn't keep it from him. That's how he got to know what she did. She needed to tell someone. But the papers were all in place to show Tracy's baby had been still-born and ours was healthy. There was no one to question it, you see. Tracy was alone in the world. Freddie believed what Ruby told him and the whole thing was passed off as just another human tragedy. But I know better. All these years, Edward, all these years. What do I do? Ruby stole a child for us!'

Edward thought for a moment before speaking. 'Nothing, Dan. You do nothing at all.' He paused. 'Tell me Dan, what happened to Jim and Ruby?'

'Ruby cracked up completely. Nervous breakdown. Gave up the job. Jim took early retirement to look after her and hit the bottle. I assume he made sure the investigation into Tracy Woodford stopped where it did of course. Now it's the other way round, the looking after bit I mean. You might have noticed. Of course, at the time none of us knew why Ruby had fallen apart.'

The two men fell into silence. The roar of the sea on the pebbles echoed round the shallow cave which had been their protective hovel, away from the storm. Far off on the eastern horizon a shaft of light indicated that the worst of the shower was over and in a few minutes the sun might break through. They took to their feet and walked the winding way back along the cliffs to Whitby. At the top of the steps, sunlight slanting at last through the broken arches of the ruined abbey, Dan stopped and took Edward by the arm. 'Edward, you're the best of men. Thanks. But should I really do nothing?'

'Nothing Dan. Believe me. You've nurtured Jane, you and Molly, you've brought her into her own world as surely as if you had been her blood parents. Now she's free to make her own way and you both should be proud. Promise me that. Let her go without a burden of knowledge she doesn't need and let Molly enjoy what she has always had. And you and I can look at each other and know you've done the right thing.'

They sat in the sunshine on the stone lid of the tomb in St Mary's churchyard, where a lifetime ago, it seemed, Edward had felt the first winds of change in his drifting life. And now he could feel pride in being called the best of men by his new-made friend. Dan held out his packet of cigarettes. 'Only two left. Let's smoke them now that the battle is over.'

'And then we can give up again,' added Edward, 'and nobody will ever know we wavered.'

When they parted at Edward's front door, the house was empty, Juliana having gone back to the shop. Monty was asleep in the centre of the table. Edward stretched out on the battered sofa and thought. It was not the first time that a tangled web had been the outcome of a human enterprise. What Ruby had done might have been the ultimate act of kindness to her sister but it was set within a framework of ignorance, of uncalculated consequences, and the drifting body of a young girl in the harsh cold tide of the North Sea bore witness to the tragedy of being human and making such decisions. And what a horror being human could be, when all we wanted was to wander the stars with the innocent angels, to find ourselves dragged down to the depths by our invincible ignorance. Edward looked at Monty stretched out on the dining table, his days and his needs so simple and honest, but with a brain the size of a walnut, while mighty

213

man strutted in the darkness, a darkness which itself shielded him from the true horror of his actions. How could God have created such a blundering tribe of imbeciles as humanity? Monty blinked in acknowledgement of the wisdom of Edward's philosophy.

Winter came early that year. First came the flurry of snow showers borne on the east wind across the grey sea, drifting to nothing on the street corners and not lasting. Then the temperature plummeted and the moors froze solid in the iron clamp of ice. The skies grew heavy and grey until one night in late November the snows came to stay. The heather disappeared under a white blanket and the sheep huddled behind walls and hurdles in the shelter of the valleys. The town became black and white, its two halves mirroring each other across the slate-grey water of the harbour. The roads out were blocked for a day or two until the council ploughs carved narrow tracks through the drifting snows at the top of the hill. In the silence of the snow-locked town, below the cliff steps and the towering abbey ruin, Edward thought often of how his life had changed. He had begun to understand how people's lives were formed, not by money or education, but by the rough rhythm of events, what befell them in the unpredictable ebb and flow of every day. He had seen this with Dan and Ruby and Molly; and he imagined the consequences for Jim; and the unspeakable blow that might fall upon Jane if the truth ever escaped. And against this he saw how people ploughed on, step by step, through the endless monotony of their lives. All else appeared froth and mere dressing; as did his past life, an unreality of misplaced daydreams.

Juliana was by his side through the length and breadth of this deep trough. He often watched her at work, her hands moving slowly over some intricate piece of work, seated at her bench, controlling and defining, while the world around him seemed to spin away in some random gyration. He had not sought knowledge when he washed up in Henrietta Street but now it seemed he carried the secrets of the tribe on his shoulders: he knew that Viktor had murdered a man; that

Ruby and Jim had committed a cruel crime; and that the little family at the *Caedmon* could only hold together if the magic circle of silence were not broken. Beyond it all, the questions remained: who was Jane's father; why had Freddie died the way he did; and was there a secret motive for enticing Edward to this little place?

Juliana lifted her head from her work and looked at Edward over her glasses. 'I spoke to Molly today,' she said.

'Oh, yes. What about?'

'I asked her about Tracy.' Edward had previously told her what Dan had said.

'Do you think that was wise?' he asked, looking up from his paper.

'I didn't mention anything about Jane. I'm not stupid, Edward! It's just that I met Patsy yesterday, in the supermarket. You know, George's new wife.'

'Of course I remember. But what's that got to do with Molly?'

'Do you remember, when we had dinner at Ruswarp, Patsy said she thought the woman who reported Tracy missing came from Egton and worked at Angelus House? Well, she told me she'd remembered her name. It was Molly.'

'You mean Dan's Molly? She was the housekeeper Malinov mentioned?'

'Exactly. Don't you think she might have known more than anyone about Tracy? I mean, an older woman and a young pregnant girl, don't you think they might have shared a secret or two that Freddie never knew about?'

'You mean, like who was the father of the child?'

'Precisely.' Julie took off her glasses, ran her fingers through her hair, and looked straight at Edward. 'Molly said Tracy had told her the father was probably a foreign guy in London. In other words, Malinov.'

'So we were right,' said Edward, 'at least, probably. What else did Molly say?'

'That Tracy's baby was still-born, and it happened when she gave birth to Jane. I said nothing, Edward, but I felt like crying.' Tears formed in her eyes as she said this and Edward

216

walked across to her, bent down and took her in his arms. He could feel the sobs shaking her body. 'And she said Freddie could never forgive himself for what happened to Tracy.'

Edward stood up, walked across the room to a cupboard on the wall, took out two glasses and a bottle and poured a couple of whiskies. He handed one to Julie. 'Drink that. It'll make you feel better.' Julie took a gulp and the burning whisky shook her back into herself. 'I've been thinking,' he continued, 'and don't say that's not like me.' She laughed. 'I need to escape from here, Julie. I know too much. I feel like one of those ancient gods from the dark ages, born to carry away the sins of the tribe but die in the process. I started off thinking this place was a haven from the chaos of my London life, an escape route. But there isn't an escape in life, is there. It's more a matter of acceptance than escape. I guess I've grown up at last.'

'What are you saying?'

'I never thought I'd think this, but the very houses of this street seem to hold out the light now. I look up to the sky and all I see is the overbearing cliff face and on the top of that the cold stones of the abbey. We should get out of this small secret world, Julie, you and me. I want to breathe the air of the hills and let the wind and the sun sweep across me. I want to stand on a hilltop and look down to the sea. I'm an outsider in this world, forever looking in but never belonging. Do you understand how I feel?'

Julie took a sip of her whisky before answering. 'You're right Edward. I've been feeling the same for some time. It's time we left this place behind. Forget about Freddie and why you're here. Does that really matter any more? We have each other. Why ask more questions?'

What she said was true but they had no money and nowhere to go; and the questions would not go away.

It was the shortest day of the year, when the sun rose above the sea at ten o'clock and sank behind the west cliff at three. Edward was standing at the french window watching the first light slant across the harbour when the telephone rang. It was George. 'Malinov's leaving,' he said.

'What do you mean?' asked Edward.

'Just that. He's gone. Sold up. Bought a club in London. Buggered off!'

'Bloody hell. That's a surprise. Did he say anything?'

'Nothing. The directors got a letter from the chief executive this morning, all of two lines long. Apparently a local businessman's bought the Boro. That's all I know.'

'So that's the end of Malinov. I don't suppose we'll hear from him again,' said Edward.

'Probably not,' George agreed. And Edward thought, 'That really does draw a line under it all.'

Later that morning, Edward caught the scent of Jim's pipe tobacco sifting through the gaps in the window frame. He threw open the windows and looked below him to where Jim was taking the air. Jim heard the creak of the hinges and looked up. 'That bloody bugger's sold the Boro. Buggered off to London, hasn't he? Sold out to a haulage contractor.'

'You mean Malinov?' said Edward.

'Aye, bloody Malinov. And that Yakult fella's been locked up for head-butting a Sunderland supporter in a night club. Accused him of unnatural acts with a yak.' George's call had been confirmed.

It was a long hard winter. There were days on end when the fishing boats could not leave harbour. And there were weeks when the raging sea broke over the east pier and fountains of white water cascaded over the stones. In February the snows were heavy and the railway line to Middlesbrough was blocked at Commondale, until a snow plough broke through from the depot at York. At last the winds of March blew warm air in from the west, the temperature rose, and the late afternoon light lasted longer. Snowdrops were already fading in the woods along the Esk and daffodils began to bloom in the flower beds before the West Cliff Hotel.

It seemed they were emerging from a winter sleep, blinking into the daylight. In the tiny cottage in Henrietta Street, one morning at the end of March, the telephone rang. It was Scrivener, the solicitor from York.

218

'I hope it's not another bank box you forgot about,' said Edward.

'Yes, sorry about that,' said Scrivener. 'No it's nothing like that. Do you remember asking me about Angelus House, who owned it?'

'Yes, it turned out not to be me,' replied Edward.

'Quite so,' said Scrivener. Edward heard a pause before Scrivener continued. 'That was then. You won't believe this, Mr Ottaway, but you do own it.'

'I don't understand. Are you joking?'

'Far from it. I have the document to prove it. The property has been gifted to you and the deeds have been amended to reflect that. The London solicitors have been acting on being of VSM Holdings.'

'Bloody Malinov!' Edward shouted down the phone.

'I beg your pardon. You know the previous owner?'

'I should think so. Victor Sergeyevich Malinov – VSM for short. He's a Russian gangster.'

Scrivener, who made his living drawing up wills and advising on trust funds, did not expect this reply and sounded flustered. 'And that's not all. He's also gifted to you a place called Ponsonby Hall. Do you know anything about that?'

'I know all about that, Mr Scrivener.'

'I take it, then, that you want me to proceed?'

Edward, who had not expected to be asked this question, merely said: 'I suppose so.'

'I'll send you the deeds in due course,' said Scrivener, glad to be back on familiar ground.

Edward put down the phone. He stood in silence, not knowing what to make of it.

'So, are you going to tell me what that was all about?' Julie asked, finally losing patience.

'It's Malinov. He's given us Angelus House. Can you believe it? And not only that, Ponsonby Hall as well.'

'But why would he do that?' asked Julie.

'One, he's sold his football club; and two, more importantly, he knows I know he's a murderer and possibly a sex offender. Maybe he's trying to buy me off! It would be impossible for me to shop him if it came out in court that I had been given such a huge gift. You could say I would be compromised in an odd sort of wrong-way-round way. I'm pretty sure he's clearing the ground before his next step up the ladder of British society and he doesn't want any messy bits of his past coming to light.'

'It's a gift. Do you have to accept it?'

'I've no idea. But think, it gives us a way out of here. I can stand on the hilltops and look down on the sea after all.'

The wheels of the legal system began to turn slowly and two months later Julie and Edward found themselves driving the switch-back road across the moors to Ponsonby Hall, a set of keys in the glove box. It was the end of May, the clouds were high and a brisk south-easterly blew salt air across the hills. As the car passed through the ornate gates at the public road, Julie looked across the sweeping gravel driveway that curved round to the front door, picking out the monstrous garden centre cement lions that stood either side. Then the mongrel architecture of the building rose up before them. 'My God, what has he given us?' she exclaimed. 'Is this his idea of an English country house?'

'Don't worry, this is the worst bit. Inside is not too bad.'

Edward stopped the car in front of the pillared door. He selected the heaviest key from the ring and inserted it into the keyhole. The levers fell with a clunk and the six-foot wide oak door swung gracefully open. A swathe of dried leaves rustled across the chessboard entrance hall, as if a window had stood open all winter while the storms had blown the leaves from the trees. It was as though the building had stood empty for an age, deserted by its placeless owner and his sinister entourage, the pretence of country living abandoned for the glitter of the city. Edward could almost feel the presence of Malinov, drifting aimlessly through corridors and empty rooms, a spectre in search of a belief and an identity. They climbed one of the two staircases to the gallery. 'I want to show you something, Julie. Follow me,' said Edward, and she followed him, wide-eyed, up the curving marble steps. At the top he paused, pointed one way, then the other, and said:

'Take a look.' Julie walked slowly past the gallery of Ottaways, just as Edward had done months before. Echoes from Freddie's journal flashed into her mind as she studied his Africa, and his Africa in Yorkshire, his obsession and his lost love. She studied the creased black faces of the tribesmen as they stood before their thatched huts; the wide laughing faces of the women washing clothes on the stones of the river and the shining faces of children, bare-legged in the African sun. And then the colonial figures, wide-brimmed hats, bridle in hand, handsome white women and men in white suits, fading into anonymity in the face of history. But one portrait stood out, that of a young English girl, perhaps fifteen or sixteen, standing by the window with the sea in the background, blonde hair and blue eyes, but with a sadness in her face.

'I don't remember seeing this one before. Who do you think she is?' asked Edward, who had followed quietly behind, unheard on the deep crimson carpet of the gallery.

Julie studied the picture in amazement. 'If I didn't know better, I would say it was Jane. Not so tall but the eyes and the hair are a giveaway. The likeness is uncanny. It could be Jane!'

'But it's not. It must be Tracy Woodford. She was pretty, blonde-haired and blue-eyed. That's what Malinov told me. And Freddie painted her picture. So now we know. And that's why we can't shop Malinov. Jane must never know where she came from. If we chase Malinov for this, who knows what will come pouring out. Remember, he knows nothing about a child. Some truths are better hidden behind lies. Ask Dan, if you doubt me.'

Chapter 8

It was ten o'clock on a Monday morning when the telephone rang. Julie put down her pencil, pushed away the drawing board and pressed the answer button on the portable.

'Julie Allington.'

'Hi, this is Sophie Desterre, arts correspondent from the *Observer* magazine,' came the London voice. 'We're interested in doing a feature on you and the Ponsonby school of design. Wondered if I could drive up to meet you. Say, day after tomorrow?'

Julie was taken aback and drew in her breath for a moment. Then: 'Sure, yes, of course. What time?'

'How about elevenish?'

'Do you know how to find us?'

'I do. Checked your website. Good then. See you on Wednesday morning.' And the phone went dead.

Just then, Edward walked in. 'Looks as if you've seen a ghost. What's up?'

'*Observer* magazine. Wants to do a feature on me. Coming on Wednesday.'

'But that's great!'

Julie had come a long way from her shop in Henrietta Street. Now she worked to commissions as far apart as New York and Delhi and six times a year ran residential courses for aspiring designers. Edward still dabbled on canvas but was happy to run front of house. At first it had been a struggle to keep Ponsonby Hall afloat but, when at last they managed to sell Angelus House to a Middlesbrough solicitor, the cash saw them through for a couple of years. Then one day Edward was glancing through a copy of the *Retail Jeweller Magazine* he had spotted on the shelves of WH Smith in the concourse at York station and persuaded Julie, much against her will, to submit her designs for the Jewellery Designer of the Year award run by the magazine. She won and doors opened.

Sophie Desterre arrived as promised. She stepped confidently out of her white BMW, followed by a scrawny looking young man with an expensive digital camera. They had come from another world. Throughout the course of a long and tedious day the incessant beeping of her smartphone punctuated chunks of conversation and spasmodic photocalls. The scrawny young man, Julian, clicked away from all angles and, when the article appeared, there on the front page was a picture of Julie, Edward's arm around her waist, smiling before the twin pillars of the outrageous front door of Ponsonby Hall. Another photo was a long shot of Julie standing in the gallery, with a background of Freddie's paintings. One week later, a letter arrived with a Cardiff postmark.

Morgane Owen's entry in *Who's Who* read splendidly: the names of the great medical institutions of the world wove with an unrelenting frequency gently between those of international organisations. This great doctor had crossed the bridge from her pure medicine to power and influence, where the clarity of the ideal became confused by the compromises of policy. But what it did not say was that she had given away her virginity to a young officer of the colonial service in a tin-roofed hut in northern Kenya one late afternoon in 1950. And that is why, when Edward received her letter, he did not recognise his correspondent for who she was. *'I saw your photograph and your surname in the magazine,'* she had written. *'I knew at once you must be Freddie's nephew. I was a good friend of your uncle and knew him in Africa. There are some things you might wish to know. Would it be possible for me to visit you sometime? Perhaps you could call me.'* Her headed notepaper included a telephone number. She signed herself simply *Morgane Owen*.

'I remember the name from Freddie's journal,' Julie had said, after Edward had shown her the letter.

'And I think Malinov pointed our her portrait to me when I first saw the Ottaway collection. She was the girl in the riding outfit, holding a horse, if I remember correctly,' Edward added.

'It's not going away, is it,' Julie added, 'the question about Freddie.'

Edward called Lady Owen later that day. She announced she would be travelling to Edinburgh the following week by car, and it would be a short detour for her to call in to see them in north Yorkshire. They fixed a date. She would stay overnight.

Edward had had little contact with the great and the good but he did remember an occasion from his city days when the Governor of the Bank of England had arrived on a bicycle to address a conference he had attended. It was not therefore a total surprise to see Lady Owen, the internationally revered humanitarian, drawing up before Ponsonby Hall in a battered VW Polo with a hole in the exhaust.

Morgane Owen was a woman in her seventies but the passage of time which in others might have ravaged the skin or bent the frame seemed simply to have bestowed a mellowness upon her inescapable beauty. She was tall and straight, with high cheek bones and deep-set dark eyes. Her hair was steel grey, short and strong. She had the self-esteem that a golden career brings and the confidence that stems from a life spent in the public eye.

After supper they sat together in a window seat looking east across the lawn which ran down to the ornamental pond. Edward thought of the Royal Worcester cups and saucers of which Malinov had been so proud, odd unexpected tools in his effort to become British. They seemed strangely to have vanished completely from the building. The three, becoming more at ease with each other, drank wine from tall-stemmed glasses and watched the dwindling rays of the setting sun draw the shadow of the hall further and further towards the distant sea.

'When I think of his life, I think of nothing but loss. Such a great talent, cut down at the point when it was about to blossom.'

'You mean Amala?' said Julie.

'I mean both. You see, she was Africa for Freddie, she drew out from him his real purpose and when she died, he never managed to replace that. It was always a search, a search, a search, and never to find.' There was a long silence.

'You said you had something to tell us,' prompted Edward at last.

'First, a question,' she replied. 'What do you know about Freddie's death?'

'Not a lot,' said Edward, 'only that the police decided it was death by misadventure, which means nothing at all. The fact is nobody knows what happened.'

'And you, Julie?' Morgane asked.

'No more, I'm afraid. The whole town thought it was just a tragic accident. Do you know anything else?'

'If you think of his life, it makes sense, I suppose. There's something cruelly romantic about the idea of drawing a line under things, when you think you've got no more to give. But jumping off a cliff seems to be a deeply unromantic thing to do, don't you think. I suppose he could have fallen.'

'You seem doubtful,' Edward observed.

'I do, and for one reason. I knew he was afraid of something. Is "afraid" the right word? Probably not. Perhaps I should say, he felt something was about to happen.'

'Did you know Freddie in his later life?' asked Julie.

'Not at all. We last met, I think, in the fifties, when I was learning my medicine in London. I'd been back to Kenya that summer to work in my father's clinic. That's how I found out what had happened to Amala and when we met in London I had to tell him. That was the last I saw of him, his back as he turned at the door of my flat and set off alone to walk the London streets. Before that I had known him very well. We were, you might say, the very best of friends, before Amala became his great love. But we never changed; we always remained that way. I believe so, though we never met again in life. The thing is, he wrote to me before he died. I have the letter here. I thought you should see it, Edward. It suddenly came to me, when I saw your face and name in the magazine, that you should see it. I knew instantly I should have made the effort to share it with you much earlier.'

She handed the letter across the table to Edward. It was

225

short and unimposing. Edward took it and read it slowly. He said nothing, before handing the paper to Julie.

My dear sweet Morgane

How the years have passed and yet I think of you still as I first knew you, fresh and full of life, about to explode upon the world. My life has fallen into the sere, the yellow leaf, while yours has blossomed into colour. Here I stand, on the edge looking down, and all I want is for you to hold me and tell me that it will all be alright. How weak and feeble of me I tell myself; and hear you thinking the same, perhaps. But the truth is I am tired of it all.

I am leaving my house here to my nephew Edward. He does not know me and I do not know him. But I made a promise to his father years ago, at a moment of crisis in his life, that I would see his son through. That I have done but it would be an imposition to have told the boy that or now to have laid any burden of expectation upon him in his manhood. My solicitor, Scrivener in York, has been told what steps to take when the time comes. I do not know if Edward will take up his inheritance. If he does not, so be it. Let things lie.

My life seems to have been punctuated by encounters with injustice. I failed Amala years ago; and now I have failed to protect another, equally as vulnerable. Her name was Tracy Woodford. There are some in Henrietta Street who will remember her.

You may ask why I write to you all these years apart. It is because I know that time has not weakened the friendship we have for each other and because I cannot think of another living being who would understand my reasoning so well as you. It is a kind of goodbye to the world, I suppose.

Your dearest friend

Freddie

'Does this letter mean anything to you, Edward?' Morgane asked at last.

'I know exactly what it means, Morgane. Tracy was a young girl who died, the result of a monstrous injustice by the people here. Yes, I know all about it. May I keep it?'

226

'Of course. You know, there is a whole room given over to his paintings in the gallery in Nairobi. Most Kenyans who care to look will think they are the work of an African. Life is full of such strange twists, don't you think?'

Morgane left the next morning. Julie and Edward stood with her on the gravel drive. There was a grey morning mist off the hills, swirling around the house and bringing a chill with it. The three seemed to share an unspoken understanding. Such days felt as if they could never be endured; as if it would be better to fall into a sleep and never awake. But they knew they had to go on and on, as life does, unpredictable and incomprehensible. Morgane embraced Julie and kissed her cheek; then she held Edward in her arms. 'You look so like Freddie. Promise me you won't make the mistake he made. Don't live in the past; always look to the future. If you look back all you see is the mistakes you made; looking forward gives you the chance to succeed, over and over again.'

'And that is how you made your life a success?' asked Edward.

'A kind of success, perhaps, but different from yours. Your success lies with Julie. I can see that. Don't mess it up. And, by the way, I forgot to give you this.' She pulled a crumpled sheet of paper from her bag and pushed it into Edward's pocket. Then she climbed into her car, slammed the door, and started the engine. They waved as Morgane drove down the gravel drive and watched as she lifted a single hand to wave, without looking back. 'She's lonely,' thought Edward. 'Who would have guessed that?' Then he unfolded the single sheet Morgane had thrust into his pocket. It was a poem fourteen lines long entitled *Sonnet 155* and at the bottom was the name *William Shake-speare.* He turned the paper over and on the back was a hand-written scribble: *Freddie wrote this out for me from memory when we were in Kenya together. I think it was some kind of student joke. Morgane*. He put the paper back into his pocket.

Edward felt desolate after Morgane had left but couldn't explain why. Then he realised the feeling came from inside himself and it was sadness, not Morgane's departure, which had brought him down. If only Freddie had told him he had become his father, in a manner of speaking, when his real father had died. He thought he could have loved Freddie, in a way he had never loved his real father, and perhaps they could have helped each other, somehow or other. But that was gone; the years had disappeared never to be recovered. In reality, he did not know what he was thinking or feeling. Before he knew it, it was mid-morning and the grey mist began to lift, and he realised he had been walking the grounds for at least an hour. His feet were sodden from the wet grass. He felt a sudden tug at his elbow. It was Julie, smiling up at him and hanging on to his arm: 'Remember what she said, Edward, don't mess it up!' He turned and held her tight with both arms round her and they stood silent for a while as the weak sunlight chased the mist away.

'Mess it up? She used a strange expression,' Edward whispered. 'Do you remember our first meeting, Julie? I was a mess, wasn't I.'

'I suppose you were, but not irredeemable,' she replied.

'You're the best thing that's ever happened to me. I'm not going to mess that up. I'm not who I was and I don't want to go back to the old me.' Then he remembered and took the paper from his pocket. 'Read this,' he said, handing her the crumpled sheet, 'I was never any good at poetry.' Julie read it and liked it; then she sent it to her father who passed it round the English Faculty at Hull. A month later he returned the sonnet, with a cutting from an edition of *The Times Literary Supplement* from the fifties, describing the whole farce of the fraudulent Sonnet 155 and the fate of the unfortunate Doctor Fotheringay. 'Whoever wrote this was a genius,' he added, 'but it wasn't Shakespeare!'

Edward thought long and hard about where Morgane's visit had taken them. At first he thought that Freddie's letter was a certain statement that he intended to end his life. Then as he re-read it, he realised he himself could have written it a couple of years ago: marriage in ruins and tired of it all. 'Goodbye to the world': couldn't he also have said that about himself, as he retreated into his quiet new ways far from the

228

failures of the city? But then he thought of the way Freddie had described what had happened to Tracy: an injustice, or was it a tragedy? Julie and he had discussed this over and over again.

'If Freddie thinks it was an injustice,' she had said, 'it must mean he knows that they stole her baby.' She had a way of telling things how they were, which Edward found refreshing on the one hand but rather chilling on the other.

'So, if he knew they stole her baby, it wouldn't have been from Dan. He only recently discovered the truth himself and why would he want to share it with me if he'd already talked to Freddie? No, it can only be from Jim or Ruby but how would he become suspicious.'

Julie looked up from her drawing board. They were sitting in her studio on the first floor, off the gallery. 'I think it's simply a matter of time passing. Freddie painted the picture of Tracy when she was sixteen or so. Isn't it possible that, when Jane hit sixteen, all those years later, he suddenly recognised the likeness and began to put two and two together? And when he put it to Ruby, let's say, she just cracked as she had done with Dan, and the truth leaked out.'

'But of course, he kept it to himself, for the same reason as we did: to protect Jane. But he knew what happened and Malinov's part in it all, although he knew he could never confront Malinov. It had to be kept secret.' Edward fell silent. After a while, he stood up and walked across to the window. There was a howling gale blowing across the treetops in the park, bending them wildly. Flurries of leaves spun in tiny whirlwinds about the lawn. Then he suddenly said: 'That picture wasn't here before. I'm certain. I would have remembered.'

'What picture?' asked Julie, in bewilderment.

'The painting of Tracy, of course, and I think I know why. Malinov bought just about everything serious that Freddie produced, no doubt without even looking at them. One day he comes back to Ponsonby and finds the picture of Tracy. What does he do? It brings back bad memories so he stores it away in a cupboard somewhere. Doesn't want to be reminded. So it's not on display when I get the conducted tour. But when he leaves, he doesn't want to take the picture with him and the best place to put it is on the wall he never plans to look at again. He doesn't know Jane exists, or of the striking resemblance with Tracy, or even that we know Jane, and that's why he can't possibly think we would ever make the connection. But for us, it just confirms the truth of the story Dan told me. It's simple. He's saying a final farewell to his past.'

'If that's the case,' Julie said, 'do you think he would want Freddie to stay alive, with everything *he* knew about him? It's the same old question: did he jump or was he pushed?'

Chapter 9

The months passed and the seasons rolled by, autumn winds falling to still cold days when the snow covered the moors and the sea lay grey beneath a leaden sky. Their life continued its routine and, before they knew it, spring arrived, swelling the hill becks with fresh water. They had sold the house in Henrietta Street and rarely set foot there or saw the people of that little world. It was a morning in May when Edward looked out of a window in Ponsonby Hall and saw the green of George's Jaguar coming up the drive towards the front door. He heard the doorbell ring and Julie's welcoming voice in the hall. A few seconds later George appeared in the kitchen, threw off his cap, for he had driven with the roof down, and shook Edward's hand vigorously. Julie followed him in and put the kettle on the stove. 'Uncle George has got some news,' she said.

George sat down in a leather chair on one side of the fireplace where the kitchen range had stood in the old days of the hall. He pulled a folded copy of *The Telegraph* from his inside pocket and slammed it on the kitchen table. 'Read that!' he said with a hiss, 'inside pages, politics section.'

Edward could see George hovering between anger and disgust so thumbed through the pages as quickly as he could, while Julie poured out coffee. There, on page five, grinning out at him, he found the familiar face of Viktor Malinov, under the headline: *Russian Oligarch Appointed Life Peer.* Malinov wore white tie and tails, an outfit that seemed to produce a further abbreviation of his stature. On his arm hung a tall slim blonde woman who had squeezed herself into a slender evening dress with such violence that her ample breasts seemed in danger of overflowing at the top. She grinned broadly at the camera and the flash had caught that inescapable sheen produced by a combination of overheating and too much alcohol. The whole effect was a perfect imitation of a page in *Hello* magazine covering the later stages of a minor hunt ball in a second-rate English county.

'But I thought you had to be British to be in the Lords,' said Edward.

'Read on,' replied George. 'The bastard has it all wrapped up!'

'Read it out,' added Julie, perching on the corner of the table, coffee mug in hand.

Edward did as he was asked: 'The Government today released a list of twenty new life peers to be appointed to the House of Lords. Prominent among them is Russian-born oligarch, Viktor Malinov, owner of the London-based Siberian mining company, VSM Holdings, and recent buyer of a Premiership football club in the south. Mr Malinov was granted British citizenship a year ago. He is currently listed as having donated £2m to Labour party funds in the last twelve months and is reputed to have been a regular guest of the Prime Minister at Chequers. On appointment to the Lords he will assume the title *Lord Malinov of Egton* and will serve on the Lords Select Committee on business ethics.'

Edward took a deep breath, tossed the paper on to the kitchen table, and cast his eyes upwards towards the ceiling. 'Christ Almighty, the cheek of the man! And he even pretends to be a Labour supporter. Can you believe it!'

'He would have been a Conservative, if the Tories had been in office,' added George with a contemptuous snigger.

'But the man's a former Soviet spy, a murderer, a child-molester and a gangster,' said Edward in despair.

'No doubt he'll fit in well in the Lords in that case,' said Julie.

'He must have been planning this for years, the scheming Cossack,' added George. 'I never liked him,' he added, as if that were some justification for being taken in.

Edward took a while to come to grips with the shock of Malinov's mercurial rise in British society. He felt no envy of the man but the cynicism with which he had accomplished his success left a sour taste in his mouth. Then he recalled his last encounter with him and remembered his utter lack of values by which to live. Malinov indeed was a lost soul seeking salvation in the only way he knew how, with money. Edward, who had once felt sorry for the preposterous little Russian, and thought he saw a sliver of goodness in him, now felt nothing but disgust. And more than that, he realised with a frightening dawning of awareness that Malinov would stop at nothing to get where he thought he wanted to be. As he lay awake that night, studying the ornate Georgian plasterwork on the ceiling above the bed, two thoughts shot into his head: first, that the gift of Ponsonby Hall and Angelus House was no more than an unarticulated bribe to shut him up; second, that there was no way Malinov would have let Freddie live if he realised that Freddie knew too much about him, such was the magnitude of his ambition to be accepted as a pillar of British society. He sat bolt upright in the bed and said out loud: 'Of course, Freddie had to be silenced if Malinov was to succeed.'

Julie woke from her sleep. 'What on earth are you doing?' she asked with a groan.

'Going to London,' replied Edward.

'But it's the middle of the night!'

'I'm going to ask Malinov why he killed Freddie. The prize he was chasing was just too big to take a risk.'

Julie by this time was sitting up in bed. 'Don't you think it odd that if Malinov did go as far as killing Freddie to shut him up, he happily told *you* about killing Terry? Why on earth would he give you information that you could use against him?'

'I've thought about that,' replied Edward, 'and it's simple. First of all he was drunk and sorry for himself. But more important than that, I'm just a nobody he thought he could buy off and, if I did claim in public that he had a dodgy past, he could easily dismiss me out of hand. His word against my fantastical stories. But Freddie shared a history with Malinov, even down to dealings with the British Security Service. That's far from easy to dismiss. There had to be a trail that could be followed. Freddie was a big problem; I was just small-fry.'

'And you think Freddie only came out of the woodwork

when he discovered what had happened to Tracy's baby?'

'Precisely. He thought it was time to put things straight. Even if Malinov was not directly responsible for what happened, he had started it all with his exploitation of the girl. Freddie must have been desolate at how it had turned out. I suppose he was naïve to think he could take on Malinov and win.'

But the next morning, in the grey light of day, what had seemed a simple proposition – to ask Malinov why he had killed Freddie – suddenly became more difficult. How did he get to a rich man? The answer was, he couldn't. Malinov had put a wall around himself to shut out the past and no matter what Edward tried, he was unable to scale the defences of that kingdom. His hammer was as putty against the adamantine castle that surrounded Malinov. It was as if the Russian had decided the past no longer existed. Edward's phone calls were received courteously by some front desk operative, their message noted, and never returned; no call could ever be put through to his private office because of meetings, absences from the office or whatever; no letter ever received more than an acknowledgement that it had been received; and emails received automatic responses that trailed on and on into the future. Until Edward realised the only way he might communicate with the man who once wanted him as a friend might be to lie in the road before his limousine until the very wheels drove over his body and the occupant was forced to alight and look him in the face; only then he would be dead.

It took a month to reach such a conclusion. In June came a distraction from this thankless disillusionment. Dan drove up from Whitby with a message: Jane had passed her Tripos with flying colours and would receive her degree on June 25th at the Senate House in Cambridge. Would Edward and Julie attend with Dan and Molly? There was only one answer possible and so on the 24th they drove down together in Edward's car and checked in to the University Arms, all at Edward's willing expense. Jane joined them in the dining room for dinner, along with an army of other successful undergraduates and their parents, at last free from the heavy weight of financial endowment, full of a kind of febrile hope and boyish or girlish enthusiasm, as they launched themselves on a world they thought they had a chance of taming. After dinner they took a stroll across the city to the Backs, through Petty Cury, across Market Square and down Senate House Passage. Edward had brought his camera and, in a strange echo of an earlier occasion, took a picture of the five of them, Jane in the centre, standing in the evening sunlight on the terrace of Trinity Hall, overlooking the dimpled Cam at Garret Hostel bridge. It was a picture of unruffled peace, beneath the surface of which only Julie and Edward saw the lurking shadows. Would they ever fade away?

It was at Christmas that a light appeared on the horizon to steer them towards a possibility. A white envelope arrived with a Cardiff postmark containing a Christmas card from Morgane Owen. On the front was a photograph of Westminster Abbey in the snow and, inside, beneath the distinctive powerful signature of Morgane, stood the printed words *From the desk of Lady Owen, House of Lords, London.* Julie, whose duty it was to deal with Christmas cards and hang them on the string across the kitchen range, took a while to react. But then the penny dropped.

'Edward,' she shouted, 'that's it! Of course. Why didn't we think of that before?'

Edward, who had been trying to avoid thinking about Christmas, heard the cry as he trudged through the six inch covering of snow on the lawn, followed by Monty, hopping from paw to paw to avoid contact with the ground as far as possible. Edward looked through the leaded kitchen window to see Julie waving a Christmas card in his direction, her mouth forming the shape of inaudible words.

Six weeks later, he was seated by the window, watching the countryside flash by as the train headed south. The hills of the north soon lay behind them as they crossed the Trent and the wide flatlands of the east stretched away mile after mile until they reached the shallow coast of Lincolnshire and Norfolk. But this was all invisible to him, with his mind's eye focused solely on the strangeness of the journey he was undertaking. It was only a few short years ago that he had stumbled into this new world but now it seemed that his whole life had been reshaped by events that he could never have dreamed about. He had started as a fugitive from the city, a bitter failure the lasting mark of his career, and had thought there could never again be a way upwards. Then the lives of others slowly began to twine their threads within his, until he had become entangled with an inescapable destiny. Had he chosen this route, or had it singled him out, as the only person on the planet who might fulfil its purpose? And then there was dear sweet Julie who had shown him what life could be when true love was involved. In this he felt he was walking in the shadow of Freddie, who had stayed faithful to his lost love all those years. How surprising it was that the past had such power to determine the future; which was why Edward was hurtling towards a confrontation he could have so easily deflected. But that is what it was to be human, he thought, to act as one must, to see it right.

His journey south was to meet Viktor Malinov. It had come about this way. When Julie and Edward had realised that Lady Owen might hold the key to the Malinov fortress, they had written to her, setting out the situation as they saw it and asking for her help. There was no reply for several weeks. Then the telephone rang one morning. It was Morgane.

'Malinov will meet you,' she had said. 'It wasn't easy, but he will meet you.'

'How did you manage that?' asked Edward, silently amazed that she had responded at all.

'I mentioned a name,' she replied.

There was a silence.

'What name?'

'An old Russian name, Edward. It comes from the old days in Siberia and Malinov thought no one had remembered it.'

'I'm not sure I understand you,' said Edward. 'What good is a name?'

'It was the name with which Malinov entered the world, before he created his false identities and his phoney existence.

Malinov was never his real name. He asked me where I found it. I simply said it was known. You see, his real name is only the start of it all. If that is known, what else will be revealed? I said to Malinov it would be in his interests to meet you. He remembered you, of course.'

'What did he say to that?'

'He asked me if I was threatening him. Then he said he had nothing to hide. He was floundering, in a bit of a panic, I suspect. Then he said he'd done a deal with British Intelligence, to wipe the slate clean. I said there was no such thing as a clean slate in British Intelligence.'

'Are you telling me he was appointed to the Lords with all this known about him? How did you know all this? I'm amazed.'

'Oh, I've been around, Edward. One meets all sorts when you've been where I've been most of my life. In and out of NGOs, working with good governments and bad. Everything is possible. Don't you think it might be useful to someone to have a file on a British peer with deep contacts with Russia? Nothing happens by chance. He'll meet you at the Lords on February 16th at two o'clock. Present yourself at the visitors entrance. Your name will be on the list. I'm afraid there's no debate about it. This is your one chance. I can't fix this again.'

'All I want is the truth, Morgane, nothing more.'

'If I thought there was more, I wouldn't have done this. It's for Freddie, you see. Nothing else. Let me know.' There was a clipped tone to her voice as she spoke these last words, as if her emotions were welling up. 'Write this down. You might need it,' and she spelled out a Russian name. Then the phone went dead. 'Perhaps she loved him all the time,' thought Edward.

It was a freezing morning in February when Edward alighted from the train at King's Cross. He had not set foot in London since his exodus some years before but the smell and the taste of the city had not changed, only much more concentrated by its unfamiliarity. He breathed in deeply and felt a shudder of apprehension pass down his spine as he realised the true nature of what he was about to do. One moment he had thought it all a dream; now it was too real and he was afraid. The last contact he had had with Malinov was a letter of thanks sent through Scrivener when the strange endowment of Ponsonby Hall and Angelus House fell out of the sky. There had been no reply and Edward could not imagine what kind of creature Malinov had become. He looked at his watch as he passed through the station barrier. He had an hour to kill so he decided to walk, partly to clear his mind, partly to slow his arrival at the scene that was about to unfold.

From King's Cross to Westminster was a couple of miles, a forty minute brisk walk in the freezing air. He zig-zagged his way through Bloomsbury, faded yellow Victorian bricks hiding behind a thin mist; crossed Russell Square with the planes and sycamores bare of leaves and shining with hoar frost; and past the white stones of the British Museum where even now crowds of foreign tourists milled around the entrance courtyard. Edward became nervous and anxious as the great city enclosed him. This had been his place, a lifetime ago; but, with a jolt, he realised he was no longer its child. He belonged elsewhere, with another life and another set of players. He wanted this over with, and then to get back home to the empty northern skies he had come to love so much. He turned up the collar of his overcoat and carried on to the top of Whitehall, past the iron railings of Downing Street and down to Westminster, where a British peer from Siberia with a false name and a dark history awaited him. 'What kind of madness is this,' he asked himself, 'for a man I can't remember ever meeting?'

He presented himself at the visitors entrance and waited in a small queue, while a pair of uniformed Metropolitan police officers checked names against the appointments list and issued visitor passes. Then a security check as if he were boarding a plane, before being directed to the central lobby to await collection. It was a strange sensation, to be standing in that quasi-ecclesiastical octagon, beneath the severe eyes of past prime ministers, like a first day at school, not knowing a soul and waiting for one's name to be called. Then, from a dark corridor on his right, he saw the unmistakeable rolling figure of Lord Malinov, moving steadily towards him, hand outstretched. 'Why Edward, how nice to see you,' he said, which Edward knew to be a lie. Malinov wore a suit of impeccable grey, with just the right thickness of stripe; his shoes looked hand-made and his shirt and silk tie spoke quality. He was no longer the shiny-suited football club owner in search of an identity; he was, in presence and attitude, the English lord *per se*. 'We should have some tea,' he said.

Edward followed Malinov down the long corridor leading to the Lords end of Westminster. They passed tall oak doors leading to committee rooms, small alcoves with photocopiers on tables as if the nineteenth century were straining every muscle to accommodate modern technology and only partially succeeding; flickering television screens, mounted high off the ground, showed in dull black and white the live proceedings of the House. Edward felt he knew the faces passing him in the corridor, retired union leaders, aged politicians kicked upstairs and purple-shirted clerics, all familiar from a myriad of TV interviews. He looked across at Malinov and wondered if his own fate might be to be thrown from the terrace into the Thames for daring to challenge a peer of the realm. They reached the sparsely populated tea room and found a small table in the corner. 'India or China?' Malinov enquired, as if the choice were an everyday request, and while they waited for the tea to arrive, Malinov turned to Edward and said: 'And now, you must tell me how I can help you.'

'I wanted to ask you about Freddie's death,' Edward began, trying to keep his calm while inwardly he was shaking.

'I know nothing,' Malinov replied, almost too quickly perhaps. 'I thought he fell; it was an accident.'

'I don't believe that to be the case,' said Edward, pushing the issue further.

'That is a strange opinion, when the police and the coroner thought differently. What evidence do you have to think otherwise, I wonder?'

'Not so much evidence as a suspicion.' He thought he

239

detected a nervous shifting in his seat from Malinov at this. 'You see, Freddie was a pretty fit chap, really. OK, he was in his seventies but he could climb the abbey steps and walk a mile without too much difficulty I'm told. He did it more or less every day. And where he allegedly fell is not a dangerous point in the cliff path. I've examined it myself. As far as I know, nobody has ever fallen to his death there.'

'Continue please, Edward. I'm intrigued. What other options can there be?' Malinov nervously picked up the silver teapot and began to top up the cups, followed by a little business with the milk and sugar. At the same time a clatter of footsteps came through the doorway as the House cleared for the end of a session.

Edward continued, unable to gauge whether he stood on thin ice or firm ground. 'He could have jumped, of course, and that is a possibility, but wouldn't he have left something for us to find? And what might have been the trigger for such an action? Have you any ideas?'

Malinov looked steadily at Edward. 'I have no suggestions to make, I'm afraid. Look, this is very tedious. What exactly are you looking for here?' He was getting rattled and Edward noticed it. He pressed on.

'Of course, there is another possibility, Viktor, isn't there? And that would be that he was pushed, done away with, got rid of!'

'That is a very macabre suggestion, wouldn't you say. Who would want to do that? Freddie had no enemies as far as I know.'

'Perhaps it wasn't to do with enemies. Let's imagine he knew something about a friend, and that friend had reasons to keep the information secret. Let's just imagine that for a moment.' Edward paused. The only sound in the room was the clink of cups. He expected heads to turn in his direction, as if his sentence had suddenly caught the conscience of all. Malinov looked nervously around.

'Edward, this is madness. I think we should move on. This conversation is going nowhere. When I agreed to meet you, I did *not* agree to an inquisition.' He rose to his feet, signalling the end of the interview. Edward grabbed his sleeve and with the sudden movement a spoon was dislodged and fell to the floor. Heads turned just as Edward hissed: 'Sit down, Malinov, or should I say Kaganovich?'

Malinov slowly took his seat again, his face losing its colour at the mention of the name that transported him back to a long-forgotten life. A steward came across to retrieve the spoon and, as he bent down, Edward heard him say quietly 'Is everything alright, my Lord?' Malinov nodded. Edward knew he had won but his hand was shaking beneath the table.

'Let's go to my office,' Malinov said.

It was a walk of some distance, through long corridors, up flights of steps, and along landings. At last they reached the corner of a narrow hallway and Malinov pushed open a door into a room the size of a broom cupboard. The sound of a water cistern filling came from somewhere behind the wall, as if Lord Malinov's office adjoined the gents' lavatory. He squeezed himself behind a small Victorian desk upon which not a single piece of paper could be seen. Edward took a chair, with his back rammed against a wall, and looked around. There was nothing, except a gilt-framed photograph of Malinov, enrobed, standing between his sponsors, on the day of his investiture. Then the sound of flushing water penetrated the wall once more.

'I take it you plan to expose me. Is that it? Or is this simple blackmail? I would have thought better of you Edward. After all, I gave you Ponsonby and Angelus.'

'Neither, Viktor. I simply want the truth. If my suspicion is right, as I think it is, the only person who needed to silence Freddie was you. Give me the truth and I'll leave you in peace. That's my promise.'

Malinov was not done yet. He thought for a while, twiddling with the end of his silk tie, rolling and unrolling it between finger and thumb. Then he leaned forward and smiled: 'But Edward, why would Freddie choose that moment to betray my secrets? We shared a past, after all. There was nothing new. I would have no need to get rid of him, as you put it. Everything was already known.'

'Except that you were in pursuit of big game this time, Viktor. Not just a football club and a mansion in Chelsea. This was your chance to get to the top in the west, to be a political figure. Not bad for a Cossack from Siberia with a lifetime of wheeling and dealing in the KGB. The rules of the game had changed, hadn't they? I'm not saying Downing Street didn't know about you all the time; but if it ever came out in public, you would be dropped like a stone. You'd worked that out, hadn't you, and that's why Freddie had to go. And that's not to mention the girl, is it?'

'The girl? I don't know what you mean?'

'When you showed me the gallery at Ponsonby Hall, there was no picture of Tracy Woodford. I would have remembered that. But when I looked again, when Julie and I moved in, there she was. You put the picture on the wall assuming I wouldn't notice. That led me to think: the stakes were raised when Freddie told you the girl had killed herself after losing your child. Imagine what the papers would make of that.'

Malinov looked shaken and held his peace for a while before speaking. 'So Edward, what is it that you want?'

'The truth.....for my silence. That's all.'

Malinov leaned back in his swivel chair which creaked under the strain. Then he reached down to a bottom drawer in his desk. For a moment, Edward half thought he would produce a revolver and put a bullet through his brain, as he had with Tracy's brother so many years before. But then, Malinov had inhabited the shadows: to kill a man was insignificant. Now he lived in a public world and the sound of a gunshot in the House of Lords could not be hidden in the noise of the city or muffled by work of his agents. When Malinov's hand reappeared it was with a bottle in its grip, which he plonked down on the desk top. Then two small vodka glasses appeared and he poured two measures into them.

'I could have had you killed, twenty years ago, Edward, and nobody would be the wiser. But now I obey the law of Britain. Na Zdarovye.' And he raised his glass to drink. 'OK. I tell you,' he said.

Chapter 10

Endings

'You're right about Freddie. After all those years, he broke silence and contacted me. I don't know what triggered it. Yes, he told me the girl had killed herself and her baby was dead. She claimed I was the father. Who knows? But something had changed in Freddie. It was as if he hated me; no, worse, was disgusted by me. It was over, Freddie and me. I felt no remorse.'

'So you killed him?'

Malinov did not answer that question. He lifted his eyes to an unidentifiable spot on the ceiling and spoke as if he were alone in the room. 'He sent a note to my people at Ponsonby Hall. He wanted to meet me, he said. I couldn't get away from London at the time and, to be honest, I didn't want to meet him. I wanted to draw a line under it all. My mind was on other things. And it wasn't until the very last moment that I made up my mind. I couldn't let him live. Would he have told all? Probably not. But I couldn't take the risk. Once KGB, always KGB, isn't that what you say? It was in my nature after all.

'I flew up north and sent a car to Freddie's cottage to fetch him but my driver phoned me to say he wasn't there. I was waiting in the West Cliff Hotel in the town, nearer than Ponsonby. I had suggested we meet there. Then my driver called back again to say the woman next door had said Freddie had gone along the cliffs for a walk. I thought it was strange, as we were supposed to be meeting. It half crossed my mind that maybe his mind had gone. Don't ask me why I thought that. My driver was a local so he knew the area and said we could head south out of town and intercept him somewhere. I went along with it. He picked me up and we took a narrow road out of the town beyond the abbey, winding up a hillside on the far side of the harbour. After a couple of miles he stopped in a farm yard. He told me the cliffs were no more than two hundred yards across a field. Once I hit the cliff path I was to turn left and, if Freddie really was walking that way, I would meet him. It was a filthy cold day and the farm yard was very muddy. Strange how these things stick in the mind. I was wearing smart leather shoes with leather soles, very English, and I slid all over the place as I walked along the path between two hawthorn hedges. I could hear the sea breaking on the rocks long before I could see it. Waves of sea-fog were blowing in, blocking the light out, then suddenly clearing again. I was at the cliff top before I realised it and turned left, towards the town, just as my driver had told me. Then I saw Freddie through the fog, on the path across the bay, a dark figure in a raincoat. He looked up and stopped walking, as if he suddenly remembered our meeting and was trying to piece together what he was supposed to do. I waved and he waved back, a single arm raised as if in salute. I could see his long grey-blonde hair blowing in the wind. We set off to meet in the middle, where the cliff path closely bordered the edge, where there was no fence, just a steep fall down on to the rocks.'

'I know the place,' said Edward. 'It's called Saltwick Bay.'

'Is that significant?' Malinov asked.

'It's where the girl's body washed up. She'd walked into the sea twenty miles north but the tide carried her all that way. That's why it's significant.'

'I didn't know that.' Malinov lowered his eyes as he spoke.

'Why would you? You couldn't even remember her name. So what happened?'

'It was very strange. I said to him we had agreed to meet, that he'd asked me. He didn't reply. He just looked at me and put a hand on my shoulder. It was blowing a gale and it was difficult to catch what he said. But he smiled at me, and I think he said something like "It's over, Viktor. The cruelty of it all." I think that's what he said. Then he went on in a kind of rambling way, saying something about the world going round whatever we do. Didn't make much sense to me. Then he grabbed my sleeve and I shook myself free. I thought he was trying to pull me over the edge. But as I shook him he fell backwards. The weirdest thing is it was all in slow motion. I held out my hand to pull him back. He could have taken it but instead he just smiled. Before I knew it, he was gone. The space where he had stood was empty. It happened in a flash. I turned and ran back to the car. I guess I killed him.'

Malinov reached down to a bottom drawer in his desk, this time with his left hand. Edward heard the drawer slide open and a dull clunk of something metal hitting the wooden side. Then he watched as Malinov placed his Makarov pistol on the desk, butt pointing away from him.

'There,' he said. 'Take it. Put a bullet through my head. That's what you would like to do, isn't it? Put me out of my misery. Shoot the Russian bastard and have done with it!'

Edward stared at the gun. 'No Viktor, that's not what I'm going to do. You don't deserve it. Take a look at this instead.' He reached inside his jacket pocket and drew out an envelope and handed it across the desk. 'Take a look. Do you recognise the likeness?'

Malinov opened the envelope and took out a small square of glossy photographic paper. He looked at it impassively, as if he were afraid to show any feelings.

'That's your daughter, but you will never know her,' said Edward curtly. It was a photograph of Jane taken that sunlit evening by the river in Cambridge. But Edward had carefully cropped away the surroundings: Molly and Dan standing on the terrace, flanked by Julie and himself. What he left was unidentifiable except for a beautiful young girl, with the blonde hair and blue eyes of Tracy Woodford.

'My daughter? But Freddie told me the baby was dead.'

'He lied, to protect her. It was another baby who died, but that's another story. The last thing he wanted was for you and your gang to track her down. But that's what triggered his contact with you, the final ghastly twist in Tracy Woodford's story. It was the injustice of the world. Think about it. You see, for Freddie, you came to symbolize the way the world had become for him, just exploitation and cruelty. And your little piece of disregard for human life, your careless thrash through anyone who stood in your way or threatened your progress, was no more than that world in microcosm. You probably are incapable of understanding that Viktor.'

'You know her?'

'Yes, I know her and she's happy and will remain that way. You'd better put that gun away. That doesn't solve anything.'

'You've become very wise,' replied Malinov.

'And you've become everything you wanted to be. Except you now know you have a daughter you'll never know. That's your life's reward. Carry that baggage as you travel the world, Viktor. You can't buy people. Money is not the answer to everything. People are free. They come to you when you love them. When you try to buy them they hide in the shadows.'

'What did you mean by that? *The injustice of the world*.' Julie was stretched out on the sofa in the drawing room having listened to Edward's account of his meeting with Malinov.

'Pretentious sentiments, is that what you mean?' replied Edward. 'Well, it just struck me that Freddie had reached the limit of his endurance. He goes to Kenya to find peace and all he sees is injustice. When he tries to make a small contribution to putting it right, the British decide to throw him out. The same injustice and carelessness destroys his only love, Amala. The England he loved turns him into a kind of traitor. And then Viktor destroys the life of a child Freddie thinks he should have been able to save. When he discovers the real cruelty of what happened, a switch seems to have been thrown in his head. A tidal wave of guilt at the harmless, innocent people he lost. But I wonder if he planned real revenge on Viktor at that last meeting or was he just going to tell it as it was?'

'How do you mean?'

'Malinov an empty man, living without feelings, without beliefs, without love; only for ambition, for money, for status, for power. When I looked at him across his little desk in the

House of Lords, in his scrappy little office next to the gents, I suddenly realised it was an addiction, this lust for influence and acceptance. But the cost of the addiction was that he would never know someone he might have been able to love. That's what I told him before we parted. He simply said it was what he was born to do. In other words, he had no choice. I said everyone had a choice and that's why I didn't pity him. He used Tracy Woodford and didn't give a damn what the consequences were. If he really did kill Freddie, it was because he might get in the way of his ridiculous ambition. As for Malinov, what can I say? I used to think there must be a tiny streak of goodness in him. Not any more.'

Julie was plunged into silent thought. After a while, she lifted her head and reached out her hand to Edward who was sitting on the arm of the sofa. 'I don't think I want to live here any longer,' she said. 'Too many ghosts walking the long gallery.'

'You're right. I've been thinking that for a while. It's time we stepped out of the shadows of the past. I never thought I had a past until I came here, nor a future for that matter. We should get married, Julie. Let's do that. Put bloody Ponsonby on the market and bugger off into the blue!' He laughed out loud at the thought.

'I haven't heard you laugh for ages, Edward, but you can now.'

Ponsonby Hall went on the market in the spring. A half-page spread appeared in the Sundays, the property went on the agent's website and word got around the locality that the house was up for sale. A few weeks later Julie was looking out of the leaded kitchen window on the wind-blown trees lining the driveway from the road. She saw a dark figure walking slowly up the slight incline, head bowed, hands in pockets, rounded shoulders. It seemed the figure dragged a foot, almost as if it had been lame. She watched in fascination as the man, for she assumed it was a man, slowly drew nearer to the house. It was unusual for a visitor to arrive on foot. Then, as he came closer, she realised it was Jim Moxon. She walked briskly down the passageway leading to the chessboard hall and reached the front door just at the moment the heavy bell sounded. She swung the door open and Jim raised his eyes, surprised at the prompt reaction to the sounding bell.

'Jim. Come in. How nice to see you,' she said. 'Let me take your coat.' He slowly pulled each arm from its sleeve and handed the coat to Julie. 'Let's go into the kitchen. We can talk there.' She led the way back along the passageway. She had noticed the grey look on Jim's face and knew this could not be a social call. It was a cold spring day with a sharp wind off the sea and Jim looked frozen and ill. She led him into the kitchen which glowed with warmth, sat him down at the kitchen table, and put the kettle on to boil. 'What brings you all the way here?' she asked.

'Took the bus from Whitby to the road end, Julie. Didn't realise it was such a haul up from there. Not as fit as I was,' Jim replied, half out of breath. The kettle had quickly boiled on the Aga and Julie made two mugs of coffee. Jim wrapped his hands around the mug and took a sip. 'The thing is, I've got something for Edward. I wanted to show him − and you − before you left, sold up, that is.'

'He's around somewhere. I'll give him a shout. I think he's next door.' She put her head around the corner of the hallway and shouted Edward's name. A minute later he appeared and joined them at the table.

'I saw you were selling up,' Jim continued, looking embarrassed.

'Time for a new start, somewhere else,' said Edward. 'Time to move on. Time to put all this behind us.' He looked at Jim as he spoke and it seemed to him that Jim knew exactly what he meant by "all this", for he nodded in agreement.

'Some people have made some big mistakes in the past,' Jim replied, and immediately Edward thought of Ruby and her secret. 'I didn't want to make another,' he went on, 'so I thought I should let you see something before you go. We should have told you before, when you were asking about Freddie Ottaway. No one else in the world knows this, only

Ruby and me.' His hand shook as he reached inside his jacket pocket, whether from drink or nerves Edward could not be sure. He pulled out a single sheet of folded notepaper, small and square. 'Ruby found this in his house, the day he died. She went in to clean that morning. She thought it was better to hide it at the time and I agreed with her. But now I know we were wrong. You need to know.' His face was drawn and tired; life had nothing left to offer him, it seemed. He handed the paper to Edward who opened the single fold and read silently. Then he handed it to Julie. There was silence as they took in its meaning.

At last Edward spoke. 'You did the right thing, Jim. I needed to know. Thanks. Tell me, why did you decide to keep it secret?'

'Oh, I suppose we thought it looked better, for Freddie's sake. He was a good man, your uncle. We didn't want people to think bad of him.' And with that Jim rose to his feet to take his leave.

'Thanks, Jim. It's much appreciated. Let me drive you home. It's a long way to the bus stop and who knows when the next bus will be along. You look tired out.'

Jim held out his hand to Edward, who took it firmly, seeing in Jim's face a vestige of relief, and Julie gave him a hug. The drive into Whitby passed in complete silence. Jim, after all, had said his piece and when they arrived in Henrietta Street he got out of the car at his cottage door without speaking more. The return journey flashed by as if in a dream, Edward's mind racing over the import of the letter he had seen. Before he knew it, he was pulling up at the door of Ponsonby Hall. He found Julie still in the kitchen drinking coffee. 'Well, what do you make of that?' he asked.

Julie had been thinking it through, for she replied immediately. 'I'm sad that Freddie had arrived at that conclusion but I can understand why. I always thought he had become tired of it all. But it strikes me as odd that he asked Malinov to come and see him and then wander off like that. I can only assume he was in such a state that he became confused.'

249

'It doesn't matter whether he meant to say something to Malinov that he hadn't already said. Who knows? By some ridiculous chance they met on the clifftop, the one seeking to end his own life, the other planning to commit murder. If it was not so tragic, it would be farcical. The savage irony of it all is that Malinov killed a man who was on his way to kill himself and that's why Freddie smiled at the end. He saw the black humour of it.'

'Will you tell him?'

'I hope never to see him again,' said Edward firmly.

They got married in the drowsy heat of August. There had been no rain for weeks and the flat fields of grain in Lincolnshire were deep yellow. Vast water pumps shot cascades high into the sky to keep the green leaves of cabbages from scorching and the levels in the irrigation ditches and channels fell far below the dykes. The air stood still and the insects buzzed lazily above the low flat mudbanks of the river. Edward had at last met Juliana's father, who studied him over his half-moon reading glasses, without shifting from his cramped desk overlooking the Humber estuary, some remote middle English text lying open before him. Juliana's mother scuttled about the small house, a kind of footnote to the main page, but nevertheless one that provided the key to its meaning. All in all, the parts added up to a whole, and Julie and Edward were pleased that their life decision would largely pass by unnoticed, except by themselves.

Dr Jane Martin, for such she had become, travelled up by train from London to perform her duties as bridesmaid and Edward picked her up from Doncaster station.

'How's Buddhism?' he asked her as they drove across country.

Jane laughed. 'That's years ago, Ed. How come you remembered that?'

'Oh, been thinking about beliefs quite a lot recently.'

'And your conclusion?'

'That it doesn't matter what you believe, as long as you believe something.'

'Believe or believe *in*?'

'Precisely,' answered Edward.

Jane turned her head to look at him, a wry smile flickering across her lips. 'You've changed, Ed. You're really quite a philosopher, aren't you?'

'And you? What are you now?'

'Still learning to be a doctor. OK, I've got the tee shirt but that means nothing. I've got a year to do at Great Ormond Street starting next month.'

'And then?'

'I want to go to Africa, to work in a children's clinic there.'

'What made you decide that?'

'We had a lecture this year from a Lady Owen. I was inspired, I suppose. She said a lot about Kenya. I'd like to go there.'

'Did you know she was a close friend of Freddie Ottaway out there, when they both were very young.'

'I didn't know that.'

'I met her. A remarkable woman. She had nothing in her life, except what she believed *in*, and she seems to have changed the world on the back of that.'

Uncle George motored down in his Jag, composing his best man's speech in his head, between chunks of over-ripe music on Classic FM, disregarding the fact that only six people would be present. Dan and Molly turned up, in their very best. When Edward shook Dan's hand, they looked each other straight in the eye, reaffirming the truth of their understanding, secret to them alone. Jim and Ruby did not reply to their invitation.

They married in the little red-brick village church of Saint Barnabas, which had no claim to fame or distinction, but its plain wooden pews and white plastered walls echoed gently to the words of the vicar and made the tiny assembly feel unthreatened by expectations that life ought to be something grander. 'For what is life, other than this?' thought Edward as he and Julie walked hand in hand down the aisle and into the bright summer sunshine. 'What more is there, than this belief in each other?' And George's speech, delivered on the little square back lawn of the church hall, went down well, if a little too long.

By October they had found a buyer for Ponsonby Hall, who had plans to turn it into a health spa. They left in November, leaving Monty under a small green mound beneath the fir trees, where he had breathed his last, and with a tiny fraction of the proceeds of the sale they bought a small black and white farmhouse in Arkengarthdale in Swaledale. Here the dome of the north Pennines ranged wide and empty under the arch of the sky in summer and the narrow roads, wedged between drystone walls, clogged with snow in the winter.

'I want no more of Malinov's money,' said Julie. 'I can earn enough from my work.' Edward had agreed and the acorn of an idea had been planted in their minds. The farmhouse came with five hundred acres of bare hillside and twenty acres of pasture. On a clear day you could look south beyond Barnard Castle and across the North York moors to the sea, across the heather and the grasses which had first seen Edward stumble into his brave new world. And such people as he had found there! It was beyond dreams.

It had been a long journey. The flight from Heathrow lasted more than eight hours and when they landed in Nairobi a wall of heat rose before them as they crossed the tarmac to the arrivals building. Now they were resting in their air-conditioned cream-and-white room at the *Nairobi Excelsior* when the telephone rang. It was reception.

'Mr Ottaway? There is a gentleman asking for you here in the foyer. His name is Porter,' came the trained African-English voice.

'Porter? I don't think I know anyone called Porter,' Edward replied.

'He said that would be the case,' the receptionist continued, 'and that I should say it is to do with your uncle.'

'I see,' said Edward, after a pause. 'I'll be right down.'

Julie had been sleeping lightly and woke at the sound of the telephone. 'Porter? Who's that? I didn't think anyone in Kenya would know us.'

'Neither did I,' said Edward, pulling on his shirt and smoothing his hair. 'I'll go down and see what this is all about.' He took the lift to the ground floor and stepped out into the cool marble-tiled foyer. There was the usual bustle. A porter with a brass trolley wheeled a mountain of suitcases to the service lift; a telephone rang quietly in the background; in a corner, sunk in reclining cane chairs two heavy African businessmen sat deep in conversation with a laptop open in front of them on a glass-topped coffee table; and through the plate glass front windows a luxury coach blew out a puff of diesel as it drew away to the coach park. It was a scene that could have been repeated in a thousand luxury hotels across the world, wherever international tourists and businessmen had penetrated, give or take a few local differences. To be honest, Edward was disappointed. He had expected Africa to be a little wilder, a little less safe, perhaps a little more threatening. He looked around him, unsure of what he was looking for. Then, in a far corner, on an upright chair by the wall, he caught sight of a very old man, European, with a slightly clerical look, in a light linen jacket and a striped tie untidily knotted at the collar. The old man raised a hand in his direction and slowly got to his feet, with the help of a cane walking-stick. Edward walked across to him. 'Mr Porter?' he said.

'Mr Ottaway. I knew it must be you. The likeness, you see. There's no reason why you should know me but I was a friend of your uncle many years ago.' Edward held out his hand and felt a bony, arthritic hand in his grasp. Porter had thin grey hair and a pronounced stoop. There seemed to be no flesh on his bones and the skin was stretched taut across his face, like parchment. He seemed to be clinging to life by the weakest of threads. 'My name is Hugh Porter, the Reverend Hugh Porter, Vicar of St Andrew's Nakuru, in the old days, that is.' He seemed a spectre from the past, wandering lost in the plastic plate glass foyer of the hotel.

'I'm Edward Ottaway. Pleased to meet you, Reverend Porter.'

'Dear boy, let's have some tea. There's a table over here,' he said, pointing to the far end of the room. He raised his arm, in a commanding fashion, and a waiter appeared, to take his order. It was a slow walk across the foyer. Porter gripped his cane hard and will power alone seemed to move his legs forward. At last they sat, the tea arrived, and they could talk. 'I saw your name in *The Daily Nation* the other day. They had an item on the opening of the new Ottaway clinic in Turkana County. I saw that you and your wife would be attending the ceremony. It turned the clock back half a century or more. It brought back so many memories. I had to meet you.'

'How did you track us down?'

Porter smiled and shook his head. 'You don't live in a place for more than sixty years without getting to know a few people, particularly in a country like Kenya. Not a problem, Edward, if I may call you that.'

'Of course, and may I call you Hugh? What can I do for you?' asked Edward, taking a sip of his black tea.

Porter thought for a moment before replying. 'I hoped you could tell me what became of Freddie. He was deeply loved here, you know. I can still recall the first time I met him. It was on the station at Nairobi. We took the overnight sleeper here. He was very young and very innocent.'

'You ask me what became of him,' Edward said. 'He died, a few years ago, I would say of innocence. But I can tell you what I know, if you have the time,' he added.

'Time is running out for me,' Porter replied, with a wry smile, 'but I have enough for today, if you have the energy after your long journey. But I tell you what, let's have something stronger than tea. I introduced your uncle to Kenya with a pink gin; let me do the same for you.' He waved his arm again and the waiter came across. 'Two of the usual, Benjamin,' he said.

'You're well known here, Hugh,' observed Edward with surprise.

'Rotary, every Tuesday,' said Porter with a broad grin. 'Old habits die hard.'

It was two hours before Edward returned to his room. Julie was rested and inquisitive. 'Edward, are you drunk?' she asked pointedly.

'A little,' he replied, falling backwards on to the bed. 'I've just been introduced to Kenya, by a nonagenarian Anglican vicar who knew Freddie. He wanted to know what happened.'

'And what did you tell him?'

'Most of it. The bare bones. He's coming with us tomorrow to Lodwar. I said we'd pick him up.'

'Why would you do that?' asked Julie, with a tone of annoyance in her voice.

'He wants to show us something, to do with Amala. That's all I know.' Then he fell asleep.

There was a green hill above Lodwar, facing north towards the Highlands. Edward and Julie had climbed it in half an hour and, when they turned to look down, they could just make out the slight figure of Hugh Porter standing, as if to attention, two hundred feet below them, his face shaded under the brim of his panama hat. Before them, on a tablet of white stone, they read the inscription *Amala Mohammed 1932-1952*.

'What did Porter tell you about this place?' asked Julie.

'That the stone was put here by her parents. Apparently she and Freddie often used to ride here. It was her favourite place.'

'I can see why,' said Julie. She looked north to the scarp slope of the rift valley, the hills clothed in emerald green, the plain yellow-brown beneath the afternoon sun. She imagined the wandering herds sheltering beneath the flat-topped trees, under the blue arc of the African sky. And to the south perhaps she could glimpse the thin silver line of the Indian Ocean, somewhere far away beyond reach, or was she just dreaming? 'It's all my fantasy, I know,' she whispered, 'but this is how I imagined humans taking their first steps when they emerged from primeval slime. An innocent world, clean and

255

shining. All lost and gone.'

'Not fantasy at all. It's a journey we all make, don't we, from innocence to knowledge, when we live a human life. I ask myself what brought me here, to this point. There's no reason to it. I used to think it was Freddie's secret plan. But it's something much bigger than that.'

'What else but love and faith and belief,' answered Julie. 'Don't ask me why it's that way. It just is.'

Edward unhitched the rucksack he was carrying and took out a heavy round object wrapped in tissue. He bent down and scooped a small hollow in the sandy earth, unwrapped the tissue paper and placed the contents in the hollow. The black sheen of the Saltwick Bay stone shone dully in the unrelenting sun, throwing into relief the name Julie had carved those years ago and the dates 1928-2005.

And somewhere else, alone, in his scheming world, without love, faith or belief, Viktor Malinov sat, ignorant of what his money had bought at the hands of others, in another continent, and by such strange alchemy. But even stranger, that a daughter he had never met, and who knew nothing of him, would work her first miracles with the children in that distant unknown place.

They were flying north at thirty-thousand feet and the sun had begun its slow descent below the cloud line beyond the tip of the port wing. In one more hour they would descend into the grey murk of northern France, cruise gently down across the English Channel and then hurl themselves into the maelstrom of Heathrow. Edward reached across and took Julie's hand in his. They were together now, he thought; they had a shared history, which passed beyond words into that mysterious land where people who love each other share a secret unspoken language.

'Thanks for coming with me,' he said. 'It was good to have you beside me.'

'I wouldn't have missed this journey for the world,' she replied.

'I'm making no more journeys,' Edward added, with a strange far-away look in his eyes. 'No more journeys because I've arrived where I want to be. It took me a long time to find it.'

Julie said nothing and they sped onwards into the arc of the spinning world, the dull drone of the engines advancing and retreating with a monotonous predictability.

'I read Freddie's sonnet, at last,' Edward said. 'It was strange. It seemed to predict so much, years before it happened. Or am I mistaken?'

Julie nodded her head. 'No, you're right,' she agreed. 'He could have written it at the end of his life but he wrote it as a prelude. It was as if his end were his beginning.'

There was a shudder of turbulence as the plane hit the first layer of cloud and began its descent into Heathrow. A labyrinth of west London roads, streets and gardens lay spread out beneath them. As the ground rose up they could make out the ceaseless flow of traffic, stopping and merging, like people moving in a crowd, afraid to touch but afraid to be alone; the endless striving for direction that only humans could endure.

Sonnet 155

by William Shake-speare

When forty summers have their courses run
And beauty's rose hath passed her golden spring;
When life's prime fades beneath the burning sun
And dying chime from ruin'd tower doth ring;
Then, love, thou know'st I shall be gone from thee
Where rippling waves in winter ice are seized
And I as wanderer cross some frozen sea
Condemn'd to voyage 'til my pain be eased.
For age my soul shall then have drowned in dreams;
Thine eyes then lost that were to mine a glass
Wherein I viewed sweet love's reflected beams
That now are dulled while I to heaven pass.
For life though sweet when love hath conquer'd strife
Sour tastes when death hath stolen my love's life.

as rendered by
Freddie Ottaway

Thanks for reading my work. You can contact me directly at
pb_north@btinternet.com
If you have enjoyed it, please write me a review on Amazon.

By the same author:

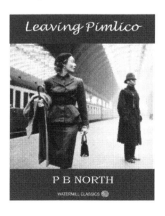

35010303R00147

Made in the USA
Middletown, DE
14 September 2016